I0709082

THE

A NOVEL

David Brent Roundsley

DBR Design
2024

design

Hardback ISBN: 978-1-7353779-3-3
Paperback ISBN: 978-1-7353779-4-0
eBook ISBN: 978-1-7353779-5-7

Library of Congress Control Number: 2024903433

First Edition 2024

Published in the United States by DBR Design

DBR Design
P.O. Box 1482
Benicia, CA 94510

Acknowledgments

First and foremost, my husband David Chamberlain, who, without his support and assistance, this never could have happened.

I also want to thank:

David L. Hatt
Gretchen Ward
Fusae & Jack Wicks
Joyce Gorham
Jeffrey & Patty Norman
Randall Watkins

For going above and beyond with their encouragement and support!

I also want to thank:

Lisa E. Paige
Rebecca Inch-Partridge

For their editorial assistance!

For Roberta "Bobbi" Piotrowski – Blay
It was the journey of a lifetime. I wish you were still here.

And Paul Carter

Contents

Preface

Homeowners Association (HOA)

In the United States, a Homeowners Association (or Homeowner's Association, abbreviated "HOA" and sometimes referred to as a Property Owners' Association or "POA") is an organization in a subdivision, planned community, or condominium building that makes and enforces rules for the properties and residents. Those who purchase property within an HOA's jurisdiction automatically become members and are required to pay dues, which are known as HOA fees. Some Associations can be very restrictive about what members can do with their properties while others may give residents more freedom.

An HOA Board (also called Board of Directors) is a group of people whose role is to run the Association. Typically, HOA Boards comprise four core members – President, Vice-President, Secretary, and Treasurer – as well as additional members to ensure an odd number of members to reduce the chances of tie votes. All Board positions are filled by an election.

In addition to the Board, an HOA often also has various committees – Landscape, Communications, Finance, Construction – staffed by residents who volunteer to support the community.

THORNWILLOW HEIGHTS

Established Nineteen Seventy Something…

Thornwillow Heights is a meticulously crafted community of two-, three-, and four-bedroom sumptuous townhomes. Artistically and stylishly designed to merge seamlessly with the natural California terrain. Uninterrupted views stretching from the south, beyond San Jose, upwards to Marin and Mount Tamalpais with the glistening lights of San Francisco reflected on the Bay. Painstakingly designed to provide luxury and accommodation through a vast array of special touches included in each Thornwillow Heights residence.

More than a home, Thornwillow Heights is a lifestyle. Along with the sleek elegance of each home comes the privilege of membership at the Thornwillow Heights Club. At the club you can enjoy the regulation-sized tennis courts, Olympic-sized swimming pool, indulge yourself in the therapy whirlpool, or you can relax with friends around the clubhouse fireplace, enjoying a smart cocktail or a game of cards. At Thornwillow Heights there are no worrisome issues as a full staff of professionals take care of everything from the grounds, building exteriors, walkways, the surrounding open space, and all recreational facilities.

The life you've always desired awaits you in the shimmering East Bay hills

Cast of Characters

Chapter 1 – Stephen and Daniel

Stephen paused to take one last look around the now empty condominium before leaving it for the last time. Running his hand over the polished granite of the kitchen he and Daniel had updated a couple of years previously, he could clearly see the condominium as it was when he first moved in eight years before. Single (since the man he was living with in the city had quietly plotted his return to his hometown out of state), this was the first time Stephen had owned his own place. Once the decision had been made to purchase a place, he assumed the process would be simple and straightforward. But it turned out to be anything but.

His realty agent, Bea, presented him with a comprehensive list of places within his budget and preferred locations. Excited at first, his exhilaration wore off very quickly as each property he viewed had issues or required major concessions. For most, if the vibe wasn't right, he knew right away. Others had potential, but there was always a nagging feeling they weren't right. Then there was *the* flat-out wrong one.

After viewing several places, Stephen had little trouble ignoring poor decorating choices, bad paint jobs, or unsightly window treatments. He could usually see past those and envision his belongings and art in their place. As they pulled up to this one, though, Bea stopped the car.

She said, "Before we go in, you need to ignore the owner's décor and items."

This caused Stephen to smile. It had never been an issue before, and he couldn't see why it would be now.

They climbed the stairs to the older four-plex with four equally sized units. After getting the key from the lockbox and entering, Stephen stopped dead. The unit, while generously sized, was covered floor-to-ceiling and wall-to-wall with pictures, papers, letters, notes, children's artwork, you name it. You could not see an inch of wall space. And then there was the furniture. At least he assumed there was furniture underneath the piles of papers and books. There were vague furniture shapes, but the owner had fully-opened newspapers spread about, with books, magazines, and other items completely covering them. Bea shot him a look that said, "I told you so."

Carefully walking through the clutter, it occurred to Stephen this was what the home of a serial killer must look like. While this was the largest place they had viewed and had potential for a home office, along with a guest room and bedroom, everything about the place, above and beyond the psychotic clutter, just screamed, "NO!" Finally daring to venture close to a wall and lifting a couple of layers of the pinned papers, he confirmed his worst fear: the entire place had 1960s paneling. He was also aware the unit was underneath someone who was clomping about loudly! Add to that, the very tall eucalyptus trees near the building made it feel like twilight in the middle of the day.

Stephen was now getting dejected, but Bea said she'd continue to cast her net. She finally contacted Stephen as he was leaving work one evening and said there were two units coming on the market in a complex he hadn't viewed before. Neither had been listed and if he was interested, she was confident she could swoop in and not be involved in a bidding war or dragged-out negotiations. Fighting the crowded East Bay traffic, he met Bea a bit after 6 pm. Looking up from the parking lot, Stephen saw two modern-looking high-rise buildings fit together like two L-shapes with the guest parking in the center space between them. Mostly cement, steel, and glass, outwardly it looked well maintained, even though it was over twenty-five years old now.

Bea got out of her car, brochures and papers in hand, and led Stephen to the front doors. Fishing about for her passkey, they came into a nicely maintained entry area. It was apparent it had once been a more opulent setting, but it was starting to look a tad dog-eared and dated even though it was still well-maintained. Bea pointed to one of the two swimming pools and a spa area on the other side of the entryway, commented there was a billiard room you needed a key for and on the top floor was a library along with a meeting room with a full kitchen, and all with lovely views of the San Francisco Bay. But then she dropped her voice as they walked to the elevators.

She said, "The average age of the residents here is death. They have nothing better to do than sit around listening to their arteries harden. I just want to give you a heads up on that."

Bea then went on to explain the two "For Sale" units were one on top of the other. One was on the eighth floor and the other directly below on the seventh floor. Going up to the eighth floor first, the unit was at the end of the hall, in the angle of the L-shape. Opening the door, a well laid out one-bedroom unit awaited. Residents could go straight into a functional galley kitchen which led to a small dining area. If they went left there was the bathroom with a full bathtub/shower, and then the bedroom. The living area had the largest amount of space, but what attracted Stephen most to the layout was the balcony running along one entire side of the unit with a partial view of the Bay through the thick grove of trees across the street. Stephen could immediately see where his furniture would go and for the first time had a good feeling about what he was seeing.

Locking the door, they took the stairs down to the unit below. As they approached the door and Bea was about to use the realtor lockbox, the door to the right flew open and a short middle-aged woman jumped out.

She looked at Bea, then at Stephen, and said, "Are you looking at the unit next door?"

Bea said, "Yes" as she worked on the lockbox.

The woman got a smile that seemed a tad forced and stuck out her hand saying, "I'm Christine. I had *no idea* Stacy was really going to go ahead and sell her place."

Saying that, her smile suddenly vanished, and Christine's face contorted into a frown. But just as quickly, she turned her gaze to Stephen and said, "Well, I hope we get to be neighbors" and shut her door smiling.

This unit had the same layout but was a bit worse for the wear. Once inside the unit, someone had thought silver-foil wallpaper that looked like wrapping for a wedding gift would enhance the decor. It didn't. The linoleum in the kitchen was well worn and the appliances seemed a bit older. But the price was also considerably less. Seeing the balcony had the same, if slightly diminished, view as the unit above, Stephen decided to make an offer on the unit.

As promised, Bea calculated what a winning offer would be and shut the sales process down before the unit could be listed or viewed by anyone else. Stephen optimistically felt like this could work. Between signing the final paperwork and the expected move-in date, Stephen had Bea take him back so he could take measurements and plan where their things would go. One of the things he had noticed on his first visit was a couch aimed at the balcony and view. It was a white couch, and in the middle was a very dark spot/stain where someone's head rested. There was a well-worn indent, and this was obviously where Stacy sat most often. On this second visit back, Stephen couldn't help but notice the dark stain had grown and was spreading outward since his first visit. He also saw it was nowhere near as clean as it was then. And it hadn't been all that clean on the first visit either.

As move-in day got nearer, Stacy suddenly claimed she couldn't get into her new place. Stephen had already contracted the movers and needed to be out of his old place, so after a lot of back-and-forth, Stephen's belongings stayed on the moving van for a week while he stayed at a hotel near the airport. Stacy ended up moving the last of her items out at 4:45 pm and Stephen got the keys at 5 pm. While it was too late to move in anything that evening, he did take a look around and discovered an old steak in the freezer with half a bottle of vodka with lipstick stains on the spout. He also noticed she had left things like a broken portable clothes drying rack cavalierly tossed in above the refrigerator, as well as assorted trash and other small items.

Welcome home!

Only after being there a few days did Stephen begin to question his decision to purchase this unit. Trying to introduce himself to anyone he met, he quickly realized the layout of the building and the timing of work schedules (for those who still worked!) meant you rarely, if ever, encountered your neighbors.

The first one he did encounter was Amira. She lived to the left of Stephen in what he had been told was very swanky and luxurious three-bedroom unit. The one woman he had talked with in the lobby said Amira was the sister of some Middle Eastern oil dynasty. She was *very* well-off and plainly also very *off*. She couldn't have been more than five feet tall and was probably short of that. Very stout.

On Stephen's first day in the condo, the front door was open as more boxes were coming in, and out of the corner of his eye, he noticed this woman scurrying past with an alarmed look on her face.

Stephen waved and said, "Hello, I'm...."

But before he could finish, he saw her furiously jam her key into the front door, rush in, and slam the door shut.

After taking a few days off from work to get settled in, on Stephen's first day back at work, he set his alarm for 5 am. At around 4:49 he thought he heard some tapping. Straining to listen, the noise seemed to stop, and he rolled over for another ten minutes. Just as he started to doze off, again with the tapping. While he had had no visitors since moving in, he wondered if the noise was coming from the front door. Looking out of the peep hole he could just make out either the top of a very large dog or the head of a very short woman.

Opening the door there stood Amira. Not quite awake and a bit disoriented Stephen asked, "Uh, can I help you?"

No longer the frightened neighbor scurrying by quickly, Amira glared up and curtly said, "I have flight in two hours. I am locked out. I need to crawl into my bedroom from balcony. I've done it several times before."

More confused than before, the key phrase that was jumping out at him was, "I have done it several times before."

Shaking his head, Stephen pushed the door open and went to turn a light on. Amira came in, looking all around with an undisguised look of disgust on her face. Opening the sliding door to the balcony, Stephen stepped aside as Amira made her way to the end of the balcony that ended where her bedroom window begins. While the balcony was about three feet deep, there was an 18-inch cement ledge running along the side of the building under Amira's three bedroom windows and living room to her balcony. Watching this four-foot-something woman furiously try to throw her leg over the balcony railing and failing several times, Stephen wondered where this farce was going.

Amira turned a furious glance towards Stephen and spat, "Cannot reach. You need to go in and open door."

Whatever vestiges of sleep were immediately shocked from his system. Looking at the balcony, the ledge, Amira, and the drop, Stephen said firmly, "I am not doing that. If you want to do that, I can get a step ladder for you."

Amira glared without blinking or saying a word. Stephen went into the living room, found a stepladder, and set it up at the end of the balcony. Now, like a cat-burglar, Amira deftly got over the railing, smoothly went to the window, popped the screen out, jumped inside, grabbed the loose screen, and firmly banged the window shut pulling the curtains closed.

Welcome to the neighborhood!

Thinking this was an amusing story, when Bea checked in with Stephen a few days later to see how he was doing and how the move-in went, he recounted the early morning saga.

Bea screamed, "DO YOU KNOW WHAT KIND OF LIABILITY YOU OPENED YOURSELF UP TO?"

And then there was Christine. For all intents and purposes, she was Gladys Kravitz from "Bewitched." Whenever Stephen left to empty trash or head out, her door would fly open, and she'd be standing there smiling and asking where he was going.

And once she made the comment, "Oh, I heard you removing wallpaper this week."

Stephen, a bit alarmed and not wanting to start out as a bad neighbor, replied, "Was I making too much noise?"

Christine smiled and replied, "Oh no. But I hear EVERYHING."

As it turned out she saw everything as well. She had proudly proclaimed she was on the Architecture Review Board. She made sure everyone knew. It also turned out she WAS the Architecture Review Board. Coming home a bit late one evening, Stephen noticed a clipboard left somewhat in the middle of the hallway close to Christine's door. Worried that someone might step on it, Stephen picked it up and moved it over by her door. While picking it up he glanced at the top page. He saw the notes:

Unit 4528 has TOO MANY TYPES OF CHAIRS VISIBLE. Send notice: MUST REMOVE ALL BUT ONE STYLE IMMEDIATELY.

Unit 5720 has STATUARY! A NUDE WOMAN! (scribbled) it's ugly and the owner is a drunk. She'll tip it over and kill someone. REMOVE AT ONCE.

The list went on and on until Stephen saw his own unit mentioned, "Christmas lights MUST BE REMOVED BY JANUARY 1. REMOVE IMMEDIATELY!"

This angered Stephen as they were NOT Christmas lights. The balconies, while large, had no outdoor lighting. He had found some delightful Chinese lanterns at a garden center. While tempted to fight this, at this point, not seeing lights on anyone else's balcony, he acquiesced and grudgingly took them down.

After finally getting the horrid wedding-gift wallpaper removed, Stephen repainted, laid down a new layer of linoleum, and slowly pulled the place together. It wasn't until a few months later, after most of the work he could do himself was done, that Stephen realized there wasn't any social life here. Having previously lived in San Francisco where everyone knew each other and interacted with each other, this was like being stranded on a desert island.

Stephen decided to post an ad on Yahoo! Personals. The following days and weeks resulted in a hodge-podge of replies ranging from inquiries about tallies of Stephen's assets (to see if they were mergeable) to ones that simply sent oversized dick-pics and nothing else.

His usual dry response to these was, "I see you have a large presence on the internet. Could you tell me more about yourself?"

His responses were never replied to.

A few days short of pulling the posting altogether, Stephen received a reply from Daniel. It was thoughtful, not too long, not too short, and addressed most of the key points in the initial posting. Stephen wrote a reply, hit send, and then… nothing. So much for adventures on the Internet!

But a bit more than a month later a reply from Daniel showed up. Even though the posting was on Yahoo!, for whatever reason, Daniel didn't realize any reply would go to his Yahoo! e-mail account and hadn't seen Stephen's reply until then. Although Daniel was apologizing profusely, Stephen wasn't in a particularly good mood that day and shot back a brief note that basically said, "Take it from the top."

To his surprise, Daniel did. And this time with more detail and insight. The messages went back and forth for a little over a month until they both agreed to meet for coffee. Things went well and they started to date casually.

After a few months Daniel was spending more than a few nights a week at Stephen's, so they made the decision to give up Daniel's apartment and for Daniel to move into Stephen's place. Shortly after the formal move-in and house-warming party together, Stephen and Daniel ran into Christine.

While Stephen had picked up a shift in her tone and attitude towards him after Daniel moved in (had she viewed him as a potential romantic interest?), this afternoon her eyes were ablaze talking about the Homeowners Association Meeting happening the following Thursday. She was now an evangelist extolling the virtues and wisdom of attending the meetings. You'd have thought she had scored front row tickets to Beyoncé or Taylor Swift. She absolutely insisted they had to attend, so, rather than try to disagree, they both reluctantly agreed to go with her to the meeting.

Stepping out into the hall that Thursday, Christine was already standing outside her door waiting for them, pumped up and ready. Her eyes had that weird glow only a true fanatic can muster. As they walked the long hallway to the elevator, Christine felt it necessary to supply the backstory, so to speak. According to her, the majority of the Board were Middle Eastern, but from different countries and tribes. And (as she went on to explain in a breathless rush) in their culture it was acceptable to lie to anyone not from their own tribe. This was all sounding horrifically racist to both of them, and neither could tell if this information was a) factual and b) if it were, where she obtained it from.

Both Daniel and Stephen were extremely quiet when the elevator finally opened on the top floor where the meeting space was. It was packed. Absolutely jammed. Christine was bobbing about, waving, saying hello, and snaking her way through the throng to get in close to the actual meeting tables. Stephen and Daniel looked around and snagged a couple of seats a bit further away. Christine had now trained her full attention on the Board, which consisted mostly of middle-aged men, as they sat down. Once the meeting came to order, it immediately devolved into a shouting match between the board members.

One man stood, pointing a finger, and loudly proclaiming, "YOU KNOW THERE ARE NO MOVE-INS ON WEEKENDS! YET I SAW

YOU MOVING YOUR WHORE IN SATURDAY AFTERNOON! YOU THINK YOU WERE CLEVER, BUT I SAW YOU!"

In response, the man being accused stood up and bellowed, "LIAR! THAT WAS MY BELOVED COUSIN OVER FOR A VISIT! THERE WAS NO MOVING IN! YOU LIE!"

This type of back and forth went on and on and on. The volume kept rising, and in looking about, it felt like watching an audience at the coliseum as the Christians were being thrown to the lions.

After a relentless amount of this back-and-forth, Daniel stood up and shouted, "SHUT UP."

The room came to a dead stop. You could hear a pin drop. Everyone turned to look at him, and Daniel met their gaze. After a few seconds, the shouting resumed, and everyone was pulled back into the accusations being flung back and forth. When it finally came to end, not a single bit of official HOA business had been addressed or dealt with. Making their way to the elevator like two clubbed baby harp seals, Christine came rushing up to jam into the elevator with them at the very last second.

Eyes ablaze, staring straight ahead, she said, "Wasn't that amazing?"

Walking back to their unit in silence, once the door was shut both Daniel and Stephen said, "Wine?"

From that point onward, talk and discussions of the HOA were limited and brief. After a couple years of being there, Stephen and Daniel realized the limited homemade fixes to the kitchen needed to be addressed with a remodel. Stephen went by the Management Office in the building to pick up the paperwork to see what the rules and requirements were for such a project. Provided permits were acquired for any and all items, and work was constrained to the hours of 8:30 am to 4:30 pm everything looked fairly straightforward.

Finding a contractor turned out to be a more challenging proposition. Assuming it would be as simple as a few phone calls to find someone, it turned out that in the red-hot housing market it seemed *everyone* was doing a remodel. And worse, major remodels of large homes. Not a one-bedroom, one-bathroom condo with a galley kitchen. Getting turned down repeatedly after several calls, Stephen and Daniel started to go into contracting offices in person to see if that made a difference. Two offices flat out said it was too small and not worth their while. The third contractor said they'd come out and give a quote. Buoyed by this, they made an appointment.

On the appointed day, the man came in, took a quick look around, and sniffed, "This is entirely too small to waste my time on. But I will do you a favor and not charge you for coming out, like I usually do."

Coming back from lunch one Saturday Daniel noticed a Kitchen and Cabinet place that was open. Walking in was a vivacious young woman, who it turned out had just started working there. She was from Sweden and had only been in the country for a few months. Explaining what they wanted done, and tentatively explaining the size of the unit and the scope of the job, Stephen and Daniel were delighted when Kerstin said no problem and pulled out contract paperwork.

Feeling like things were *finally* on track Stephen and Daniel stopped by the cabinet place to give them a deposit the next day. Kerstin wasn't there.

The man behind the counter looked at the contract and check and chuckled, "Ah, Kerstin's little job. She just started and this was the first thing she's ever booked."

Daniel exchanged a look with Stephen that implied, "What are we getting into?"

A couple of weeks later Kerstin asked if they would like to go with her to select the granite for the kitchen. They met her at the shop and got into her SUV. Kerstin merrily regaled them with taking her girlfriends from Sweden to the Exotic Erotic Ball. She said her girlfriends weren't sure what they should wear.

Kerstin said, "I told them, you wear what I'm going to wear. High Heels!" Laughing heartily, she then asked if they wanted some Ecstasy.

Now with a contractor in place, work had begun. While very disruptive in such a small space, it went fairly quickly. The downside was the occasional note from the 'HOA' (Christine) accusing them of drilling or something equally ludicrous at times when it was impossible to be happening. The project wrapped just before Christmas that year, and a combination holiday party and "The kitchen/bathroom remodel is done" celebration took place.

For Christmas, Stephen and Daniel had gone up to Washington state to spend the holiday with Stephen's parents. Upon returning, after stepping into their place, Stephen felt a *squish* underfoot, and stooping down, realized the carpet was saturated with water. A little beyond that spot Stephen found a damp note. The note was from a neighbor on the other side of the hall that they rarely saw but were cordial with.

The note said, "I don't know if you know this or not, but Christine has been doing an illegal remodel on her place for the past few months. I know you both work in the City, so you're not around to see and hear the mess and noise. Well, the cheap-ass idiot she hired broke the water pipes in her bathroom when he was redoing the shower. And her bathroom abuts your entryway closet. Check your closet. I know she would never tell you, but I'd start some fans and maybe call a mold remediation company. She's a real piece of work."

Stephen was FURIOUS. No wonder Christine hadn't been popping out whenever they walked by, and why casual conversations had yielded the fact there hadn't been any architectural warnings handed out for a while. Stephen and Daniel pulled out all the fans they had, a space heater, and turned everything up full blast. Stephen suspected the fans would annoy Christine, but tough. Thankfully they had gotten back just as this happened and things dried out quickly and completely.

From that point on, it was very quiet with the HOA. There were newsletters sent about every two months. For the most part these were only about benign subjects but sometimes (buried deep inside) were warnings about the age of the elevators, which were now over thirty years old, and the possibility of a special assessment. This along with the fact both Stephen and Daniel had a lot of belongings and had taken on a storage unit at a not insubstantial cost was worrying. So, every other weekend or so Stephen and Daniel started looking at open houses.

At first, they went looking at older stand-alone houses. The first one, in Hayward, looked promising in the listing. As they drove up, there was an odd vibe to the place. As they entered, the realtor gave them a pitying look and rather mechanically handed them the flyer. The first thing both Stephen and Daniel noticed was a smell. Earthy, damp, possibly agricultural? It permeated the entire house. The home was older than it had appeared in the listing, and there was something off about the flow. As they made their way around, they arrived as the master bedroom.

What stopped them both cold was there was a deadbolt and padlock on the OUTSIDE of the bedroom door. It was so menacing and sinister looking, neither of them bothered to ask to see inside of it.

As they were turning to leave, the realtor gave a pitiful shrug and resignedly said, "Thank you for coming."

Neither Stephen nor Daniel had ever smelled a dead body, but both were pretty sure the odor in the house is what one would smell like. They couldn't get out there fast enough.

The following weekend, a house was listed a bit closer to where they were currently living. Pitched as a "view home," they found their way around the winding streets the led to the address. Seeing a group of parked cars, they assumed they had reached their destination. The front was VERY 1950s with faded turquoise stucco and dated "artistic" brickwork.

As they stepped inside, they were standing in the main living room with a group of other open-house attendees. Everyone had just stopped and stared. The floor was raw cement that sloped down to the very center of the room where there was a very prominent drain directly next to a power outlet on the floor. Frankly, it felt like the set for one of the "Saw" movies. There was no staging or furniture. Just this large room with the floor angling down to a big drain and a power outlet. No one seemed able to move past that.

With more questions than answers, Stephen and Daniel continued in. Once past the raw cement living room, the remainder of the house felt like it was made of cardboard. As promised, there was a view, but they both realized the back of the house was standing on very thin uprights hanging over the edge of the very steep drop. When another couple stepped into the room, it noticeably shook. Everyone got wide-eyed and backed out of the shaky room as quickly as possible. Passing through the dungeon/living room, they couldn't leave the house fast enough.

Stephen was tempted to lean into the mortified onlookers and whisper, "They're still looking for the body."

They viewed a few more homes, but all had either major architectural flaws (including one that had a massive visible crack on the foundation when you stepped out back) or were in neighborhoods that were completely unacceptable. The worst was on a very steep hill surrounded by a lot of dead or dying trees and vegetation. When they walked in, they were greeted by sun-bleached, orange shag-carpet. Some mildly interesting stained glass, but the most curious item was a spiral staircase that went upstairs but had a padlocked trap door at the bottom!

The agent, sensing their gaze, spoke up, "That goes to the tenant downstairs. In fact, there are four tenants. Three live in this building in the levels below, and the fourth lives in the studio out by the garage."

She was pointing through the window and about fifty yards up the street was a very dark and decrepit building, mostly hanging over the steep drop-off, and held up by spindly supports. At the end was a VERY DARK and somewhat disturbing looking room with peculiar metal and wood items stacked up against the windows. Nodding, they explored the rest of the house, which felt like it was pulled together from scrap plywood and cast-offs from a Home Depot. Also, with the stained glass all around and the fact that none of the windows opened, on this moderately warm day, the house felt like was over 100 degrees.

Hard pass.

With the housing market heating up and the pickings in their price range obviously limited, they reluctantly started limiting their searches to other HOAs.

One Friday Daniel mentioned there was going to be an open house at Thornwillow Heights the following Sunday.

Stephen was working on a project and offhandedly said, "We could drive by Saturday while we're out to see if it's worthwhile to bother going."

So, that Saturday after lunch and after finishing some errands, they started driving up the hills toward the address. The first thing both of them noticed was the elevation. They were significantly higher up than they were at their current location. No longer were tall trees obscuring the dazzling views of the Bay. They kept climbing and climbing until they came to the street with the listing. This wasn't a large building with people stacked on top of each other, but groups of townhouses. Some with two shared walls, but many with only one. The architecture was definitely dated by now, but the street looked maintained. But it was the view that got them both. While not all that high up, being that much higher than the surrounding areas, it felt like you were on top of the world. Just by driving past the unassuming location, they both agreed stopping by for the open house wouldn't be a bad idea.

Pulling onto to the street early Sunday afternoon, there were a fair number of cars parked in the driveway and nearby. Walking towards the unassuming unit, it seemed nice enough, but nothing special. But when they walked in the door, the "wow factor" hit them both. Unobstructed 180° views of the San Francisco Bay all the way from San Jose, across to the Peninsula, and on up to Marin. And as it turned out, this was a remarkably clear day. Stepping into the townhouse, the layout impressed both of them.

Going down into the living room Stephen noticed the entire width of the place had a fabulous view. There was a modest living room with an area off to the side that would be perfect for two desks and makeshift office. Walking upstairs, again the "wow factor" hit when Stephen realized the guest room and master bedroom both had the same dazzling views. The guest room had its own full bathroom, as did the master bathroom which also featured a Jacuzzi® tub along with a separate shower. Downstairs had a half-bath just off the entryway.

The price was more than either felt truly comfortable with, but when they left, both Stephen and Daniel said, "That's the one."

Exhaling, Stephen said, "Should I call Bea and see what she thinks?"

Daniel agreed, so they went home and called. Bea told them she knew the agent selling the place and they'd be accepting offers on Monday.

She asked, "If you think you want this, I can pull together an offer I know they'll accept."

Although a bit more over the asking than either Stephen or Daniel were expecting, reluctantly (but with some excitement) they both agreed to move forward.

Monday rolled around and the phone didn't ring. Neither Stephen nor Daniel commented on it, but by around 7:30 pm, with no notice from Bea, they both felt a bit dejected and decided it hadn't gone their way.

They were both commiserating and saying, "It was probably for the best," when the phone rang. It was Bea. "You're new homeowners, congratulations!"

Shit! Realizing they had no financing lined up, a mad scramble went into place to get the down payment by the close of business Tuesday. While Daniel started looking at loan options, Stephen went down to the bank he had been at since his first job in 1972. He nervously stood in line where there was one man ahead of him. Not intending to listen in, the man in front was getting very irate and loud.

The man shouted, "YOU DO NOT UNDERSTAND! THIS CHECK HAS TO CLEAR TODAY! I'M BUYING A HOUSE AND THEY ABSOLUTELY MUST HAVE THIS CHECK IN HAND TODAY!"

The teller behind the counter pushed her glasses up a bit, and then tilted her head downward so she was looking over her glasses at the man. She said, "I'm sorry sir, but a check this size needs to have a four-day hold put on it to make sure it clears."

The man shouted, called her vile names, and threatened to speak to her supervisor. Nothing he said or did ruffled or upset the teller. After ten minutes of not getting anywhere, the man stormed out, slamming the front doors loudly.

Looking over his shoulder at the exiting man, Stephen turned to the teller and smiled and nervously laughed a bit, "Hi. Uh, I'm doing the exact same thing he was doing. Uh, minus the shouting and swearing. We chanced upon what we think is our dream home Sunday, and if this check doesn't clear by tonight, we're going to lose it."

The teller smiled back and took Stephen's paperwork. She punched his account number into the system, made a few mouse clicks, and smiling said, "I see you've been with us since 1972. I don't see any issues. I'll put this in right now and you should be good to go. Enjoy your new home."

Whew…!

The check did clear, financing was acquired, and everything seemed to fall into place. One of the first things was the discovery packet. Stephen and Daniel sat down with Bea and went over it. Stephen noticed there was an acute lack of any HOA newsletters. The few that were in the package went back three, maybe four, years.

He thought, thinking of Christine, "They seem to be quite hands-off with the residents but that isn't a bad thing at all."

Everything thing else looked good. They would have a place with their own private entrance and garage. They no longer had to worry about running into Christine or having their weird next-door neighbor knock on the door with yet another lockout. (The last time Amira had tried to make the same balcony pitch, Daniel had stepped in and said, "NO. That's far too dangerous. You need to call a locksmith.") And this looked like it would be a significant upgrade from the current HOA.

And Stephen thought about all of this as he was taking his last look around the condo that had been their home for the last eight years. While there had been a lot of "firsts" and good memories there, there were also a lot of hassles and issues to deal with on an almost daily basis. Saying goodbye felt like the right thing to do.

Chapter 2 – Andrea

Andrea woke up with the sun streaming in through her bedroom window. Not prone to setting an alarm, she stretched and stayed in bed for a while, listening to the birds sing. She remembered a time when she first lived here when there weren't many birds. There weren't many trees either. Or landscaping to speak of. But that had changed over the last few years. She needed to be at the semiconductor company's office building in Fremont at some point today. One of the perks of being a contractor was she went in when she felt like it and left when the mood struck. On the few occasions she had been questioned about her tardiness or early departure times, she'd simply state, "I have an emergency with another contract I'm working on and needed (or need to) deal with it immediately." There were never any follow-up questions.

Petting her German Shepherd, she slowly got out of bed. Wrapping a thick robe around herself, she made her way into the bathroom and threw some cold water on her face. Staring into the mirror through somewhat bloodshot eyes she was starting to see the lines and sun-damage that comes with spending a lot of time outdoors. Rubbing a squirt of Nivea over her face and hands, she fluffed her greying (with a bit of mouse-brown peeking out on the sides) hair and made her way downstairs. Filling the water dish, she got a treat down for her dog and put some water on to boil. Filling her favorite mug, she made a steaming cup of chamomile tea. While the tea was steeping, she removed her robe and put on a bulky cable-knit sweater and headed for her small patio area. Since moving in, she had made this her private oasis. Adding pots and carefully planting flowers and herbs, it was her very own personal Eden. Gathering her tea and grabbing her things, she bundled up a bit more as the morning chill hadn't burnt off quite yet. Sitting out back, she started her day the way she started every day: journaling.

Looking over at her almost-empty cup of tea she opted to make another cup before getting the day fully started. As the water was boiling, Andrea thought about the circular route life had taken her on to get back up to Thornwillow Heights. She recalled being mostly happy living with Tamara when the two of them lived three streets over shortly after the development opened. Yes, they certainly had their differences and Tamara studying for and taking the California Bar Exam definitely put a lot of stress on both of them. But it seemed like a companionable groove had been struck, when out of the blue, Tamara announced she was going back to her husband. Andrea had been totally blindsided. She knew they had parted *"as friends,"* as the saying goes, but she had no idea they were still in close contact or even that this could be a possibility. With little to no discussion, Tamara was gone, and Andrea couldn't maintain the residence alone.

That necessitated the move to Union City and a much less desirable neighborhood and living situation. The apartment wasn't very far from the noisy freeway and the area and the tenants were... riffraff. Moving in, Andrea had turned a blind eye to her surroundings and neighbors and kept to herself. But then *that couple* moved in next door. She couldn't even remember their names now, but she could still see the woman. Jet-black hair styled with Bettie Page bangs, always wearing a slutty looking crop-top, showing off her flabby stomach and back tattoos. Eye make-up like a goth-cartoon, and more piercings and metal on her face than you'd find in a hardware store. When the goth queen had said hello to her that one day, Andrea had been startled, but kept her reply dry and brief. For whatever reason, this seemed to set some type of war situation into motion.

The woman was coming and going at all hours of the night and early morning, doors slamming, arguing that could clearly be heard. Rather than say anything directly, Andrea had written an *anonymous* note and left it on the woman's car. It quickly became clear, though, that the note wasn't that anonymous. Trash and refuse started showing up outside Andrea's door, and then she found her precious Land Rover (inherited from her aunt) keyed. Twice. The final straw was coming out to four flat tires. It was then that she knew she *had* to get out and saw the listing at Thornwillow Heights. The listing was on a different street, on the opposite side of the *view homes.* The price, while a bit steep, was just this side of doable. The private back patio had more than made up for the lack of a view, but she still was able to take the view in with her long walks with her dog or just hiking the various hills and trails surrounding the place.

After journaling for more than an hour, Andrea roused herself, and headed for the kitchen. She finished washing the dishes from dinner, dried everything, and then put it all away. She then decided to stick her head out the front door and pick some fresh flowers. She tried to always have them throughout the house, and at the moment the kitchen was missing that essential component. Taking a deep breath, she realized there wasn't much more she could do to kill any more time, so she threw her sweater onto the dining room table and went upstairs to knock out a shower before heading out.

What was making her more resistant to leaving this morning was her new contract. Or more specifically, the person she not only had to share very close quarters with, but "collaborate" with, Luke. With that thought alone, she shivered a bit and got back into bed. Pulling the covers all the way up, she remembered when the contract had come in. It was not only lucrative but also had a lot of potential. Not a terribly long drive down to the facility office, Andrea felt this could really be a professional turning point.

She recalled that first day. Taking a bit of extra time to dress carefully, somewhere between office casual and new-tech chic, she gathered her notes and notebooks, and made sure to grab her new designer eyewear as she headed south anticipating this new challenge. What she enjoyed most was the open-endedness of her position, part project manager, part marketing specialist, part SEO advisor, and part content manager. Walking in, feeling confident and excited, she was introduced to Suzanne, the head of HR. Suzanne was very warm and said they were all looking forward to her joining the team and felt her involvement would really enhance the project they were currently prioritizing.

Once signed in, Suzanne led her through a maze of desks, which Andrea looked at warily, not being a fan of open-office settings. But she brightened as Suzanne took her down a hallway that clearly had individual offices. Andrea thought, "Yes! This is more like it." Stopping in front of a doorway, the first warning sign was how much furniture was jammed into what had clearly been a single-use space. There were two massive workstations, face-to-face. And behind the one furthest into the room sat Luke. And all those new-job fantasies came to a screeching halt.

Sitting behind the workstation was one of the most repugnant men she had ever seen. A small, flat, greasy face plastered onto a giant head, sitting on top of a morbidly obese body. Thin, lank, greasy hair peeked out from underneath a dirty trucker's hat, that shockingly had the outline of a naked woman, like you'd see on trucker's long distance mud flaps on it.

Andrea thought, "In what universe would ANY company allow that type of apparel to be worn on the job?"

She was about to find out. His dirty T-Shirt said, "Winners Do It Every Day," but the "a" in Day had a big piece of pepperoni obscuring it. How long it had been there was up for debate. She was further appalled by the filthy, baggy shorts, which you could somewhat look up, as he had his VERY dirty feet up on the desk. A pair of rubber beach sandals were laying askew by the foot of his desk. His small beady eyes were enlarged by a pair of Coke-bottle lenses in frames that looked like refugees from a 1950s health video.

Seeing Suzanne enter the room, Luke had shot up from his sprawled position far too quickly and frantically turned his monitor off. Andrea shivered and couldn't begin to imagine the horrors he had probably been looking at.

Suzanne gave Luke a pale smile and said, "Luke, this is Andrea. This is the consultant we told you would be joining the team. She will be sharing this space with you. I KNOW you will BEHAVE YOURSELF and do everything possible to make Andrea feel welcome and get her up to speed on the project."

With that Suzanne gave a disapproving glance at Luke, as she turned to Andrea arching her eyebrows with a "What can I do?" smile and left them alone.

Andrea, now with a sickly-sweet smile on *her* face, nodded at Luke, who grunted some type of acknowledgement and jockeyed back into place, tilting his screen, making sure only he could see it. With a slight shudder, Andrea set about trying to create her own barrier, and set up her workspace. She already knew she would be having a lot of "the other client has an emergency" situations on the horizon.

Thinking about driving every day to sit opposite Luke gave her pause. As much as he brought up deep waves of revulsion within her, Luke seemed oblivious to how she felt about him. Long ago Andrea had mastered the art of appearing to listen to someone, even while she had her own internal dialog taking place. And even more useful, with a few well-placed sympathetic nods and the occasional "Uh-huh," people felt she was not only listening *but cared.* She couldn't figure out why people always referred to her with phrases like "She's SO NICE!" but came to realize her lack of replies was perceived as concern in what people were saying and in turn, the perception that she *was* truly interested in them. Knowing she possessed this hidden super-power, Andrea enjoyed playing with people. More often than not, she'd smile and offer a cheery "Hello" to people she quietly loathed and despised.

And now Luke was yet another one of those clueless saps. While he was a textbook example of what women were NOT looking for, Andrea now found herself on the receiving end of long monologues about not being able to find the right woman (It was a woman right? Not a man?), past failures, both professionally and personally, and his fears and concerns with the current project they were both now working on. While Andrea didn't relish hearing more of Luke's complaints, he was foolish enough to tell her more than he probably should about not only the project, but the company overall.

Andrea had been looking for a situation where she could jettison her contracting status and come on board full-time. With the information she had gleaned from Luke, she just might be able to swing the situation in that direction. And get rid of Luke in the process…

After one more look around her comfortable and inviting home, she felt it would probably be for the best if she got herself organized and went into the office. Before getting everything in the car and heading out, she decided to take her dog out for a quick walk. She heard the moving van coming down the street before she saw it. She had noticed the two men going to the open house a couple of months earlier and had seen one or both at various times afterwards. Both appeared to be in their 50s, one with a beard, the other with a big bushy mustache. Based on their attire and the costs of units up here, she assumed they worked in tech. And now it appeared they were moving in. It had been a very long time since there had been any shifts in the neighborhood. She hoped this wouldn't upset the established balance.

Chapter 3 – Sandra

Sandra was up every morning at 3:30 am sharp each and every day. Weekends included. Right out of bed, CNN was turned on as she got onto her elliptical machine with the Wall Street Journal propped open in front of her while she did a relentless 1-hour workout. This was followed by half an hour of yoga while she tuned into MSNBC, followed by fifteen minutes in the custom steam room she had built adjacent to her master bathroom, and then a brisk ten minutes in the custom shower with its twenty-four nozzles specifically designed to hit each and every square-inch of her body.

Out of the shower, Sandra went to her walk-in closet, where everything was meticulously stored by type, style, and color. The color part was negligible, as her entire wardrobe went from light grays and tans to charcoal and black. Nary a sign of any bright colors. The materials ranged from tweeds to wools to silks. No filmy chiffons or polyesters. The silk blouses she had were either black or charcoal with a smattering of off-white or cream. Oddly, with the limited color palette, her wardrobe never came off as severe. A sort of stylish business-chic, her single concession to any overt feminine accoutrements was a single strand of white pearls, or more often than not, a simple sterling silver chain with a stunning piece of malachite dangling from it. Her strawberry-blond hair was generally pulled back into a business-casual bun, and her face went sans make-up. Sandra strove to radiate control and a no-nonsense business appearance.

Out the door before sun-up and rarely home until late in the evening, Sandra had her life as fine-tuned as a racecar. Many years ago, she joined a new bio-tech company, the odds not being in the company's favor when they launched. But perseverance, talent, and drive pushed them forward. And Sandra's steely resolve and steady hand had helped navigate that climb to success. Granted, her degree was in Liberal Arts, but it didn't impede her path from General Admin up to a Senior VP reporting directly to the CEO. A not inconsiderable accomplishment, but Sandra was more than a bit bitterly aware that without sexism, she would not only have been President long ago, but probably CEO and then Chairman of the Board. Still, the hard work, hours, and a limited social life had yielded their rewards.

As she was zipping up the soft-leather boots she was opting for today, she looked around her house. She liked her home. She had created it from the ground up. Some felt it was a bit sterile. The soft cream of the paint didn't deter from a gallery-like effect for the well-chosen and sparsely placed pieces of art. Each with their own UV safe halogen spot-light, while the living/dining area featured sturdy, but extremely high-end pieces of furniture accumulated over the last twenty years.

The kitchen, spotless and gleaming, was as much of a chef's kitchen as anyone could want. The most high-end cooktop, oven, and appliances gleamed in the sunlight-bright spotlights. High end pots and pans hung from the Avance Tabco® SCT-36 rack. The wine refrigerators were home to a very carefully cultivated collection of every type of wine available. Not visible to visitors, was a cabinet off to the side that hosted an expansive selection of very high-end scotches, bourbons, gins, and vodkas from around the world. Sandra was seldom in the kitchen, but that didn't stop her from having the cleaning service come in three times a week to keep it in that "It looks like it's never been used" look.

Yes, Sandra really loved her home. Until she didn't. Why did that Schuster man have to buy the place next door and move in? She felt herself grinding her teeth with this thought and had to mentally stop the action. She remembered when Lavonne and George lived there. It was perfection. Quiet retirees, Lavonne would come over occasionally with extra lemons or limes from her bushes, as well as some of the home-grown herbs and vegetables she liked to grow. George would wave and say hello, but he kept to himself.

The only time there had been any sort of intrusion was once when Lavonne had asked, "Are you doing woodworking now?"

Sandra, confused, said, "No. Why would you ask?"

Lavonne, smiling said, "Oh, George said he's heard what sounded like a sander or some shop item coming from your place. He said he heard you grunting and moaning, like you were really pushing into it. You have such exquisite taste in art, we thought if you were getting into wood working, we'd love to see what you're doing."

Sandra smiled tightly, her cheeks flushing a bit, and said, "I'm just taking care of some small areas in the house. No woodworking to show." And she thought, "Note to self; look into soundproofing the bedroom and look for something quieter the next time I'm up at Good Vibrations."

And then George had the fall. It looked like a hip replacement was all that was needed, but that opened a Pandora's box of medical issues, and before anyone knew it, the house was on the market. If Sandra could do one thing in life, it would be to go back to that moment in time and offer to buy their house herself. Still, not really anticipating big changes, the house sold within two days. Lavonne and George were gone to a retirement community and there was that Schuster man.

Ugh! Sandra recalled seeing him for the first time. She saw him get out of his black BMW 7 Series. Emerging from the shiny vehicle, glossy black hair, a tanned face, and a smile that looked like the most expensive (and obvious) set of veneers she had ever seen. She had assumed he was the realtor. To her dismay he wasn't. Charging over and introduced himself as her new neighbor he got way too close and was way too smarmy. Smiling tightly, she welcomed him to the neighborhood and then dashed into her front door, pulling the front curtains tightly shut, and turning the security system on.

It was less than a month later when Sandra realized her oasis and castle was no longer her cherished sanctuary. When Lavonne and George had lived there, they never as much as peered out their second story window, either into her living room through the massive floor-to-ceiling windows Sandra had customized, nor into her backyard, where Sandra would often sit out to mediate, read business prospectuses, or on an especially nice day, sunbathe. Suddenly Sandra was VERY aware of that Schuster man's sleazy smile greeting her as she walked into her living room, wearing only her Versace luxury spa robe, or that VERY UNFORTUNATE TIME, nothing at all. Feeling VERY exposed, she now felt it necessary to have drapes installed. But this was just the start. She discovered he started to build a deck. A VERY LARGE DECK, which would allow him total visual access not only to her backyard, but to her bedroom as well!

When out working in her meticulously laid out garden one weekend, she heard THAT VOICE bellow, "Hey neighbor!"

Looking up, she stated very flatly, "You know, I wish you had asked me about the deck. I believe it is oversized to the property, and frankly, it makes me feel very exposed."

The smile vanished instantly from his face as he said, "Tough. It's a done deal. It cleared permitting at city hall. Maybe you'll want to avoid the backyard more in the future. Also…" now smiling again, he said "You don't have to put curtains up on my account."

Sandra, flushed with anger, got up and marched into her home. She picked up the phone and called her lawyer. Barely containing herself she told her lawyer in no uncertain terms he was to use each and every legal weapon at his disposal to make her neighbor's life a living hell! In the meantime, she consulted a construction firm and had an oversized fence installed, hoping to mute the view into her back yard.

Unfortunately for Sandra, she underestimated Schuster until she received the restraining order based on the illegally constructed fence and saw he had an equally aggressive legal team that would not only call her bluff but raise the stakes. Holding the summons in her hand, she was shaking with fury. She immediately contacted her contractor, who had done all the work on the house. On more than one occasion he had expressed interest in the home, should she ever want to sell. She brokered an all-cash deal that would close immediately.

As things were unfolding quickly, Sandra realized an HOA would be the answer to her problems. People cannot do just whatever they want. It's all governed by a set of rules that everyone has to adhere to. Pulling up several realty sites, she saw the listing for Thornwillow Heights. A call was placed to her realtor.

Chapter 4 – Settling In

Moving into Thornwillow Heights had thrown a few learning curves at Stephen and Daniel. After years in apartment settings and then in condos that were, for all intents and purposes, apartment settings, the townhouse took a little getting used to. While there was no one living above or below, the walls were so unexpectedly thin you could clearly hear everything going on in the units on either side.

Stephen and Daniel had found out the couple on the right side both worked in tech. Not having seen them or met them yet, it sounded like a football team doing their daily training when they were home. You could hear their garage door open, and then, "BAM!" The door into the house would slam loudly, causing some of the items on the walls to vibrate. And then it would sound like a group of husky athletes were racing up and down the stairs as fast as they could run. Stephen was rather shocked when he discovered the main "runner" was a VERY petite younger woman who couldn't have weighed more than 105 pounds and stood a hair over five feet tall. And her husband wasn't that much bigger!

And then on the other side there were the dogs. One of the rules at their previous HOAs and apartments had been that no pets were allowed. As Stephen and Daniel worked a lot, it hadn't crossed their minds to get one. The new HOA allowed pets. No more than three dogs or cats. The couple next door had two dogs, one was a Rottweiler and the other a Chihuahua. To their amazement and extreme displeasure, it was the Chihuahua that was the source of continual noise. Despite the fact the unit had double-paned windows, even with the sliding doors shut tight, if either Stephen or Daniel were on the phone the inevitable question was, "Oh, you have dogs?" What made this worse were the owners of the dogs.

While still unloading things as they were moving in, a car had pulled up next door and the most morbidly obese man Stephen had ever seen wrestled his way out of the driver's seat. The man was immense. If someone had said he was starring in one of those reality shows about a person so large they had to cut most of the wall away to get them out, Stephen would have believed them.

Waving and saying, "Hello," the obese man completely ignored Stephen and made his way into his garage.

"Probably the only opening to the house big enough for him to enter easily," Stephen thought.

Shortly thereafter another car pulled up and a severe looking woman got out. Bearing more than a passing resemblance to Roseanne Barr when she starred in *She Devil*, large mole included. Again, Stephen waved, and again, was completely ignored.

What soon became obvious was the man was far too large to take his dogs for a walk and who knew what "Roseanne's" thing was, but the result was their dogs did their business on the deck behind their house. Not only that, but once they did their business, it stayed there. On the deck that only Stephen and Daniel (and the owners) could see. It was also obvious neither of the animal's owners even bothered opening the screen for them as you could see it was completely pushed out, like the coyote from the Roadrunner cartoons had dashed through it. Between the tattered screen, the dog shit, and the non-stop barking, Stephen and Daniel were not very happy. Trying to be *good neighbors*, they had held off filing a complaint with the HOA, but their patience was nearing the breaking point.

A couple of months after moving in, Daniel's parents came to visit. They had gone out to dinner and had gotten back later in the evening. As Stephen was stepping out of the driver's seat, the nasty little Chihuahua came rushing out and nipped at Stephen.

Not frightened, but VERY ANNOYED, Stephen bellowed, "GET THE FUCK OUT OF HERE!" as "Roseanne" suddenly appeared, scooped the yapping dog up in her arms and scurried into their garage.

Throwing a fearful look over her shoulder as her garage door noisily shut. Annoyed, but not giving it much more thought, the next morning the doorbell rang. Standing there was "Roseanne."

Stephen tightened up and was ready to unload several months of frustration when "Roseanne" said, "Sorry about last night. It won't happen again. We're moving. My husband's mother will be moving in. She's very quiet. And she makes jam."

Hearing the word "moving," Stephen's face relaxed. Opening the screen door, he was handed an incredibly tiny jar of something resembling jam. After he gave a brief, "Thank you," "Roseanne" turned and walked away quickly.

Very shortly after that, "Roseanne," the man they assumed to be her husband, and the two dogs were gone. In their place a very frail looking, elderly woman. Things seemed like they were looking up. The incessant barking had stopped, someone had cleared up the dog shit, and they had even replaced the shredded screen door. But the next Sunday, around 9:30 am, Stephen went out to get the paper, and there wasn't one there. Assuming they were late, or had missed the street, Stephen called, and a replacement showed up around 11. Then the next Sunday, the same thing happened. And the following Sunday after that. Assured the delivery person had not bypassed their place, despite wanting to sleep in a bit, Stephen set his alarm for 5:30 am the following Sunday, wrapped up in a warm robe, and stood in the walkway, just out of sight of the street, or neighbors.

A little before 6 am Stephen heard a vehicle driving up the street and heard the sound of a paper landing in the driveway. Just as he was about to step out and retrieve it, he heard the garage door open next door. The little old lady scurried out onto Stephen's driveway. Before she could reach the paper, Stephen stepped out of the walkway and looked her square in the eye. She met his gaze, and faster than anyone would have expected, she darted back into her garage and the door closed quickly. That was the end of the paper thief.

The only other neighbors they had actually met were the couple, Jane and John, across the driveway in the next building over and another woman, Thelma, who would just appear out of nowhere from time to time. Jane was retired and her husband John was semi-retired. They were very friendly and welcoming. Unlike the vast majority of people they saw out and about wearing tank tops, shorts, sweats, and in many cases, pajamas, Jane's hair was always done, and she was always wearing something that didn't look like it was plucked directly from the dryer, and John wore actual long-sleeved shirts and trousers. They had been part of the initial group that bought into this section of the development and had lived there ever since. Jane made mention of John being on the Board of Directors once upon a time, but it had not been very pleasant, so they'd been more than happy to keep to themselves after that. While not seeing them much, both were always friendly and would stop for a chat if they happened to be out front at the same time.

In the meantime, between leaving early and generally getting home late in the afternoon, Stephen and Daniel rarely, if ever, saw any of their neighbors. And other than an unexpected leak at the kitchen window a few months after moving in, they had no interaction with the management company or the HOA for a several years.

It had been a very trying month at work for Stephen. The marketing company both he and Daniel now worked at together had been sold at the end of the previous year. Despite claims things would continue "as is," in February they abruptly fired Daniel from his position as well as most of the support staff that had all become a bit of a family unit. Daniel had pivoted quickly to becoming a consultant and was working a long-term contract in the city. But more surprising to Stephen was they kept him on.

However, while he had been the Creative Director responsible for web design, product verticals, sitting in on business meetings, and all collateral materials and branding for the company, he was now relegated to only creating a mind-numbingly large number of Internet banner ads designed to trick people into clicking on them and then supplying their personal information.

Shortly after this abrupt change and bored beyond words, more as entertainment for himself than anything, Stephen created an obviously fake mortgage calculator graphic. He included it with the myriad number of other ads he had churned out that day. To his amazement, and that of the new overlords, the ad did spectacularly well. It out-performed all the other ads combined, including the ones created by the new owner's team in New York. While good news, of sorts, this now felt like indentured servitude to Stephen, as these were the only types of ads he was tasked with making now. He'd make them in blue, maybe green, change a button from red to orange, shift some aspects from top to bottom, then back again. But all of them were a variation on the original one he had created in a fit of boredom. All of them worked and all of them bored Stephen out of his mind.

On top of that, the previous head of the company had had a penchant for hiring dysfunctional people and seemed to enjoy the discord and flare-ups that clashing personalities created. The most egregious hire was the airhead "salesperson" they found when the company two floors below had gone out of business and was selling off their office furniture. What Tallulah did for the previous company was hard to ascertain as she didn't have the common sense to come in from the rain. Almost literally.

A few weeks after joining the company as a salesperson Tallulah had drifted into Stephen's office and asked, "So… I'm housesitting for a guy in Pacific Heights. The one thing he asked me to do was to make sure I covered the grill outside if it started raining. Well… I go out a lot at night and often don't get back until early morning. If you know what I mean? Anyway, I got in last night and it had been pouring. I mean, water was everywhere outside. The grill was soaked, and the rain just kept coming down. So, my question is, as long as it's raining and the water is just running over and through the grill, it won't rust? Right?"

Stephen had been talking to the woman from Accounting and they both looked at each other, stifled a giggle, and the woman from Accounting said, "Uh, yes. Right."

Mollified, Tallulah walked away smiling, while Stephen just rolled his eyes.

Not too long before the changes that would pigeonhole Stephen into the hateful banner ads, he had been tasked to expand one of the offerings in a new vertical on their site. And unfortunately, Tallulah had become the default salesperson for it. Against his better judgment, he had asked Tallulah to provide a list of current and potential clients in this vertical and also supply a list of keywords and any write-ups for use on the website.

To Stephen's shock and dismay, Tallulah instead sent him an Excel spreadsheet, where she had inserted pictures, backgrounds, and an immense amount of unrelated (and ugly) clipart in her attempt to design *her* content. In the first place, the website had a uniform look-and-feel across all the offerings. In the second place, what she had created was completely different (and frankly 3rd grade level hideous) from that look-and-feel. And finally, Tallulah's vertical was the smallest of all of them and provided the least amount of revenue.

After sending her effort to Stephen, Tallulah walked into his office with a triumphant smile on her face extolling the virtues and "ability" to *design* in Excel. Stephen was beside himself, and said, "Firstly, we are NOT redesigning your vertical or any other part of the website right now. Secondly, Excel is a spreadsheet. Not a design tool. Lastly, you didn't provide one single item I asked you for."

Smiling like the village idiot that she was, Tallulah said, "I just thought it would be a fun challenge to try and design in Excel."

At a loss for words, Stephen replied that this wasn't what was asked for and was unacceptable. Stephen reiterated that he only wanted the list of partners and potential partners, keywords, and any write-ups applicable. Again, Tallulah kept that stupid smile on her face, and restated how "incredible" it was that she was able to pull a new design together in Excel. The circular conversation went on for what seemed forever but was probably only a few minutes.

After Tallulah had tired of extolling her virtues as an Excel designer and departed, the woman from Accounting stepped in with a piping hot cup of tea.

She said, "I heard. Sorry, there isn't any alcohol around, but I thought you could use this."

And then there was Sabrina. Not teenage, but most definitely a witch. Despite being well into her late 40s, Sabrina dressed like she was going to a teenage goth-rave. Fishnet stockings paired with shiny Doc Martens, short black vinyl skirts, crimped hair dyed flat-black and a massive nose-ring that drew attention to her blotchy skin and messy lipstick, à la Robert Smith from the Cure. Hired to work on the most lucrative vertical, they sadly put her in the office next to Stephen's that had been Daniel's office. While they had doors, the walls only went three quarters of the way up to the ceiling, leaving the top area open so you could hear any and all conversations nearby.

Stephen generally came in a bit after 6 am to get an early start and not be bothered by idiots like Tallulah.

One day, as he turned his laptop on, he could hear Sabrina, already in the office making calls. At first it was business as usual, or so he thought, as he overheard her slur, "So, we will be committing to six weeks? And then we'll go fully online? Ummm, uh-huh. Yes. Yes. That sounds good." (Was she moaning now?) "You know what else sounds good? Your voice. So…uh what are you wearing?"

Stephen stopped what he was doing and looked up towards Sabrina's area.

Sabrina continued, "What? You don't want to know what *I have on*? How do you know I have ANYTHING on?"

("OMG… please, please, please let her be wearing clothes," Stephen thought.)

Then it got very quiet, when suddenly he heard, "WELL, I WAS ONLY BEING NICE! WHO THE FUCK DO YOU THINK YOU ARE? YOU'RE PROBABLY SOME FAT MIDDLE AGED TROLL WITH NO HAIR AND MISSING TEETH."

After another pause, "GO AHEAD. THEY WON'T BELIEVE YOU. FEEL FREE. ASSHOLE!"

After the sound of the phone angrily being slammed down It then sounded like Sabrina had thrown the phone across her office as a loud thud hit the wall between herself and Stephen.

At this point Sabrina must have realized Stephen was in the office and there was a low-key "Sorry. I was talking to my pharmacist."

What???

Not sure if it was her pharmacist or a client, it became obvious this type of call was not a one-off. Very shortly after that, a couple of weeks later Stephen came in on a Monday. He found Sabrina's desk cleared and empty. Raising an eyebrow, he asked the Head of Accounting what had happened.

Trying to control a smirk, she said, "They came in and calmly explained that her behavior had not been appropriate, there had been complaints and they were letting her go but would give her a recommendation to allow her to file for unemployment. Sabrina immediately shot up and told everyone she was a witch and was going to place a dark curse on the company and everyone in it. She then proceeded to walk throughout the entire floor, stopping at each and every desk muttering some type of mumbo-jumbo sounding curse before gathering her things and stomping out. Aren't you sorry you took Friday off now?"

(The curse must have worked as the office was shuttered nine months later.)

So yes, things had been stressful at work and all of this was going through Stephen's mind as he turned onto their street. Stephen could see the mailperson had just finished loading the community mailboxes and was pulling away as he came down the street. Smiling and waving as she passed, Stephen jumped out of the car and grabbed the many letters and small packages wedged into the tight mailbox. Jamming everything into his computer bag he pulled into the garage and shut the door. Daniel wasn't home yet. Once in the house he tossed his computer bag onto the kitchen counter where all the mail came spilling out.

After changing, washing his face, and checking the front area for packages, Stephen took a cursory look through the mail. Bill, flyer, bill, package from Amazon, reminder from the dentist, bill, flyer for a new pizza place, and at the very bottom, a letter from the HOA management. This caught Stephen's eye as they had had very little correspondence over the years they had been up here. The only items received were a very rare newsletter, which mostly looked like a grade-school mimeograph with scolding notes about where and where not to park, the yearly budget summation, and in the years, they had elections, ballots.

While Daniel always used a letter opener on each envelope and then looked at all of them in order, Stephen just ripped the envelope apart and read the single sheet of paper; "We've run out of money."

There was a bit more, but the phrase **"We've run out of money"** stopped him in his tracks. Their monthly dues were not inconsiderable. In fact, in many areas that amount alone would have been rent for a very nice apartment. Stephen suddenly wanted to talk this over with Daniel, but he wouldn't be home for another hour or so.

Looking at the time, he realized it was nearing dinner time for Jane and John and he didn't want to interrupt them, but despite the fatigue from the day and week at work, he found himself suddenly very energized with the need work off the anger and surprise of the letter. Not really thinking about it, with the letter still in his hand, he grabbed his keys and decided to go for a walk. As usual, the street was deserted. Or so it seemed. Walking quickly up past the mailboxes some movement to his right caught his eye. It was the woman who lived close to the mailboxes with her German Shepherd. During the time they had been up there, they had never spoken or really acknowledged each other, but Stephen had seen her out walking her dog or out alone. He decided to go over and introduce himself.

As he got closer, he smiled and waved. He sensed the woman was around his age, maybe mid-50s or so. Comfortably dressed in a dark, baggy sweatshirt, jeans that either were so worn they now had holes or were the "buy them distressed" style now popular paired with well-worn Doc Martens on her feet. Her straight hair loose, blowing in the breeze, she had a kind of Mona Lisa type smile as he approached.

Introducing himself he said, "Hi, I'm Stephen. My husband and I moved into the unit over there a while back…"

Before he could continue, she said, "I know who you are. I saw you move in. I'm Andrea. I live over there," gesturing over her shoulder.

Stephen then realized he was still gripping the letter in his hand and asked, "Have you seen this?"

Andrea frowned a bit and said, "No, I haven't. What's it about?"

Stephen flattened out the letter and let her read it. The look on her face was rather neutral, then she handed it back to him.

Stephen said, "Did you have any inkling about this?"

Andrea paused, shook her head, and said, "I don't really pay much attention to the HOA."

At this point, Stephen realized he and Daniel were guilty of that as well. Still, a bit worked up, a bit worried about the ramifications of what "no money" might mean to homeowners (with flashbacks to the threat of a special assessment from their previous HOA lurking in the back of his mind), he said, "We should go to the next HOA meeting. I believe it's a week from Thursday."

Andrea, still in a somewhat distant space, seemed to mull the statement over, paused for a second, and then replied, "I agree. I'll go with you."

For whatever reason this made Stephen feel a bit better and they made an agreement to meet out front on the street and head to the clubhouse together the following Thursday.

A short while later, now back home, Stephen heard the garage door open and greeted Daniel with the letter and a big glass of wine. Usually, Daniel liked to come in and get settled before doing anything else, but seeing how riled up Stephen was, he put down his messenger bag and read the letter. Twice.

Stephen then updated him about running into and meeting Andrea, and how they had agreed to go to the HOA meeting next week.

Daniel's face darkened and he said, "Do you remember the last HOA meeting we attended? It was a complete shit show."

Stephen agreed, but pointed out this could be serious, and we owed it to ourselves to at least see what was up and what might be coming. He also pointed out meeting Andrea and getting to know another neighbor wouldn't be a bad thing. Somewhat reluctantly Daniel agreed.

As Stephen and Daniel were discussing attending the Board meeting, the same letter was being delivered to everyone else in the Association. Many sat unopened, more than a few went directly into the trash, but of those that were opened and read, anger and outrage came roaring through. Lively discussions broke out in many of the households as well as a flurry of phone calls, emails, and texts.

While these discussions were going on, mostly without notice, a group of people were quietly posting notices on all the community mailboxes as well as on the door to the clubhouse. The notices read, "IT IS IMPERATIVE THAT EVERYONE ATTENDS THE NEXT BOARD MEETING! The reckless spending on landscape to the neglect and ruin of the actual buildings has to come to an end. Join us next Thursday as we confront the Board on their profligate spending! JOIN US IN TAKING BACK OUR COMMUNITY!"

Chapter 5 – The Board Meeting

An hour or so before the meeting, Tom gathered two notebooks and a folder with pictures taken around the community. A relative latecomer to living in Thornwillow Heights, Tom was energized and focusing on what needed to happen this evening. Being in construction for many years and owning his own successful company, he knew what he was talking about. At this moment, holding the letter in his hands, mixed emotions were going through his head. On the one hand, with his background and knowledge, he really should have paid more attention to the overall state of things before purchasing. On the other hand, he and his wife had been looking for over a year and with another child on the way, there was a certain amount of pressure to find a place and move. And between the demands of his flourishing company and a third child coming, he really hadn't had the time or energy. But then he started noticing things. The lack of upkeep on the buildings… Visible dry-rot, peeling paint, damaged siding… The list was long and Tom knew if he could see this, there was probably a lot worse hiding underneath. From his understanding, there was a maintenance schedule that was to take place with all the phases of the community every six to seven years. And Tom knew for a fact his phase was now pushing ten years without any upkeep.

His queries to the management company were deflected or outright ignored. The one bit of useful information he could glean was they had a construction supervisor. Tom now undertook the task of driving around the complex weekly to see if he could spot said maintenance supervisor. The first few weeks on his scavenger hunt were rewarded with nary a sign of any upkeep. One thing that came to his attention was he never found any sign of their landscape vendor, "Landscape Dreams," in the older sections, but found two, or more, always in the newest addition.

After a few weeks of searching the Association grounds, Tom finally spotted some of the *maintenance work*. What he saw was a crew of workers, most either sitting in their cars or trucks, music blaring, a not insubstantial amount of open drinking, and someone sound asleep in a truck with the HOA management logo on it. Once this "work" was complete, Tom noticed areas where they had simply painted over obvious dry-rot, and other areas where they replaced some of the siding but not in others in obvious need of replacement.

With that, it didn't escape Tom's sharp eyes that the newer part of the community did not seem to exhibit the signs of age and wear that the rest of the older buildings were showing. Verdant landscape, walls, and roofs showing no signs of neglect were in sharp contrast to the peeling paint, sagging rain gutters, rough asphalt, and dying landscape evident in the remainder of the Association. All in all, it was presenting a very grim picture.

Finally attending an HOA Board meeting a few months ago, he was stunned at the rudeness and dismissive attitude of the various Board members. With looks ranging from bored, to peeved, to out-and-out angry, he was told the Board would take his comments into consideration and quickly dismissed him. Tom in his early thirties, a boyishly handsome six foot one, spoke with confidence and passion and was accustomed to being listened to. At the next meeting he attended, the hostility radiating from the Board was stunning. Tom noticed his concerns were not on the agenda as promised, and when he got up to speak, he was abruptly cut off.

When he did get in the question about the construction supervisor he was told by Sylvia, "We were paying the supervisor $80K a year, he really wasn't supervising, things got away from us, so we felt that it was a waste of money, and no longer have a construction supervisor."

Not one to let things go, Tom then took it upon himself to walk the acreage and streets of Thornwillow Heights and made every effort to meet and engage with everyone he met. What was gratifying was almost everyone he talked to was aware of the same issues, some more than others, but all agreed: they were all overdue for a change. As a result of his efforts, Tom became good friends with an older woman who lived across the street: a grandmother whose looks could be very deceiving.

While it would be easy to dismiss her as a kindly old lady, behind her tri-focal glasses were a pair of razor-sharp eyes that didn't miss a thing. And she was nobody's fool. Mathilda not only listened intently to Tom, but she also mentioned she had been on her own fact-finding mission of late. In her encounters with other residents, she had built up a short list of volunteers who were able and willing to get information out to everyone when and if needed.

With that, a small gathering of like-minded residents gathered informally at Tom's place with the consensus being more people needed to attend the meetings and see what was really going on. The letter arriving only underscored the seriousness of the situation. Grabbing his things, Tom ran a hand through his dark hair, took a deep breath, and headed up to the clubhouse.

Roger slowly washed his dishes from the Stouffer's frozen dinner he had just finished. Methodically drying the plate, the glass, and then the silverware, he put everything away in their proper place. Finishing that, he stepped into the bathroom giving himself plenty of time to allow for his enlarged prostate. As he patiently waited, he wondered how bad the meeting would be tonight.

At that last meeting things had gotten a bit heated. Renaldo had been particularly uppity. Stating that not only were there not enough funds to keep the lights on for another month, literally, he was also quite emphatic, "That's just the way it is."

Renaldo was an odd one. An accent you couldn't cut with a chain saw and as prickly as they come. Often lately, he would just stand up and abruptly leave early without saying a word. Oddly enough, there wasn't much discussion amongst the remaining Board members following his startling statement and no discussion of a plan forward. Once Renaldo had left, it was as if the statement had never been made, and the group dove back into ridiculing some of the more eccentric, and let's face it, "not right" neighbors. It was lucky that uppity Tom-person had left before Renaldo made his financial pronouncement!

Coming back from that meeting, Roger, as Vice-President of the Board, thought about what had been said and summarily drafted a to-the-point note flatly stating the Association had run out of funds and instructed the HOA management company to send out a letter to all residents. It isn't like they sent much out to the homeowners. In fact, the last time they had bought stamps in bulk, postage rates had gone up so much they had to double the postage on the envelopes. And they still had stamps left over. While not expecting happiness and joy, the shitstorm that came afterwards was unprecedented. Between all the letters and the calls, the woman who got all the correspondence at the management company sounded like she was going to jump out of a window. Granted, a ground-level window in her case.

Roger yawned. Flushing and then zipping up, he knew the Association had hit the skids financially before and had bounced back. And with a much higher quality of landscaping than had previously existed, thank you very much! Considering how few people ever showed up for meetings and how the turnout for the annual Board elections had been so low they'd often had to do multiple ballots just to get the minimum, it was surprising how many people suddenly showed up to complain at the last very ugly meeting. Sadly, Roger knew the coming one would be far worse.

In the aftermath of that horrible meeting, Roger felt it best to run things by Rosemary. Rosemary had been on the Board of Directors many years ago, and while she hadn't been active on the Board in years, she'd been VERY active behind the scenes. A former City Council member, for years she played a very large role on the city's Planning Commission as well as being involved in almost all aspects of how the city functioned. Definitely a "power behind the throne" type of person… Rosemary found she was far more effective in offering guidance and advice as opposed to being the public person in charge. Once Rosemary retired, her drive and energy to "keep things moving on a smooth path" resulted in her maintaining very close ties to Rebecca and the other core Board members. Well, except Renaldo. Oh, and Durusha. Talk about a seat-filler.

Rosemary was also, in Roger's estimation, a *very comely* candidate for more than just committee meetings. A widower, Roger was unaware of any other suitors who might get in his way. Never missing an opportunity, Roger would step outside his front door and scurry over to Rosemary's front door directly across the street, offering her fresh cut flowers (taken from the HOA landscaping), or home baked cookies, along with continual offers to "have dinner at my place." Rosemary always shut these overtures down tersely and quickly, but this time, it might be different.

Of course, Rosemary had received the same letter as everyone else and had instantly been on the phone with Rebecca and Sylvia. She was furious with Roger for sending it out without having run it by anyone but was also curious as to why Roger had done this. Rosemary knew Roger coming over was going to open a whole can of worms, but she had to get to the bottom of this quickly. There was a knock at the door almost as soon as Rosemary had hung up after calling Roger to ask him to come over. She often wondered if he was always standing by at the ready in case some opportunity would present itself for them to meet or talk?

As he ambled into her home with that half-wit smile on his face, she felt like she was really looking at him for the first time. Her granddaughter would call him a "hot mess." What seemed like an infinite supply of flannel shirts, in various shades of brown or gray, and those pants oh the pants! – pulled all the way up to his chest. And if that weren't bad enough, suspenders to make sure they stayed up there. With his propensity to only wear brown pants, it almost looked like one of those cartoons from the early 1900s of a poor person wearing a barrel. And with that thought, his shape wasn't that far from a barrel as well. Even worse, the (possibly) five or seven very long hairs on top of his head in the world's worst comb-over. Roger was continually licking his lips as if he had been lost in the desert for years and was about to get his first drink of water. The ever-present spittle around his mouth gave one the feeling he was a predator ready to devour you. That thought made Rosemary shudder as she shut her front door.

An amazingly repellent man, but if you got past the buffoonery of his countenance, there were two very shrewd eyes continually sizing you and everyone else up. Rosemary always suspected it was a bit of a contrivance on Roger's part to come across as the simpleton so people would let their guard down and underestimate him. It had obviously served him well as a top sales executive before he retired fifteen years previously. And now he was the Vice-President of the Board.

They sat apart from each other. After dispensing with minimal social pleasantries and any idle chit-chat, Rosemary cut to the chase and fumed, "What the hell did you think you were doing, sending that letter? And written LIKE THAT?"

Roger looked downward like someone had scolded a puppy for going on the carpet. Looking out the window a bit past Rosemary rather than make direct eye contact he said, "Well, it's true. We ran out of money, and no one seemed to want to address the issue when Renaldo brought it up. I kept expecting someone, Renaldo, Rebecca, Sylvia, to call and get our arms around it. But no calls took place. As Board Vice-President, it seemed like the right thing to do. In light of the blow-back and how unhappy everyone is, I probably should have just ignored it like everyone else."

Rosemary's eyes hardened as she gave Roger a withering glance. After a few moments, she cleared her throat and said, "Well, what is done is done. Sadly, everyone is pretty much up in arms. I haven't seen this level of unrest and discord since the construction lawsuits back when we pulled this place from the brink of insolvency. We did it before, we will do it again. So be it if it means a special assessment, or higher monthly dues. Or both. The important thing is to NOT loose traction over the major gains we made in getting this community fully landscaped, so it actually looks like something, not some trailer park in the desert."

Clearing her throat Rosemary continued, "Now, more than ever, it's vital we all pull together to get through this. Remember, my name is NEVER to be mentioned! In fact, I won't be attending the meeting tonight. I have people who will be taking complete notes and updating me. Once Rebecca, Sylvia, and I convene and have a game plan, we will update you."

After sitting for a few more minutes with nothing being said, Roger realized the visit was over. He got up and waddled to the door, which Rosemary was now holding open.

As he turned around and started to say, "Would you be interested in…"

Rosemary shut the door very loudly and firmly in his face.

Stepping back into her living room she cast her gaze about at the various oil paintings of the English countryside, figurines of kittens and cats, and then noticed the rumpled doilies left in the wake of Roger sitting there. She strode over and started to smooth the doilies out when she caught a whiff of… Roger. The Costco-sized bottle of Febreze was dispatched once again.

Sylvia did a quick once-over in the floor-to-ceiling mirror in her entry hall. Her burnished, hennaed hair had been her trademark for years now. Short in the back, curly on the top with not-quite-wispy bangs cut on an angle. Shorter on the right, allowing the left-side free rein, she felt the asymmetrical haircut had always projected determination as well as style. What Sylvia didn't know was coupled with her "the 80s called and want their shoulder pads back" wardrobe and driving her Datsun 280ZX 10th Anniversary Edition, she screamed *power-lesbian anachronism*. Also, the henna, while definitely striking, coupled with her thin frame, and pointed nose, gave off a distinctly Woody Woodpecker vibe. Tallish and trim, with an angular face, her only concession to femininity was a bit of eye liner and shadow. Thin, masculine lips almost seemed to repel lipstick the three or four times she had gone down that path.

Moving into Thornwillow Heights shortly after it was constructed had seemed like the beginning of a sleek 80s nouveau lifestyle, but it sadly never seemed to catch fire. While everyone assumed she was a lesbian, she never made any public pronouncements as such. She had certainly had "close" girlfriends, even going as far as to allowing Yvette to move in with her "while her house is being painted." But that close proximity and the inability of either of them to really confront who or what they were to each other ended with a friendly wave, a fruit basket, and a "I hope the new color in your living room works out" as Yvette drove away in her 1985 Toyota MR2.

From that point onward no other woman (or man) ever lived with Sylvia again in her two-bedroom condo tucked into the end of Nightshade Court. Sylvia gave an approving glance around the living room taking in the chrome-and-leather furniture, the floor-to-ceiling mirrors, the Nagel print of Duran Duran's Rio album hanging above the fireplace, and the matching liquor bottles above the wet bar that had been THE signature design motif of the early Thornwillow Heights designs. The glass coffee table with custom chrome support had an artistic array of "Architectural Design" magazines fanned out on it along with a tasteful abstract statue of a nude woman. Still recalling her mother's disapproving tsk-tsk, she had stated emphatically "MOTHER, IT IS ART!"

Having graduated at the top of her class at Smith, Sylvia had done very well in the world of publishing. Retiring early at the start of the 80s, she had a very comfortable nest-egg, but alas, also a lot of time on her hands. And then the whole homeowner lawsuit fiasco hit. Sensing this was something she could apply her talents to, she went to one of those early sparsely attended meetings and her eyes locked in on Rebecca. Both of them instantly sensed a kindred spirit and the two of them became joined at the hip in their quest to turn things around.

And now there was this uprising to deal with. The days, months, yes, the years, spent improving the Association with nary a thank you, and these upstarts think they know it all. Well, they have another thing coming. Despite some arcane rules (or were they laws?) about not meeting outside of the posted meetings, the Board, such as it was, did meet regularly and had been brainstorming furiously these past few weeks. Roger was at every meeting. What Becca saw in him was beyond her. If he wasn't such a drooling old coot, she'd almost think he was a dirty old man. Thankfully, Roger never gave her the time of day, which was fine with her. But Becca seemed to have a soft spot for him probably because he had given her his unswerving loyalty and dedication. Consistently voting along with the other hand-picked Board members on each and every item Becca championed. Until the letter.

But that letter! What on earth was he thinking? And the phrasing? Of course, everyone is in an uproar. "We've run out of money." Really? There were ways to phrase the diminished funds by framing it with all the various accomplishments the funds had supported. Had anyone asked her, and they most certainly *did not*, she wouldn't have agreed to send a letter at all. Most of the residents were like mushrooms: keep them in the dark and throw a bit of shit on them from time to time and they would be just fine.

One final glance in the mirror with an approving nod at herself, she adjusted the Tabra earrings she had found at the Skyline Art & Wine Festival in '87. A quick squirt of Jean Naté, armed with copious amounts of numbers in a thick binder – more than most people could ever comprehend – she strode quickly to the door hoping her temperamental alarm system wouldn't go off and she would be able to start her car without calling AAA again.

Fishing for her keys, she remembered to grab an unopened roll of Certs breath mints.

Melva had barely gotten in the door when her adult daughter came rushing up to her talking a mile-a-minute. "Mom… can you believe THAT woman parked in HER spot again?? It's the only spot that has shade. I've been parking there for weeks. She keeps yammering at me that it's not our spot and to park in our designated area. MOM! You're on the Board. DO SOMETHING about that horrible woman. I swear she has it in for me. If she isn't telling me where to park, she's frowning and throwing shade my way every time I encounter her and her yapping dogs."

Melva exhaled, dropped her bags, and turned to her daughter. "I couldn't agree with you more about that woman, but things have gotten quite out of hand with the Association. Now is NOT the time to try to settle scores or create any more unrest. There's already far too much of that to deal with right now. And to make matters worse, the Board elections are coming up soon. *That woman* is nothing more than a boil on the butt of one of her mangy mutts. Ignore her and keep parking where your beautiful car won't be scorched by the sun. Maybe you should get up a bit earlier to make sure you snag the spot?"

"MOM… you've got to be kidding? Getting up earlier is JUST. OUT. OF. THE. QUESTION! I say you should just confront the bitch and let her know who the sheriff in town is and shut her down NOW!" Whirling around she dashed up the stairs, slamming her bedroom door loudly and suddenly the house was filled with the sounds of Katy Perry warbling about kissing a girl.

Melva exhaled, sat down, and poured herself a tall glass of Absinthe. Savoring the drink and trying for just a few minutes to forget about her daughter, the HOA, or anything else unpleasant. Once she had caught her breath, she called Sylvia to see if there was any new bullshit to deal with before she arrived at the meeting. She was a bit taken aback to hear several of the rabble-rousers had signed up to speak again tonight. Anticipating their rancor, she closed her eyes and murmured "It will work out in God's hands."

Thinking back to just a few months ago, Melva couldn't believe what a difference there was between then and now. Then the Board meetings had almost been like a coffee klatsch. Just a few friends getting together, discussing the laundry list of items on the agenda, dispensing with the crybabies who would show up from time to time, and then getting down to the real fun of discussing all the neighbors they truly despised. Making fun of their looks, homes, anything, and everything was fair game. And all the laughter! So many nights she returned home with a slight ache in her side from laughing so much. But now, at least for the time being, those meetings are on hold. This insurrection needed to be dealt with first.

Running a brush through her wiry hair, she noticed a few more long hairs jutting out of the prominent mole on the left side of her cheek. Reaching for the ever-present tweezers, she yanked them out. Deciding a more determined look was called for this evening, she grabbed her MAC Eye Kohl eyeliner, Smolder Intense Black, adding a thick raccoon line around the existing pile of eye makeup. Throwing a quick smile into the mirror, she noticed she had lipstick on her slightly crooked front tooth. Running her finger over her teeth she got most of the lipstick. After one last gulp of her drink, she grabbed her dark purple pashmina, flung it around her neck with a determined flourish, patted down the flyaway hair, took a deep breath and headed out for the meeting. As she put the key in the ignition, a small burp came out of the blue. Having had garlic pesto for lunch, Melva hoped Sylvia would have a Certs in her purse.

Renaldo was finishing his third glass of wine, looking out the window at the view. It was one of those clear days they got each year, and he could clearly see San Francisco in the distance. Watching the planes take off and land at OAK, he couldn't help but wish he was on one right now. Renaldo's best friend who lived in the Loire Valley in France was going to call this evening. Renaldo made up his mind, regardless of how horrible or contentious the meeting was, he was leaving promptly at 8:45, and that was not negotiable.

Not one for regrets or dwelling on the past, Renaldo pondered how this whole homeowner mess came about. He had moved up to Thornwillow Heights so he wouldn't have to worry about maintenance or upkeep. He was retired and wanted a nice home in an environment to enjoy that retirement in. The first few years had been exactly what he had asked for. He drove into his garage, shut the door, and thanks to the addition of a five-foot cement wall around the front area of his home, including a locking gate, he never saw, nor interacted with, his neighbors. Which was fine by him.

What his neighbors saw was a little hunched over man, sometimes using a cane or walking stick, who had more than a passing resemblance to the goblins portrayed in the "Lord of the Rings" films. On the very rare occasions Renaldo encountered someone at the mailboxes, he was curt and dismissive, coupled with an undecipherable accent that at best would be called "European."

The status quo was just fine until that time when Renaldo had stepped out onto his deck. The board he had stepped on was unmistakably "soft" when he put his weight on it. After further exploration, he realized several areas of the deck, where potted plants had been for years, had obvious water stains and the wood was mushy and soft. Fine. The HOA was responsible for the care and upkeep of everything from the walls outward, so he contacted the management company.

No reply was forthcoming from his email, so he called the management office. The woman taking the call sounded like a bumbling idiot. She mumbled all sorts of, "Well, according to the bylaws in section 10, subsection 19, paragraph 12..." but never really got around to saying anything specific or giving any indication his complaint would to go anyone who was empowered to actually deal with the issue.

So, after one more round of back and forth with the management company, Renaldo, pictures, and correspondence in hand, attended his first Board meeting. The meeting had some tables placed together with five people sitting behind it. There were only two other people sitting in the audience and there was a woman he correctly guessed was the inept voice from the management company sitting to the side. She was taking notes and she looked like she would rather have been anywhere but here. What piqued

Renaldo's interest was the vast majority of the meeting seemed to be centered around landscape issues. There was very little time spent on anything else. When it came time for him to air his grievance, he received a rather indifferent response, but after firmly stating his case and displaying his evidence, agreement was finally given to the management company to address and correct his deck issues.

While his intent was to leave once his deck was dealt with, he noticed they had no one designated for finances. The woman Sylvia was fielding some of the questions about it, but it seemed to be kind of a black hole. After staying to the end, which he noticed seemed to peeve the five Board members, he inquired as to why there was no Finance Secretary or Treasurer position. Vague mention of someone who had recently vacated that position and that there would be an open seat in the upcoming elections.

Renaldo thought it over, and when the call for applicants came two months later, he submitted his name. Much to Renaldo's surprise he won the seat. Even more surprising, no one else really cared if he was Treasurer or not. He found he held an unacknowledged, and often annoying position, on the Board. They would drone on about the aesthetics of the community, with scant interest given to the more substantive issues such as building maintenance or street repair. But always with the landscaping. It was a mania! In a perverse way, Renaldo enjoyed being that little squirt of lemon in their otherwise flowery discourse.

Renaldo noticed Rebecca completely dominated the meetings. He also noticed the incredibly large diamond that kept catching the light. It was large enough to look more like cheap costume jewelry, but he knew by her demeanor it wasn't. He also picked up right away that she not only had money but probably came from money. And as such, money, well not *her* money, but other people's money, meant very little to her. It came, it went, there was always more. It informed his perception of how she, and *her Board*, viewed the Association.

Renaldo kept his own schedule. He would often show up to find the other Board members deep in conversation, often giggling like a bunch of teenagers. Minus that Durusha woman. She always sat there, off to the side, looking like she just smelled herself. He would sit, and more often than not, read messages on his phone, and chime in only when it felt prudent. He did go over the numbers presented by the management company. Sometimes they were up. Most times they were down. And once he read them and they were entered into the minutes, the conversation pivoted back to landscaping. Once the clock neared 9 pm, regardless of where conversations were or where the meeting was going, he would abruptly get up, gather his items, and make his way slowly out of the hall. This had been standard practice for his time on the board. Renaldo felt tonight *might* be a bit different.

Durusha looked at her watch again. Traffic had been a nightmare. Getting out of the management meeting at Fitness Vitamins and Super Foods had taken much longer than usual. There was some upset over a weight loss supplement that seemed to incur a rabid bout of canker sores on users coupled with explosive diarrhea. Oddly enough, the diarrhea component seemed to be providing the desired weight loss proclaimed by the product. But everyone was sniping at each other pointing fingers and placing blame. One of the perks of being possibly the plainest and most unobtrusive woman in the company, was Durusha almost never got tarred and feathered for mistakes. Conversely, being the plainest, most nondescript woman in a company, a company where everyone from the front desk person up to the CEO look like ab models, Durusha never got any of the accolades either.

Pulling up to her home, Durusha stopped and weighed her options. Did she have time to go in, clean up, and pull herself together before the Board meeting or should she do whatever she can with the tight mass of curls that had gone more awry on the drive home and head over to the clubhouse? Knowing what a volatile freak show tonight would be, and knowing, too, other than being a silent partner on the Board whose only job was to keep the vote at 100 percent, she opted to decompress before heading over.

Durusha could never quite figure out how or *why* she got on the Board. Definitely the odd woman out, she realized she had never really thought about it until now. Rebecca was most definitely the queen bee, with Sylvia and Melva her ladies-in-waiting. The three of them were less like a close-knit group of friends and more like a coven. They were constantly huddled together, and she always knew when they were talking about her. The muffled conversation would stop, three heads would turn her way, then the three would huddle together again, and the sniggering would commence.

Durusha knew she didn't belong in this clique. This was just like school, all of her schools: grade, intermediate, high school, and even college, combined. Early on Durusha knew she didn't look like the other girls in her class. They all had shiny hair either in pig or ponytails, often with bright ribbons. Durusha on the other hand had hair with a mind of its own. Wiry, wavy, and no shine whatsoever. Nothing could tame her wild hair. Despite using lots of hair product, blow drying it, setting it in curlers, and even one very unfortunate stab at having it chemically straightened, her hair was like Freddie from the "Nightmare on Elm Street" movies: you couldn't kill it. The one time her mother tried affixing a bow somewhere in the tangled mess someone in class said she looked like she just came from the circus. But the one comment that had cut through them all was on her first day in high school. The cheerleaders were all smoking out back before class began, looking cool and hot as expected, and as she walked by, she clearly heard "Oh, it's pubic head."

While the other three women on the Board in their corner weren't as *openly* hostile, she felt the same venomous vibe coming from their side of the room from time to time. She hadn't really thought about how or why she was selected to join the Board. It had been quite a long time. And it wasn't like she had a riveting social life going on or had really connected with her neighbors or workmates. So being asked to run had seemed like a compliment and maybe the start of making some friends at Thornwillow Heights. She remembered that day she ran into Melva at the communal mailboxes. The conversation had started benignly enough, but after a few minutes she was being asked to run for a seat on the Board.

Melva said, "It will be fun. There are two other women on the Board along with me, and we have such a great time. And we're also helping improve our community and neighborhoods. You should run."

And Durusha did. And to her shock and surprise she got on the Board.

But that's when the narrative shifted. At first it was exciting getting to know her fellow Board members and the potential of friendship, but it soon became very clear any dissent from Rebecca's agendas would not be tolerated. She clearly recalled *that* Board meeting when the vote had come up to completely dig up the almost-new plantings around the clubhouse to replace them with a *"fall palette."*

Durusha had raised her hand and said, "Well, we only put the plantings in maybe, two, three months ago? And I mean, well, I think they are coming in nicely and while a *few* of the plants are no longer flowering, there is still a *lot* of nice color there, and ummm, considering the costs and time, might there be somewhere else better to spend those funds on?"

OMG… It was like time stopped dead. The silence was deafening, but the looks on everyone's face – well, everyone minus Renaldo, whose face had long ago settled into a stone etching of someone in a continuously bad mood – was, well, the message was received. Not loud, but clear. After an agonizingly long pause, Rebecca cleared her throat, completely ignored what Durusha had just been saying, and put the new fall palette up for a vote. Watching everyone vote yes, with all eyes on Durusha, she reluctantly and slowly raised her hand as well. And after that, the die was cast.

After splashing some water on her face and going through the motions of trying to flatten her hair, Durusha took a deep breath, turned around, and started to head out to the clubhouse. Seeing she had spilled marinara sauce on the grey wool sweater that matched her grey wool slacks, she frantically opened her closet looking for anything else to wear. Already ruffled, stressed, and running late, she grabbed the first thing she could find. She knew the Hawaiian print shirt clashed with the grey slacks but hoped no one would notice or comment. Looking at her mismatched apparel and flyaway hair in the entryway mirror, she knew she shouldn't have watched *Mean Girls* again last Saturday night.

Chapter 6 – Rebecca

"FUUUUUUCCCCCKKKKKK!" echoed throughout the entire house. Jonathan let his newspaper dip as he cast a wary eye towards the bedroom. For the first time ever, he was appreciative of the overstuffed, oversized furniture Rebecca INSISTED they had to have. At this point, he was wishing it was one of those magic chairs from Harry Potter and he could completely vanish into it. Pulling the newspaper up as high as would look reasonable, he quietly prayed for invisibility or a natural disaster to sweep him away. Sadly, disaster had struck, and Rebecca was completely caught up in it. Jon would just be collateral damage.

Staring intently into the bathroom mirror, Rebecca had been pondering the meeting that was about to start in forty-five minutes to such an extent she forgot to remove the curling iron. It wasn't until she smelled and saw the smoke coming from it that she realized what was happening.

"Shit! Shit, Shit! SHIT, SHIT, SHIT!"

Her face flushed, her jaw clenched, and her nostrils flared as the anger went coursing through every fiber of her being. She couldn't stop herself from replaying everything leading up to this moment. Relaxing a bit, a small smile coming over her face, she retraced things back to the *good old days.*

Prom Queen. THE Prom Queen. It hadn't taken a lot of effort. Admiring her raven-black hair in the mirror offset by her ivory skin and her eyes, still bright blue, like blazing sapphires. She recalled being compared to Rose McGowan in her prime and pulling the loose skin around her cheeks and neck back, and tilting her chin up, yes, she could still see it. And all that promise after graduation. Being a legacy student had all but ensured her admission to Stanford. And there had never been a question about Jon getting in. With a GPA in the stratosphere, that and a combination of grants and scholarships ensured both would be moving to the next phase of their lives together

But it hadn't been all rosy at the start. Mom and Dad said they liked Jon and were fine with them marrying, but she heard the murmured regrets and saw the disappointment in their expressions. But she KNEW Jon would prove them all wrong and they'd become the king and queen of the metaphorical prom of their adult lives!

Yes, she could have married Bret. Captain of the football team, scholarship in Lacrosse, guaranteed to make partner in his father's law firm, but deep down, despite Bret claiming she was his one-and-only, Rebecca knew in her heart he was a player off the field, as well as on it. So, Jonathan was the one.

And the promise was there, and it hadn't been bad. In fact, some would say idyllic and wonderful. Up until a point… Jonathan HAD excelled and started to fulfill his promise early on. With patents under his belt, think tanks were after him. Larger corporations came sniffing around and were soon throwing offers at him like confetti raining down on a parade. Our parade. But Jon had had different ideas. He didn't want to be a company shill or beholden to a Board of Directors only looking at the bottom line. Despite her tears and pleading and the many, many arguments, he steadfastly decided to find backing and start his own company. Eventually, as backing was found, there was promise the venture could rise from its humble beginnings to take its rightful place among the Hewlett Packards, Apples, Googles, and Oracles. But that isn't how it unfolded.

Things started out according to plan, but something shifted early on. Instead of outsourcing, Jon started dealing with the importing and exporting of the components necessary for the business directly. And it was then things started to change. He discovered he enjoyed the negotiation process and almost overnight went from a fledgling tech start-up to an import-export business. Well, this wasn't what Rebecca had envisioned, but seeing the seismic shift in Silicon Valley, managing chips and processors, this could be quite lucrative. Granted, not the prestige she was looking for.

Sadly, on an early trip to the East, Jon's attention was caught by some tchotchkes on display. Little did Rebecca know at the time but his offhand comment, "Hey, I bet I could sell these in the States for ten times their value," would irrevocably change the future she had so clearly seen and mapped out in her mind. And yes, she sadly admitted to herself, he did exceedingly well selling the tchotchkes to the major importing outlets as well as the second- and third-tier retailers. He also turned a very handsome profit aligning himself with several major online retailers. But… the *King and Queen of Tchotchkes* was not what she had envisioned… or wanted! While not insubstantial, the income was NOT anywhere near the upper echelon of top-tier Silicon Valley movers-and-shakers.

Going into "their" offices infuriated her. There was Jon with all the promise in the world joking and chatting with the help like they were their equals. These were people who couldn't make change for a five-dollar bill if you held a gun to their heads. Everyone would scatter to their respective desks and corners when she came in. As she thought they should! But it was demoralizing coming in seeing boxes of plastic Buddhas, incense holders, and some hideous items she had no idea where they came from or what they were good for stacked to the ceiling. She was not about to be the one putting "RUSH" stickers on boxes and waiting for the UPS man.

Rebecca threw herself into charity and alumni work. Sitting on Boards, chairing committees, and bringing some focus and drive to organizations and events that just didn't move. But there were changes with her college friends. The social ramifications started to sink in once the nature of "their" business became known. The invites to Atherton became further and further apart, until at last everyone was busy with the latest mergers, acquisitions, and partner switching (marry up or wither on the vine). (She recalled Tabitha's biting comments about their sorority sister after her SVP husband opted for a younger wife, "Go back to that Winnebago in Modesto, Charlene! It's over and you're done!") And then, gradually, the phone calls ceased, the invites stopped, and the committee work vanished.

It was time to move, literally and figuratively. Atherton, Hillsborough, Los Altos, and Woodside were off the table. San Francisco was a world unto itself, and North Bay was completely out of the question. Though Sausalito would have been lovely…

Then they heard about Thornwillow Heights. The development had been established in the mid-70s, slowly building outward in phases over the years. While the original floor plans and layout weren't anything to write home about, the selling point was its proximity to two bridges and all the destinations that mattered along with dazzling views of the San Francisco Bay.

The first rounds of construction were at least a decade old. Actually, much older now that she thought about it. VERY pedestrian, absolutely nothing to merit praise. Thankfully by the time they became aware of Thornwillow Heights, a new developer had created a small new subdivision, more opulent and architecturally alluring than the earlier ones. Even the streets themselves were several cuts above the asphalt and curb design of the earlier phases. Initially the developer intended it to be its own standalone development (and even at one point considered making it a gated community, which would have been HEAVEN!), someone realized it would be more financially prudent to merge with the existing Homeowners Association, and so the new subdivision was merged with the older one. One very fortuitous turn of events was the new subdivision (with the newer, much bigger, and (dare she say?) more costly to maintain development) was grandfathered in with the same homeowner dues as the smaller, older, and (let's face it!) dumpier buildings.

In looking at all the options, Rebecca thought this seemed like the best one available while "their" new company was getting established, so they moved in. Ignoring the fact there were shared walls and it wasn't a full-sized mansion, once the front door closed, inside it "felt" like a mansion. Of course, they had to furnish it to the max and beyond. She hadn't been sure she'd be able to get Mr. Stefán to do such a small job but…

("Ummm… I think you're in luck, Rebecca. The estate in Los Altos Hills I was just about to start on sadly went into foreclosure. Some risky stock trades, and then Mr. uh… Well, *you-know-who*, had that dalliance with the nanny, and then his wife. Poor Francesca. The whole pool-boy, pills, and a truly unfortunate Botox event… well, let's say, I don't see that one coming back, so I think I can undertake your *little project*.")

And it was nice. There were some surprisingly like-minded people near them, and while not the life she had envisioned and dreamt about for years, life was good. Until it wasn't… The damned HOA! Who knew that with any new construction, if there are defects or issues the owners have a tight window of time to sue the developers and builders? And motherfucker, did the old stuff have problems! And with those problems, came those goddamned lawsuits! And who pays for those? EVERYONE! Here she and

Jon were in their nice, brand-new home and these pissants who couldn't afford to live in their enclave all come out of the woodwork, hat-in-hand, demanding everyone in the HOA pay for THEIR lawsuit.

And oh, the cause and effect of THAT Herculean task. The landscaping (or what you could call landscaping) went from barely there to non-existent. She would swear, the place looked like a trailer park but without the trailers! There was next to no money in the HOA coffers, and she insisted she even saw a tumbleweed roll down one of those older streets once. The legal case seemed to drag on forever and their once-new-and-wonderful home just seemed so… well, absolutely not what it should be.

Since she was going into the office less and less, one night as Rebecca was complaining to Jon about the lawsuits, the lack of landscape, and the expenses to the HOA, Jon casually suggested Rebecca might want to run for the Board. And after going to the next meeting, Rebecca realized no one had any drive or killer instinct. So, she submitted her name and ran for the Board. And got on it. Not that it took any great effort. No one was really running because no one wanted to do any of the real work. The Board position was just there for the taking.

And take it Rebecca did. The lawsuit eventually ended and some of the money was back! No one else had much interest in doing anything in the aftermath. First and foremost, she established a Landscape Committee. One street looked like they were waiting to do a remake of Green Acres. There was just nothing there. In looking at the various buildings and streets, she realized there was this amazing opportunity to bring color, life, and a bit of dignity to streets that were, honestly, downtrodden. Surprisingly, it took an amazing amount of work and research. Constructing watering systems, selecting the trees (there were no trees… WTF was up with that?) and plants… Well, one area that was going to command her COMPLETE attention was HER street! It was going to become a gardening showcase.

And she found the right partner: Landscape Dreams. During the interview process, they said and did everything right and far exceeded her expectations. And even better, they would be at her beck and call, no request too small or too large.

And dammit, she did it! She turned the sinking ship around. Trees finally in place and flourishing (okay, so some of them were bigger or had more aggressive root systems than anyone could have foreseen resulting in raised and cracked sidewalks and driveways, but still, wasn't it better to have some kind of landscaping rather than to have nothing at all?). It finally started to look and feel like the quality development it should have been all along.

Yes, there had been missteps. All those gorgeous flowers planted around the clubhouse devoured by the greedy deer. Not to be deterred, she would dispatch Raul to replant it instantly. She didn't know how the Association got along without Raul and Landscape Dreams. Available anytime with a simple phone call, when something needed tending to, Raul was always there in an instant. She wasn't going to have anyone accuse her of allowing the entrance to the complex to fall back into the state it had fallen to prior to the lawsuit. But did anyone there appreciate all her hard work? Hardly. The miles she and her faithful committee members walked weekly while keeping their watchful eyes alert to issues were unacknowledged and most certainly unappreciated.

And now, after serving the community and staying on the Board selflessly all these years, everyone was up in arms! Did they NOT understand the costs of maintaining such vast acreage? Landscaping was the ONLY thing keeping the property values up! So, they had hit some bumps with the reserves? It happens. But it's true, Sylvia assured her these hiccups would happen and would be resolved shortly. While it might be mandated in some bullshit laws governing HOAs to maintain a minimum amount of reserves, not letting people know what was up had served the Board quite well up until this point. Granted, if five people showed up at a Board meeting, it felt crowded. And usually of the given five, four of them would have some immediate peeve, be it a leak, a neighbor parking in their space, or that one insipid woman who claims a feral cat held her and her husband hostage in their home for over a week! She could swear that woman's husband was a stunt-double for Jabba the Hutt in that *Star Wars* movie.

Rebecca KNEW it was a mistake for Roger to send that letter out to all the homeowners alerting them to the dismally small amount of money in the reserves the second it arrived. And the fool hadn't even passed it by her or anyone else on the Board before sending it. Idiot! Just a tersely worded note would have been sufficient basically saying, "Well, we've run out of money." And he's surprised by the uproar?

And then there was Tom Fields. He had only lived in Thornwillow Heights for a few years and suddenly he's standing up questioning and challenging the entire Board. He acted like they were common criminals. Rebecca thought she had put him firmly in his place, but not one to be outdone, the bastard ran around posting notices on the communal mailboxes and even going door-to-door!

The meeting after that letter was packed to the rafters. (Rebecca had been stunned to realize an African American couple actually lived here. When did that happen?)

And now suddenly the room was overflowing with the outrage he had stirred up. It finally got to her, so she stood and bellowed, "SHUT UP!"

In retrospect, Rebecca realized it hadn't been her best move. And then marshalling the Board to storm out so they could huddle was probably a tactical error, too. So, the meeting tonight was going to be the big showdown!

It wasn't like Rebecca and her partners on the Board hadn't tried to mitigate the damage before this meeting. They had gone out and ripped down as many of the offensive notices on the mailboxes as they could find. From the items listed on the agenda tonight, it was obvious it wasn't enough.

Smoothing down the burnt part at the end of the part of the hair that had escaped the curling iron, Rebecca did a once-over in the mirror and thought, "Thank goodness I have dark hair! No one will really notice, but maybe I'll go a tad heavier with the perfume in case someone thinks I was smoking."

Still fuming, she added another layer of eye shadow to emphasize the blue of her eyes and grabbed a tube of the "power-red" lipstick she only wore on those occasions when she really meant business. Glancing down at the oversized diamond she had insisted Jon purchase to seal-the-deal, she wondered if resetting it would show the stone off more prominently. Going to the closet, she fished about for her tried-and-true, go-to La Croix jacket she had bought on their honeymoon in Paris. It was time for the "I MEAN BUSINESS" go-to ensemble.

Taking a deep breath, tugging the jacket on, not only did she hear the ripping sound, but felt it too! Letting out another "FUUUCCCCKKKKKK, fuck, fuck, fuck!" her voice rang throughout the house.

She knew she'd been stress eating a little bit more lately, but she'd noticed more than a few of her garments were significantly tighter and shorter these days. She was going to have to let Consuela go! She'd always been very clear that all those designer items had to go the dry cleaner, but she'd long suspected Consuela had been throwing things in the washer and dryer to save herself a trip downtown. Heaven knows what that old Kenmore dryer had done to such magnificent pieces of clothing. Grabbing a less wanted, but still a "I MEAN BUSINESS" suit, it was time for one last check in the mirror.

In the meantime, Jon began to realize it would not be to anyone's advantage (especially his!) if he were still in the living room when Rebecca emerged. Initially, he was relieved and then happy she had found a place on the Board and an outlet for her organizational skills. But soon it became apparent this was more than a casual volunteering situation. More and more time was consumed with more and more projects, which meant more and more meetings, which meant more and more of everything. Not wanting to bear the brunt of her rage and disappointment, he quietly got up and out of the overstuffed chair.

Frantically looking for his shoes, he quietly slipped into them as he quickly moved toward the front door. His foot collided with a small handheld weeding tool. The weeder clanked loudly on the tile. Looking behind himself nervously, Jon grabbed the weeder and dashed out the front door. Placing the gardening tool on the porch, he power-walked up the street, trying not to draw any undue attention. John thought to himself, "That's the fourth time this month one of Raul's tools has been in the entryway. Rebecca must be finding them on her landscape walks and bringing them inside for safe keeping."

Chapter 7 – THE MEETING

Looking out her kitchen window, Thelma could see some of her neighbors starting to walk up the street. Looking at the clock, she realized tonight was THE meeting. Taking another deep drag off her ever-present Virginia Slims cigarette, she turned towards her husband who was sitting on one of the recliners in front of the TV. She was going to draw his attention to the parade of people, but realized he was asleep. Again. While not the very first person to move to Thornwillow Heights, Thelma and her husband were definitely in the first wave. Now one of the few remaining original owners, looking out the window at the small army of residents walking past, she saw history repeating itself. Again.

Thelma thought, "Category 2 Shitstorm incoming."

Smirking as she exhaled, she thought, "Heads in the sand 99 percent of the time, then only coming up for air and showing any interest when money is involved. Once this resolves itself, they'll all go back to pulling their curtains tight and shutting the garage door as quickly as they can once they're home."

Just like last time! Thelma wondered who would still be standing when the dust settled this time and who might be sent packing…

The modest clubhouse was situated in the center of the many phases of the Association. Generally, when driving past, all but one or two parking spaces would be open. About the only time there wasn't any parking was when all of the tennis courts were booked, there was a pool party, or someone had rented the clubhouse out for a private event. Tonight, the parking lot was jammed. Along with no spaces open in the parking lot, the street – again normally open and empty – was clogged with vehicles. And there was a massive amount of foot traffic as people made their way up to the clubhouse.

This was the first time Stephen and Daniel had been up to the clubhouse. Taking in the clubhouse and surrounding area, Stephen paid a bit more attention now. Having a distinctly 1970s feel and a bit of an Eichler influence, it was not an imposing structure. Beige wood, beige-painted bricks, big beams, and a fair amount of glass were the main components. What gave the structure any character at all were the angles. While the main entrance was perpendicular to the street, you could see the larger wings of the building going off at twenty-degree angles.

Stephen noticed an abundance of flowering flora and wondered how they were maintained or even survived when anything remotely floral in front of their place was instantly devoured by the deer. Joining the queue to enter, once inside, while nice enough, it was clear the building was never intended to hold this many people. The 1970s feel continued once inside. Bleached wood beams, large tiles on the floor, rattan furniture, and a couple of scraggly palms looking as if death was imminent. A couple of watercolor paintings of boats hung on one wall along with a couple of end tables and a coffee table in front of a large stone fireplace. If there had been some hanging ferns and a ceiling fan or two, it would have been an archetypical early 70s singles bar.

There was a crush of people milling about in the entryway. Overall, the age range leaned more towards 50s and up, but there was a smattering of people in their 30s and 40s. Everyone was talking excitedly amongst themselves in tones of disapproval and dismay. People were looking around questioningly, and Stephen suspected many of the attendees hadn't been there before, much like himself and Daniel. Aside from Andrea, who had decided to go with them, Stephen didn't recognize any of the faces in the room. One decidedly older woman – if she was eighty, she was a day – seemed to be in her element. Bright red blotches of rouge on her cheeks and poorly applied turquoise eye shadow, she was the most animated person around. Stephen could see her talking to this person, then that person, then moving on to yet another person. She seemed to be the belle of the ball and enjoying herself immensely. In mid-sentence, she'd suddenly wave wildly to someone across the room. More often than not, the waves were not reciprocated.

Finally maneuvering through the crowd into the larger room, Stephen could see seats. At first it looked as if everything was already taken, but after entering further, Stephen was pleasantly surprised to find three empty seats.

Waving Andrea and Daniel over, they sat down. Unfortunately, Stephen realized after sitting down the woman next to him had used some kind of an overpowering perfume that was not dissimilar to the scent of a Raid bug bomb. Immediately his sinuses started to plug up, and worse, he realized he didn't have a handkerchief or anything with him to blow his nose. What started out as small sniffles became rather loud and obvious noises of trying to keep the massive mucous flow in his nose rather than out. After a few minutes of the rather loud sniffling, the woman next to Stephen cast an evil glance his way, and then got up and moved. Stephen fully expected to find dozens of dead flies and mosquitos around the seat the woman had just vacated.

Almost immediately his sinuses returned to normal, which was a relief. Out of nowhere the animated older woman he had spotted early on scurried over and took the now empty seat.

She smiled widely and then placed her hand on Stephen's leg, leaning in she said, "I'm Sarah. I was a social worker for fifty years and am now retired."

Leaning in quite close and encroaching into Stephen's personal space, smiling widely she said "My, but you're a nice-looking young man. Is this your first time here?"

Stephen could clearly smell the gin on her breath and was quite thrown off by this aggressive introduction. At first looking over for support from Daniel or Andrea, he realized they were talking and were oblivious to the woman to his left. Clearing his throat, he introduced himself, making it a point to introduce *his husband*, Daniel, and their friend, Andrea. Once he said "husband," Sarah pulled back, removed her hand from his leg, and stared straight ahead.

While this had been going on, Stephen hadn't noticed the shift in the room. The Board members had entered and begun to take their seats. He noticed the nameplates in front of each chair, and at the center the nameplate said "Rebecca Mayfair-Jones, President," and the woman sitting behind the nameplate absolutely fit the name and title. Sitting stiffly upright, her eyes tightly scrutinized the room while the remainder of the Board took their seats and shuffled some papers. As she shuffled the papers in front her, her jaw locked tightly, radiating displeasure. An older man, who seemed to be a bit on the confused side sat to Rebecca's left. His nameplate said, "Roger Beaman, Vice-President." Smiling as if someone had just told him a joke, he kept looking around the assembly as if searching for something or someone.

Stephen noticed a bit of excitement in the crowd now. Looking around to see what the cause might be, he was somewhat surprised to see an older, bent-over man make his way along the side of the crowd and take the seat next to the Vice-President. Looking for all the world like a scowl etched into stone, the little old man had a walking stick which he placed by his chair.

Unable to see his nameplate from where they were at, Stephen heard a couple of people in front of him murmur, "He's the only one who told things the way they really are at the last meeting."

Another woman kept throwing her pashmina over her shoulder dramatically as she made her way to the front. Sadly, at least for the elderly woman sitting in the front row, the pashmina caught her squarely in the face, causing her oversized glasses to go askew. Behind this rather flamboyant woman, a much mousier, dowdy woman followed. Appearing older than she probably was, she had a rather glazed look on her face as she ignored the packed meeting room. Her bright Hawaiian print blouse was in extreme contrast to the heavy grey slacks and her mousy appearance. Stephen couldn't read their nameplates either.

Finally, an older woman with flame-red hair strode in, taking her seat. Giving a dispassionate glance at the room, she then nodded at Rebecca and gave a cursory nod to the other two women. Sitting a bit further away was a frumpy young woman. She had all sorts of binders, clipboards, and stacks of paper.

Someone nearby whispered, "That's the useless toad from the management company. She hasn't a clue as to what she's doing and is afraid of her own shadow. Worthless…"

The meeting was called to order, the minutes from the last meeting were read and approved, and then the agenda was laid out. Like the vast majority of people in attendance, Stephen and Daniel hadn't been to any of the previous meetings. As such, it was interesting to hear so many mundane items from the previous session as well as those on the current agenda. But the energy in the room caught fire when the mention of Tom Fields speaking was mentioned.

Before Rebecca could say anything, a young man stood up and loudly said, "What is going on with the issue of no funds for the organization?"

With that, the room erupted in chants of agreement, a scattering of "Sit down and wait your turn" and even a couple of "Boos" from the back of the room.

Sarah leaned in towards Stephen and excitedly whispered, "That's Tom Fields. My, oh my, isn't he a strapping young thing? He's the one who brought everyone together tonight. Ummm, I'd love to take him home for the night."

Stephen, completely blindsided by this proclamation, looked at Sarah in disbelief. Shaking his head, Stephen was now looking at the Board members, then at Tom, who was still speaking, then back at Sarah.

Stephen and the rest of the room now were fully focused on Tom.

Annoyance was radiating from Rebecca and the rest of the Board, as she banged her gavel and said frostily, "We will be holding this meeting in accordance with the rules and regulations the way it has been run for years. This item is on the agenda, and we will get to it when we get to it. DO NOT SPEAK OUT OF TURN AGAIN!"

Everyone turned to Tom, who did not sit down as he met Rebecca's steely gaze said, "That's all well and good but look at this room. You and I know the funds or lack thereof is the *only reason* anyone is here tonight. You blew me and everyone off at the last meeting, and frankly, I think I speak for everyone when I say, we are fully expecting some type of explanation for the depleted funds as well as a fiscal roadmap to rectifying this completely unacceptable situation."

At this point the room exploded with applause. Everyone started talking amongst themselves, creating a thunderous wall of sound.

Beyond enraged, Rebecca stood up and shouted "ORDER! ORDER! ORDER! EVERYONE NEEDS TO BE QUIET NOW!!!!"

Taking longer than Rebecca would have liked, everyone eventually quieted down, but a certain amount of buzz continued among the assembled neighbors. At this point Stephen noticed a woman two rows down across the aisle. She had dark, almost black hair with big bulging eyes. Even based on the high level of excitement in the room, she was notably agitated. She would start to stand, then would sit, then would start to stand, all the while, looking about wildly, her hair askew. Even from this distance it was obvious she was flushed and possibly quite possibly on the verge of hyperventilating.

As things settled down, her agitated hand shot up in the air.

With questioning glances from the assembled group, Rebecca looked her way and said "The floor recognizes Audrey Simpson. Yes, Audrey?"

Audrey stood up, trying to compose herself, but still looking about wildly, she took a deep breath and said, "I do not believe anyone here recognizes or understands the selfless work and tireless effort this Board has made to enhance and enrich our community."

With this being said, many people started whispering and an audible grumble could be heard from the back of the room.

Faced with this response, Audrey took a deep breath and seemed to flush even more saying, "AS I SAID, this Board has been tireless in their efforts, and no one here appreciates their dedication and work. It is obvious from the turnout tonight that most, if not all of you, have never set foot here before, nor understand what it takes to keep this organization functioning properly."

Breathing deeply, Audrey continued, "That being said I think we need to create a Communications Committee to update and inform everyone in the community, as well as to educate and enlighten so people fully understand and grasp the enormity of everything that is done. I propose a kick-off meeting next Tuesday. Umm, it will be at *my house*, and those of you who know me and are interested are welcome to attend."

Sitting down, Audrey looked as if she was ready to faint, but pulled herself together.

Everyone looked around, looked at Audrey, and then the murmuring began again. Snippets of conversation could be overheard...

"WHO IS SHE?"

"What the... I don't know who she is, I don't know where she lives, how on earth could I show up even if I wanted to?"

Such whispers went on until Rebecca angrily called the meeting back to order. It was no challenge for the crowd to see how Rebecca was reacting to Audrey's impromptu announcement.

Once past this flashpoint, the meeting settled back down and droned on with the mundane items that occupy the lions-share of most homeowner meetings. You could see people were losing interest, many openly yawning, and a few getting up to leave.

But that all shifted abruptly when it got to the Finance report, the hunched over man, Renaldo, clearing his throat said, "As I have stated previously, we have run out of money. The reserves are at a historic low. That is all there is to state!"

And with that stark pronouncement, Ronaldo gathered his papers, pocketed his phone, grabbed his walking stick, and walking down the center aisle, exited the building.

The group, stunned and caught off guard, looked at one another and the murmurs and whispers began again in earnest.

Stephen overheard one couple say, "He's the only person up there who's speaking the truth."

Another person murmured, "Him I like!"

Tom stood, much to the visible annoyance of Rebecca, Melva, and Sylvia and again stated, "This is serious, and as residents of Thornwillow Heights, we demand to know how the Board is going to address this issue and what sort of timeline are we looking at?"

The crowd, having already sat in the overcrowded and hot room for over two hours applauded loudly! Calls of "Yes, I second that motion" and other nods of agreement went round.

Rebecca stood, called an end to the meeting, and stated the discussion would be on the agenda and continued at the next meeting. Then without notice, the remaining Board members stood and filed out the back door, which exited into the pool/spa area of the clubhouse. It appeared the remaining Board members were huddling together discussing the meeting.

Stephen, Andrea, and Daniel sat there and finally Andrea said, "*Well*, that was certainly interesting."

At this point Sarah leaned in, far too close for Stephen's liking, and said, "WASN'T THAT FUN?"

Smiling from ear to ear, she abruptly stood up and looked around saying, "Where's that Tom person? I'd like to personally thank him for standing up."

And in a slightly lower voice she said, "And I wouldn't mind giving that tight tushy a little squeeze either."

As she rushed off, they could hear, "Tom, hello? Tom. Yes, over here…" as she merged into the exiting crowd.

As they left, they noticed people breaking off into groups of between two and six people, all huddled together talking animatedly about the previous few hours. Andrea, Stephen, and Daniel walked back to their respective homes, and the only thing that any of them could muster was, "Well, that was indeed *very interesting*."

Andrea's place was first, so Daniel and Stephen said their goodbyes and continued to their place. Out front of another unit a bit further down, they could both very clearly hear a radio tuned to a conservative talk show and were met with a hearty wave from Michael. Daniel hadn't met, nor seen Michael before, but Stephen had encountered him often when getting the mail. Michael, as he had learned, worked for the state. Stephen forgot the specific job title, but his job was to go in after any sort of catastrophe had occurred, be it a bridge falling down, a gas line exploding leveling a building, or just about anything where there was wide-spread devastation and/or casualties and figure out what went wrong and how it happened. His line of work was in stark contrast to his ever smiling face and friendly manner. A constant along with Michael's good cheer was the non-stop of conservative talk radio. At this moment whoever was talking was tearing into somebody.

Tonight, Stephen really wanted to just head home, but Michael, waving them over, asked how the meeting went.

Stephen asked, "How come you didn't attend this evening?"

Michael chuckled heartily and said, "Oh, I NEVER go to those. They're way too dark and negative."

Stephen raised both eyebrows and after introducing Daniel said, "It was kind of a mess. Everyone was up in arms about the lack of funds, but other than temperatures running hot, nothing seemed to have been cogently addressed or discussed."

Michael, giving a deep, hearty chuckle said, "Ah. That's nothing... Wait until we have a good shaker up here. Come over here. See those pipes coming from the garage and under the walkway? They should NEVER have been built like this. It just takes one good shove of earth, and all our homes are going to go up like kindling. "**Ka-Boom!**" followed by a very jolly laugh.

Making eye contact and faces at each other Daniel and Stephen said their goodbyes. Once in the door, they both looked at each other and said, "Wine?"

Chapter 8 – The Communications Committee

About two weeks after the meeting, it came to Stephen's attention there was an online community for the Association. He signed up for it and discovered a post from Audrey at the top; **"Communications Committee Meeting Disappointment!"**

Audrey had written, "I can only say how disappointed and unhappy I was that only a small handful of people showed up at my kick-off for a potential Communications Committee. There were less than nine of us, and no one appreciated the quibbling that led to one member abruptly leaving after only ten minutes. As I've put quite a bit of work into this effort, I am posting this as we will try to have a second kick-off meeting this coming Tuesday at the clubhouse this time. All interested parties feel free to show up. 7 pm"

Stephen thought about this for a few moments. He had been doing graphic design since college, web design for over fifteen years at this point, and had been on social media from the earliest inception of MySpace, then on into Facebook, Twitter, etc. He had also done a wide variety of online and print media. When Daniel got home that night, they discussed going to the meeting. Daniel was much less enthused but figured it wouldn't hurt to check it out. But he still warned, "Remember how the Board meeting went."

So, on Tuesday evening, a bit before 7 pm, Stephen and Daniel headed out for the clubhouse. In stark contrast to the Board meeting, there were only three cars in the parking lot and the building was only partially lit. Walking in they noticed the main area they had all met in last time was dark, but to their left as they entered was a smaller lounge area, the area that had rattan furniture in front of the large stone fireplace. Entering the room, Stephen noticed there were six women there and no men. Audrey was sitting on the right side of the fireplace, with everyone in a loose circle. Their arrival had stopped an obviously animated discussion dead in its tracks. Everyone turned to see who had entered. Moving to the only two open seats, Stephen took one to the left of Audrey, and Daniel took the seat to Stephen's left.

The older woman to Daniel's left held up a hand that quieted the room and introduced herself. "Hello, I'm Rosemary Stoddard. To my left are Elena

Petrov, Christina Lanford, Betty Jean McMillan, Mathilda Townsend, and I suspect you already know Audrey Simpson, who called this meeting."

When she mentioned Audrey's name, there seemed to be a slight facial expression of disapproval that quickly vanished.

After introducing themselves, Audrey, who seemed annoyed about something, took a deep breath, and wasted no time picking where they had obviously left off.

Looking to her left directly at Stephen, Audrey made a small motion as if shaking off something undesirable and said, "Well, I just do NOT have the time to run this committee. I've said it before, and regardless of how many times you ask, I just cannot take on ONE. MORE. THING."

This resulted in the all the other women, minus Rosemary, to start talking at the same time.

Christina spoke up and said "Well, it's absolutely vital we finally start hearing about what's going around here. It seems like too much has already happened that none of us knew about. We need to get the word out."

Stephen noticed Rosemary seemed to take umbrage at this remark, and was about to say something, but Rosemary stayed silent.

Elena then spoke up in heavily accented English, "Well. I am developer. I make app. We should make app for Association, so people know."

Christina turned, a bit exasperated, and said "Elena that just isn't a possibility. We have a LOT of elderly people who don't have computers let alone cellphones. Plus, heaven knows what the costs of creating and maintaining an app would be. NO. We need a newsletter!"

Betty Jean turned around to Christina and said "I agree. Why the hell can't a simple newsletter be produced?" as she turned her gaze to Audrey.

Audrey, again getting agitated, started to flutter her hands saying, "WELL DON'T LOOK AT ME. I ABSOLUTELY CANNOT UNDERTAKE THAT. WHY DO I HAVE TO DO EVERYTHING?"

So, the conversation kind of went round and round when Stephen raised his hand tentatively.

He said, "Uh, well, I'm a web designer, I've been active on social media for quite a while now, I've worked in publishing and with small businesses…"

Before he could continue, Elena said loudly. "Good! He's our man. He can chair committee."

Looking a tad alarmed, Stephen looked over at Daniel, who shrugged and made a bit of a face, and then at the others. Rosemary had stayed quiet and inscrutable up until this point, but he noticed that Elena, Christina, and Betty Jean were nodding in agreement. At this point, all heads turned towards Audrey.

Already flushed from her previous outbursts, Audrey was now getting red and blotchy around her neck and upper chest area, and it was obvious her breathing had become heavy. Looking around with her nostrils flaring, it appeared she had tears in her eyes. After several deep breaths she said "WELL! I guess that is THAT!"

With her eyes now murderously trained on Stephen she said, "So what is the name of this stellar publication that is going to wow us all and win journalistic accolades? The Thornwillow Tattler? Thornwillow Times? Something else incredibly clever? Do tell us?"

Stephen was VERY uncomfortable but turned to face the group. He said, "Well, before we jump to publication titles, I think it would be best to brainstorm to figure out our target audience, what specifically they need to know and want to hear, how to access the correct information, and then look at the most expedient and financially prudent manner to get the news out to everyone in a timely manner."

Nods along with low level noises of approval took place all around, with the notable exception of Audrey, and to a lesser degree, Rosemary.

Now on the verge of hyperventilating, Audrey's eyes grew large, and glaring ominously, she perched precariously on her chair, almost looking like she was ready to pounce or collapse. All eyes turned to Audrey as she stood up abruptly while clumsily grabbing her purse and a few pages with her notes on them. As she got up, her purse fell to the ground and a variety of prescription pill bottles came tumbling out, along with two sets of keys, a wallet, and what might have been an airline-sized bottle of vodka. Getting down on her hands and knees she scrambled furiously to return all the contents to her purse.

Muttering under her breath she said, "FUCK! … If I've lost the keys to the clubhouse there will be hell to pay."

Finally standing, she turned to face the group, her voice catching she said, "Well! I can see everything is in FINE HANDS and there's no real need for ME to be here any longer."

Without another word she dashed for the door. With a VERY LOUD "BANG!" the door was slammed shut. It was a miracle the glass hadn't shattered. Everyone sat there, openmouthed, looking at one another, when out of the silence the sound of a car revving over and over could be heard and then a very loud screeching of tires as a car roared out of the parking lot. Following that were the sounds of horns and screeching brakes. Some kind of yelling could be heard, but not clearly, and finally everyone could hear the car everyone KNEW was Audrey's fading into the distance.

Everyone sat there for what felt like eternity. Finally, Mathilda broke the silence and said, "I've been talking to neighbors about creating a volunteer group. People who could be street ambassadors and help spread the word. I have a group ready and waiting. If we can get a newsletter printed, I can get it out and they would hand-deliver them on their streets and save us on postage."

This resulted in nods of approval, and with Audrey now gone, everyone seemed a bit more relaxed. Ideas were bandied about, energy levels rebounded, and it was agreed they would have another meeting in two weeks to hash things further.

As everyone got up to leave, Rosemary grabbed Stephen's arm and said, "Would you and Daniel be so kind as to walk me home? It's gotten dark and I'm not as young as I used to be."

Both readily agreed, so after Rosemary locked the clubhouse and the lights were turned off, they slowly walked Rosemary down the two streets to her residence.

Rosemary said, "I'm truly sorry you had to see that. Audrey is… Well, she's highly strung," giving a little laugh, "and I know she somehow viewed this committee as her baby. I can tell you, there's been talk of this for months and nothing has ever happened. One failed meeting after another."

As they approached her front door she turned and smiled saying "Please, if there is ANYTHING I can do to assist or be of help with, do not hesitate to ask. And DO keep me informed about EVERYTHING you'll be undertaking."

As Stephen and Daniel walked back to their place, after a long silence they both walked in the door and simultaneously said, "WINE!"

Chapter 9 – Changes

Once the dust had settled after the VERY unexpected Communications Committee meeting, Stephen pondered what the next steps *should* be. When he went out front to water, he found his neighbor Jane was doing the same thing. He walked over to her garden area so they could discuss both the contentious Board meeting as well as the bizarre Communications Committee meeting. After a brief discussion about the Board, Jane and Stephen chatted about current events and politics. They both had a few chuckles. As they said their goodbyes, Stephen spotted Andrea heading out for a walk with her dog.

Sprinting over, he rather breathlessly recounted the previous night's meeting. Again, Andrea seemed to be in a somewhat distant space, but came to life chuckling about Audrey's curious behavior at both the Board meeting and what Stephen relayed from the Communications Committee gathering. Stephen asked if she would be interested in becoming involved in the committee.

Pausing for a few moments, again with a somewhat distant and unreadable look on her face, she said, "Well, I've worked in tech for years, and often do editorial overviews and some writing for projects. I think I'm a fairly decent writer. Umm, yes, I think this could be interesting. I will attend the next meeting. Please let me know. I need to get into the office sometime today, so I'll catch you later."

They said their goodbyes, and Stephen was starting to feel a bit better about the unlikely circumstances that were unfolding.

When he got back into the house Stephen reached out to Mathilda, Christina, and Betty Jean. He reluctantly included Elena in the message but had a feeling she might be more of a hindrance than an asset moving forward. And for a reason he couldn't put his finger on, he felt reluctant to include Rosemary at this point. Mathilda reassured the group that her team of volunteers were standing by and raring to go. Still not completely sure how to proceed, everyone emailed back and forth with thoughts and ideas. But the input was good, and things seemed to be moving forward in a positive direction.

Later that day, Michael, seemingly forever out in his open garage gleefully listening to conservative talk radio, waved Stephen over. He informed Stephen he and his wife Brenda had decided to sell their place and move about a quarter mile up the way into a different development. Surprised and a little bit sad, as he was only now really starting to get to know his immediate neighbors, Stephen asked why they were moving. With the radio still angrily blaring in the background, Michael, grinning and jovial as ever, said Brenda's mother was probably going to sell her place and move in with them. While they *could* accommodate her at their current home, they had found a place not too far away with a very separate bedroom/bathroom situation so they would not be living in each other's pockets. Despite his preferences in radio, he seemed like a genuinely nice person and Stephen felt it would be a loss for the neighborhood.

It was stunning how quickly the "For Sale" sign went up. What was even more startling was how quickly it was covered with a "SOLD" sign. Moving at warp speed, Michael's garage, which seemed to have had every inch of floor space filled with odd pieces of metal, car batteries, electrical components, and who-knows-what-else, was now completely empty as furniture and household items were now being staged in anticipation of their move. After living on the street for several years, this was the first home sale Stephen and Daniel had witnessed.

A few days later, when Stephen stepped out to water a newly planted wisteria, he noticed an immense moving van covering a vast portion of the street. Movers were coming and going at a frantic pace. Michael, standing out front in a T-Shirt and cargo shorts, was answering questions, pointing to this and that, and generally overseeing the process. From time-to-time, Michael's wife Brenda would come out. Much less grounded than Michael, she seemed like she was on the verge of a nervous breakdown. Her glasses askew on her face, she had missed the buttons on her blouse, so it was hanging on her at an odd angle.

Stephen could hear her shouting, "OH NO… NOT THAT ONE. THE OTHER ONE. I SAID THE OTHER ONE OVER THERE" before she would disappear into the house again.

Stephen was just about to wrap the hose up when he heard a loud shriek! "MICHAEL!! They've packed the pet carrier!"

Michael seemed to be paying more attention to one of the movers and the clipboard in his hand. Brenda ran over screaming, "MICHAEL. DID YOU HEAR ME? I SAID THEY'VE PACKED THE PET CARRIER! WHAT ARE WE GOING TO DO? WHAT WILL WE PUT MITTENS IN?"

Michael waved the mover away and chuckled heartily. Just as he was about to speak, a wide-eyed black and white cat came charging out of the garage and began frantically climbing up the tree Michael was standing next to.

Michael, with Brenda now moving around frantically behind him, started yelling, "MITTENS. MITTENS. MITTENS. GET DOWN NOW! DO YOU HEAR ME? MITTENS."

Mittens now more than halfway up the tree looked murderously down on them and hissed. Undeterred, Michael kept repeating "MITTENS. COME DOWN HERE NOW."

With the repeated pleas to the incensed cat not working, Brenda was now getting more worked up, pacing back and forth, looking up from time to time, now pleading with the cat to come down. Mittens was having none of it, wildly looking about for an escape route from the tree.

Despite needing to leave shortly for an appointment, Stephen was mesmerized by this obvious bit of theater. Brenda kept getting more and more distraught, but Michael had had enough and started to try to get up into the tree. Not the most physically fit specimen, he began to try to climb up into the tree. What ensued were several minutes of him clawing, panting, jumping, and grabbing at branches, and making absolutely no headway, as Mittens stared down at him venomously. Considering his girth and obviously not being anywhere near in-shape, just watching him attempt to get any type of leverage into the tree was entertainment enough. But then, unexpectedly, Mittens darted down the tree, claws fully extended, running down Michael's back! Michael called out in pain, but pivoted shockingly fast, and grabbed the cat. Stephen wasn't sure who was more surprised, Mittens or himself. Mittens was hissing and flailing with its claws, as Brenda appeared from the garage with a large paper grocery bag. Attempting to put the bag over the flailing cat, resulted in Michael AND Brenda both sustaining a massive number of scratches and bites. And then in a moment of hesitation on Mitten's part, Brenda got the bag completely over the cat. Michael wrapped his arms around the bag. From the noises and movement, it was obvious Mittens was beyond enraged, as Michael kept shifting around, trying to gain some leverage and hold onto the moving bag. Suddenly, the bag ripped apart in an exposition of paper and Mittens darted away, running up the street.

Michael standing there, blood oozing through his T-Shirt, his arms and face covered in scratches and bites, turned to Brenda, who looked as if she was about to cry, chuckling, "Don't worry. We'll get her eventually."

Mesmerized by the show unfolding in front of him, Stephen didn't notice Thelma now standing by his side. The smoke from Thelma's cigarette, smoked down almost to the filter, alerted him to her presence.

Squinting for a moment, a wry smile on her face, she said, "They've lost nine cats since they've been here due to the very hungry coyote population up here at Thornwillow Heights."

Stephen didn't really have a reply to that. Hearing the mention of the community's name, it occurred to Stephen Thelma had been here longer than anyone and asked, "So, why do we have that rather ugly stone Thornwillow Heights logo with the snake?"

Thelma took a drag off her cigarette and said, "Well, before this was developed the only things on these hills were a willow tree, brambles with thorns everywhere and a lot of snakes. Once they started developing the place, people started calling it Thornwillow and it stuck. I guess they included the snake as an homage to the original inhabitants. Though frankly, even with it being developed, there are still a lot of snakes. And more than a few thorns. Or at least thorny issues to deal with." And with that, Thelma proceeded to walk away, in a literal puff of smoke.

At the end of the day as the moving van pulled out, the "SOLD" sign was taken down. Stephen wondered what their new neighbors would be like.

Chapter 10 – A Sense of Community

Some changes in Stephen's life corresponded with the new Committee work. With Daniel established as a consultant and the marketing company's longevity very much in question, Stephen quit. Having a handful of smaller side-projects, he now had more time to devote to the Committee. At the next gathering, Stephen introduced Andrea to everyone, and it felt like this group would coalesce well.

And little by little Stephen and Andrea got to know each other better. It was not uncommon for Stephen to just drop in on Andrea where they'd talk about the Homeowners Association, but just as often they discussed music, movies, or politics. They had a shared sensibility and a similar sense of humor. They were now emailing several times a day. Sometimes Andrea would just show up at the door first thing in the morning and Stephen would have her in for a cup of tea. Or in the evening after Daniel got home, they would have her over for a glass of wine. It became casual and comfortable enough that when Stephen was making a big pot of spaghetti sauce, they would often invite Andrea over on the fly. With their shared sense of humor, they had lots of laughs over the eccentric, peculiar, and just plain weird neighbors populating their community.

While this new world of community involvement was starting to take shape, Stephen felt like he was living in an actual neighborhood for the first time in a very long time. The only other time previously had been years and years ago when he was living in San Francisco. The apartment building was a block off of Noe Street, and it felt less like an apartment and more like living in a friendly sitcom. Compared to the world people live in now, back then no one locked their doors. Granted, you had to get through a security gate to get into the building, so it wasn't completely open, but once in, you could go anywhere and everywhere at will. And everyone did. One of the more eccentric residents worked for the morgue. He was also a drag queen, with the stage name Chrissy Cadaver.

There would be many nights when you'd hear the loud click, click, click, click of Chrissy's (very) high heels tentatively making their way down the cement stairs, then the sliding glass door would fling open and an exuberant voice would say, "Cranberry and vodka?"

This was generally just the first drink before the actual evening would begin, as he'd totter down the rest of the stairs for a night on the town.

Then there was Sasha. You couldn't forget or overlook Sasha. In fact, Stephen was warned about Sasha by more than one of the residents of the building before they had met.

The neighbor next door said, "He's, uh, quite a handful. I'm not sure the two of you will get along."

And the first time Sasha strode into the living room, all conversations stopped. There he stood, all five foot six of him, with the thickest mane of hair Stephen had ever seen. His hair went down almost to his waist, a healthy tan, and eyes like a cat, taking everything in. VERY androgynous, but with an alpha-male energy, Sasha stopped, scrutinized Stephen, and said something incredibly bitchy and insulting in a (what Stephen eventually found out was a faux) British accent. Unfazed, Stephen tossed an equally lethal barb back, and before anyone could say "Shall we go to Twin Peaks?" the two of them were thick as thieves. This actually made some of the residents nervous. (As it should have done!)

Sasha was living upstairs with Oliver, but no one ever really saw Oliver. Occasionally a tall, very quiet man with dark hair and glasses, would scurry past on his way out or back, but seldom did he stop in and join in the camaraderie. One night the apartment was reasonably packed with a lively game of cards taking place.

Sasha had lost several hands in a row, and with a theatrical hand to his forehead, he said, "I have THE GHASTLIEST HEADACHE. I'm going to call it a night. I MUST LIE DOWN!"

Less than twenty minutes later the sounds of Sasha and Oliver having incredibly loud sex was all but drowning out the conversation over the card game. At first everyone's eyes got big as they looked up at the ceiling, then massive waves of laughter broke out as Sasha was screaming at the top of his lungs, "DON'T STOP, DON'T STOP, DON'T STOP!" (Sasha could get quite loud!)

But things, circumstances, and people change. Sasha, for all his wild unpredictability, went on to meet an established older man, had a fairly (for its time) outrageous wedding ceremony, and moved out of state. The man Stephen was living with had grown unhappy with San Francisco, and unknown to Stephen, had begun the process to move back to his home state. And there was the city itself. There was no parking for the complex, so Stephen's car parked on the street was broken into. Several times.

One time he was home and heard his car alarm go off! He got up and dashed for the door.

His friend grabbed his arm and forcibly said, "SHOES!"

Stephen, was trying to break away, saying, "But my car…"

To which his friend tersely replied, "Needles. There are all kinds of needles out there on the street. PUT YOUR SHOES ON FIRST."

For a far too brief period of time, there had existed an idyllic sense of friendship and community. Regardless of what petty tiffs people got into, when push came to shove, everyone was there for everyone else. Sadly, that era came to an end, but now for the first time since then, Stephen was starting to feel that happening again.

As Stephen had gotten to know more people, not just on his street, Andrea was also now meeting and talking to people out on her walks. There was most definitely displeasure with the current Board, but there was still some uncertainty as to how to proceed.

What everyone did know, though, was the annual election was coming up. Rebecca, Roger, and Melva were all up for reelection, and had made it known they were most certainly going to run again.

In the meantime, Tom was having his own gatherings. Mathilda was the one who introduced Stephen and the Committee to Tom and his group. While it was a bit unclear who came up with the idea, talk was going round about finding three people to run against the incumbents.

In a short period of time, two visitors attended one of the Communications Committee meeting: Carol, who many years previously had served on the Board, and Timothy, who had also served a while back. With a bit of trepidation, both agreed to run. This meant they only needed one more person to run.

Stephen seriously considered throwing his hat into the ring, but he knew the right person to run was Daniel. Daniel was a good public speaker, had worked in executive positions, could read a spreadsheet, and was able to condense and simplify complex pieces of data into a more easily understood format.

When Stephen broached the subject, Daniel's first reaction was, "NO WAY! You've been at those meetings. Those people are crazy."

But Stephen explained why Daniel was the better choice, and even enlisted Andrea to help plead the case. Very reluctantly, Daniel agreed to run. In going to the next Communication Committee meeting, this was put forward and everyone heartily agreed. So, now there were three candidates to run against the incumbents, but now they needed to figure out how to proceed.

As it happened, Carol reached out to Daniel and Stephen extending an invitation to meet for lunch. Carol mentioned her husband, Sam, might be joining them as well. Very bright and accomplished, she was an SVP with a global software company. She explained that her previous time on the Board had been during the infamous lawsuit period. This was also when Rebecca first joined the Board. Being incredibly tactful, she explained Rebecca was not the person we witnessed at the meeting when she first joined. While definitely smart and no one's fool, Rebecca had initially sat back, taken notes, was respectful, then figured out how and why things worked. Or didn't work, as was the case. At about the same time, Rebecca then drafted her friend Sylvia, and the two became a force to be reckoned with.

Carol admitted the Association didn't look too good at that point. What minimal landscaping the original construction company had put in had pretty much died off. At first everyone was pleased Rebecca and Sylvia were interested in creating a Landscape Committee. The first efforts showed promise, and everyone seemed pleased. But in a very short time Rebecca brought Roger onto the Board, and *everything* became focused on landscaping. As landscaping began to override everything else, one by one, everyone who had been on the Board quietly left when their term was up.

But Carol realized it was now time for a change, and while not overly thrilled, she recognized she had experience to bring to the table. She said Timothy felt the same. After a bit of brainstorming, the idea was to create a campaign flyer. Carol very quickly sent Stephen a good headshot and concise biography. Daniel was able to create one that matched in length and tone. The fly in the ointment? When Stephen reached out to Timothy, he politely declined to be a part of the flyer. This made Daniel wonder if Timothy was aligned with Rebecca?

Everyone pondered these questions as Carol said, "I cannot imagine where Sam is? He said he'd join us. Oh well, it was a very nice lunch, and it was lovely to get to know you both."

As they said their goodbyes, Stephen could hear Carol on her phone, "Where are you?" as they walked away in different directions.

In talking this over with Andrea, it turned out she knew a bit more about what was going on. She said Timothy lived in the newest section, just around the corner from Rebecca. She then intimated that she was privy to some of the family drama and turmoil Timothy and his very high maintenance wife, Shayla, had going on. Stephen, uncomfortable, steered the conversation in another direction, as he didn't want to get caught up in salacious gossip when he was starting to feel connected to the community.

In some ways, having Timothy pass on the flyer opened the brochure up to being able to present the two candidates with enough space remaining to explain why there was a need for new leadership. With everyone on the Communications Committee being connected online, they all had a chance to participate in workshopping the brochure. Once Stephen had a comp made up, he created a PDF version and sent it out to everyone in the group for review. Minus a few wording tweaks on the main platform subject, it was approved. One of the women in the group said she had access to a color printer at work and shortly thereafter, a stack of flyers was waiting on Stephen's doorstep.

Stephen sent Mathilda a note and she asked him to drop the flyers off at her place, one street over. Greeting him a massive smile, Mathilda assured Stephen every resident in the Association would have a flyer either hand delivered or left on their doorstep by that evening. Stephen had withheld the flyers for the street he and Andrea lived on, as he and Andrea had decided to hand deliver those personally. As expected, the majority of people were either not home or not answering their doors. The few that were home were introduced to Stephen and Andrea as they explained why they were handing the flyer out and encouraged them to vote for the new candidates in the upcoming election.

While unsure how it would be received, nary a word of any negative feedback had been reported from anyone. Now the candidates had officially thrown their hats into the ring, and the flyers were out with their intent to take on the Board, a bit of nervousness settled in. Everyone was nervous about what Rebecca and the Board might do as a means of retaliation. Would they mount their own campaign? No one really knew. But excitement was building on every street.

While all this was going on, instead of a moving van pulling up to Michael's now vacated home, an army of contractors showed up. While someone redoing the kitchen or the baths after acquiring a new home was not unheard of, everyone very quickly discovered this was to be a "down to the studs" renovation. As it was a few doors down from Stephen and Daniel, the construction and mess weren't much of an intrusion but more of a curiosity. While Stephen thought back to their modest remodel at their previous place, the number of contractors running in and out, and the sheer volume of building supplies, this was going to be a massive project.

One day, spotting Andrea out on the street, she excitedly flagged Stephen down to inform him a *very* attractive woman was the new tenant. Stephen suddenly flashbacked to a low-key conversation the two had had a while ago.

While discussing a variety of subjects Andrea had said very casually one day said, "Oh, you know that I'm a lesbian?"

Stephen hadn't really thought about that after meeting her. He did notice she was not a "girly-girl" type. Her hair was never styled *per se* sometimes she'd emerge from her home with it still dripping wet from the shower. She never wore a trace of make-up and her wardrobe seemed to be exclusively baggy sweaters, sweatshirts, jeans in varying states of "stylish distress," and either sneakers or shoes that looked like a variation on Doc Martens boots. Yet none of that had actually telegraphed a lesbian vibe.

Andrea was now clearly aflutter. She had already spoken to the new neighbor, Sandra A. Miller, (Andrea being very emphatic about knowing Sandra's middle initial: maybe she thought it stood for Andrea and that signaled some type of connection?) and couldn't stop going on (and on, and on) about her. She was petite, VERY FIT, with long strawberry-blond hair, and intense deep-green eyes. Andrea then mentioned she was a very senior VP with a biotech company. She was currently living in Berkeley and had now acquired Michael's old place. The way Andrea was going on, Stephen assumed there was some sort of reciprocal vibe.

The only thing Stephen could think to say was, "You go, girl!"

Andrea, beaming, walked back to her place, throwing continual glances back at Sandra's soon-to-be-new home.

A couple of days after that conversation, coming back from getting mail, Andrea was standing in the street with a woman that *had* to be Sandra. Andrea, fawning and bubbly in ways Stephen had never seen, waved excitedly, and introduced Stephen to Sandra.

What struck Stephen right away was not so much a lesbian vibe, but the feeling of someone who worked very hard at not only controlling her own outward demeanor, but seemingly trying to control everything and everyone else's around her through sheer force of will. Appearing taller than she actually was, her Manolo Blahnik heels combined with her very trim figure gave her a stature and gravitas other women of a similar build lacked and would envy. Wearing a tailored black suit with a grey silk blouse underneath Stephen noticed a silencing glance directed at Andrea that at once subdued her overly animated efforts at introducing them. A cool dry hand was extended as Stephen welcomed her to the neighborhood.

In a controlled cool tone she said, "It's a pleasure to meet you." Steely would be the adjective that best applied to Sandra. A polite, but tight smile followed.

Andrea then interjected with, "I've been telling her all about the current board and the uprising. Guess what? She said she can have *anything* we need printed, including full color, at her place of work! Isn't that WONDERFUL?"

Stephen smiled and agreed.

Sandra went on to say, "There is still a lot of work to be done, but once the initial demolition is over, I will be hosting some type of housewarming party."

At the end of that statement, without so much as a word or motion, Stephen knew he had now been dismissed. With that he headed home saying, "Welcome to the neighborhood!"

Glancing back, he noticed Andrea kept moving into Sandra's personal space, only to have Sandra give her a disapproving glance and move a bit further away.

Stephen thought, "Andrea is certainly a smitten kitten."

While not put off or having any bad vibes, Stephen wasn't completely sure how he felt about Sandra. She came across as *very* controlled. Between the amount of money spent on her new home and the vast amount of work she was embarking upon; Stephen knew she had some serious money. She seemed nice enough, though, and Stephen hoped she would become a welcome addition to the neighborhood.

As Stephen walked back to his place, Thelma appeared seemingly out of nowhere. And her ever-present smoldering Virginia Slims with its precarious amount of ash hanging on for dear life.

Tilting her head towards the receding figures of Andrea and Sandra, Thelma said, "THAT IS GOING TO BE INTERESTING."

Stephen arched an eyebrow and asked, "Why?"

For the first time Stephen could recall, Thelma just smiled like the cat who ate the canary. Another glance at the receding figures and Thelma waved goodbye as she kept going towards her own place.

Over her shoulder she called out, "Oh, and good luck with the election."

Daniel recalled the first time they had met. Cigarette firmly in place, she had commented, "I *love* recycling. I know how much everyone drinks and know what liars a lot of them are. Some claim to have that holier-than-thou macrobiotic vegan diets. Ha! Bullshit! The woman who used to live next door to me went on and on about how her body is a temple. Then I found all the pizza boxes, Twinkie wrappers, and more Ben & Jerry's than you could imagine. Along with all those vodka bottles. CHEAP VODKA!"

Stephen had laughed nervously, but it also gave him pause about what their trash and recycling might be saying about them?

Chapter 11 – The Housewarming

With the proper paperwork for the upcoming election filed, everyone seemed to be walking on eggshells now. While the tension had been building for weeks, now with the actual election just a few weeks away, it felt like living in a pressure cooker. What made the situation that much more intense was no one had any idea what the current Board or its incumbents would do. Would they retaliate? Would they mount their own PR campaign in opposition? Talk was going on everywhere about all the possible "What ifs?" And Rebecca had become the main topic of conversation with Andrea.

Now when Stephen and Andrea (and Daniel if he was around) got together, Andrea ALWAYS steered the conversation to Rebecca. And something that troubled Stephen on a subliminal level was he could see the same fire in her eyes Christine used to exhibit when talking about the Board at their old HOA. Stephen noticed an excitement level he wasn't sure was warranted or healthy. One of the *facts* Andrea trotted out one afternoon was Rebecca had purchased ALL three units in her building and knocked them together into one massive mansion. Having nothing to go on either to refute or confirm such a statement, Stephen found it dubious. Knowing the prices of the individual units, if someone were going to layout that much money, surely they'd purchase an actual stand-alone mansion, wouldn't they?

Andrea also began to drop hints and aspersions about Rebecca being serviced in more ways than just landscape by the Landscape Dreams on-site manager, Raul. Andrea was often spotted out either alone or walking her German Shepherd frequently, so Stephen assumed she had caught sight of an interaction implying something beyond property owner and landscaper. But thankfully, these types of conversations didn't dominate and were often just part of larger discussions.

The day the election packet arrived from the Homeowners Association, Stephen wanted to open it immediately, but a part of him was fearful of what he might find lurking inside. Brushing aside his concerns, he ripped the envelope open to discover six candidates. Of the six, there were Timothy's, Carol's, and Daniel's names with thoughtful biographies and background information stating why they were currently running. To Stephen's surprise,

Rebecca's was just the same bio that had appeared on countless ballots before it, Roger's was incredibly thin, and Melva's was non-existent. Baffled and confused, Stephen dashed over to Andrea's place. She had just got home so they both looked at the packet. And they both had a feeling they were missing something. Surely, the incumbents were going to do more than this after the contentious meetings and the length of time they'd held power. They were baffled at the lackluster biographies and the complete lack of any type of campaign effort. It wasn't as if they hadn't received the campaign flyers Stephen had made, as those were personally delivered to each and every residence.

While the lack of effort on the part of the incumbents should have calmed people down a bit, instead it served to ramp up the anxiety and tension more so. Everyone had the feeling a grand gesture or some kind of massive retaliation was imminent. At this point Tom, Mathilda, Stephen, Andrea, and everyone else involved did their best to engage with their neighbors to stress the importance of not only voting but voting for much needed change as well. It now felt like the pressure cooker was turned all the way up.

During this period, the work on Sandra's place seemed to be progressing. Or at least expanding in scope. From the start it had seemed like there was a small army working in the place, but over the last couple of weeks, the army seemed to have expanded. The amount of lumber and building supplies seemed to multiply daily, and the number of items removed from Michael's former home also seemed to increase. After four weeks and two very full dumpsters, Stephen couldn't believe there could possibly be anything left to remove from the unit.

And now, along with the topic of Rebecca, Sandra's name was coming up in every conversation with Andrea. With all her gushing and fawning, Stephen felt like he was witnessing one of those shows aimed at teenage girls on the CW, just exchanging the leading man for Sandra. While Sandra apparently had no problem finding storage for her furniture and other belongings, the same didn't appear to apply to her clothes.

Dropping in on Andrea one afternoon, she proudly opened her closet door to show Stephen it was now nearly 100 percent full of clothes. Not her clothes, but Sandra's clothes. Smiling wider than Stephen had ever noticed, Andrea proudly proclaimed, "Sandra asked if she could keep clothes and things like that here while the remodel was going on." Looking again at the massive amount of clothes, Stephen recalled being over once before when he and Andrea were going to go to a meeting. Andrea had stopped at the hall closet to get her coat, and Stephen had noticed it was almost entirely empty at that time, save for a coat, sweater, and a few items for her dog.

To add to the surreal moment, Andrea then proudly led Stephen to her typically empty garage where there now stood four very full clothing racks. The way Andrea made her "Ta-da!" movement, he felt like she was about to make an acceptance speech.

Not really knowing what to say, he finally mumbled, "This is very nice of you to let her keep her belongings here."

But an old joke came to mind and he couldn't resist sharing, "You know what two lesbians bring on a first date?"

Andrea got a very nervous look in her eyes as she tentatively said, "What?"

Stephen smiled and said, "A U-Haul."

Andrea gave a nervous laugh.

But what Stephen was really thinking was what an oddly intimate thing to ask someone, who was for all intents and purposes a complete stranger, to do: ask them to keep your clothes at their place. And thinking further, intimate gestures, and the icy façade he'd met previously just didn't seem to go hand in hand. Obviously, there was more going on here than Stephen was privy to.

Stephen only caught occasional glimpses of Sandra either running into her home or driving away for the next few days. From what Andrea was saying, the interior of Sandra's place was now completely down to the studs. Not only that, but they were making major structural changes as well. Stephen, familiar with the four basic floorplans in their area, couldn't imagine what Sandra could be doing to the interior space.

About a week later, Andrea announced Sandra was having a "To the Bare Walls" party. Curiosity was tinged with a bit of anxiety. Sandra hadn't moved in but was already altering the energy in the neighborhood. Not sure what the attire for such an event would warrant, Daniel defaulted to a button-down shirt, no tie, jeans, and a blazer. Stephen went the same route but opted to wear a tie as well. By this point in time, ties had completely fallen out of fashion. He rarely saw them, even when he was in an office situation downtown. In fact, it oddly felt a bit "punk rock" to wear a tie nowadays. Stephen asked Andrea if she wanted to go with them and she agreed to meet up out front at 7:30 pm.

A bit more, okay, really a *lot more* put together than either of them had ever seen Andrea before, both Stephen and Daniel were caught off guard. While still technically "casual," tonight she had opted for a more studied version. Her Doc Martens seemed shiny, if not new, and her jeans, while still "stylishly distressed" also had a "designer distress" look, versus an older pair of hers that had developed tears and holes naturally. Even Andrea's turtleneck sweater had a "new" feel, now with a dark-patterned silk scarf cavalierly wrapped loosely around her neck with the long ends showing front and back. Instead of the older pair of glasses she had on most of the time, she now sported newer designer frames. And her hair even had a hint of styling. Still loose and free, there was a bit more curl and was that Wella-Balsam Stephen could smell??

The entirety of the work Sandra was doing was interior, so minus the skip full of debris, the was no inkling anything was happening while walking up to her place. Lining the walkway, artfully arranged tea-candles placed every few feet led up to the open front door. Instead of being blinded by overhead ceiling lights, the dark interior had a warm glow as there were more tea-candles around the edges of the entry hall and on each step of the staircase leading down to the now-cavernous open living area. The original floorplan for this model had led down into a somewhat narrow living room opening to a wider area by the windows with a dining area. The kitchen was walled off with an entrance by the stairs and another to the dining room. All of that had been wiped away, including the previously lower ceiling, to present a giant great room.

Still mostly empty, there were two frames for counter islands that were draped with expensive looking tablecloths. Tea candles flickered along the walls and floor and gave the unfinished room the feel of a chic restaurant or bar. On top of the counter was a lavish spread of cheeses, gourmet snacks, cold-cuts, high-end desserts, French bread, crackers, and a huge array of wine and liquor. Stephen noticed she had real plates and crystal instead of paper plates and plastic cups. She even had cloth napkins. Very nice!

The room was more crowded than Stephen had anticipated. Most of the people appeared to be in their mid-50s and up, but there was a smaller group of younger women (perhaps in their late-20s?) congregating in the furthest corner. And the music caught Stephen's attention. At that time, there was a radio station broadcasting from San Francisco, Energy 92.7. They had a VERY GAY identity and seemed to only play very Hi-Energy dance tracks. Hearing that channel being played, Stephen felt there might be more clues to Sandra than he had previously thought.

Finally, they found Sandra standing with a small group by the wine. Seeing them, she turned and walked over. More understated than on the few occasions when Stephen had seen her coming and going, tonight she had on form-fitting black jeans over black leather boots with an expensive looking cream-colored sweater. And her hair was now pulled back in a ponytail instead of her usual more business-like bun. Smiling firmly, she extended her hand and welcomed them to her gathering.

Sandra looked to her immediate right where a small group of over-60s was standing. Introducing the group, Sandra drifted away.

After names were exchanged, the oldest of the group, a woman closer to eighty than seventy said, "We lived on the other side of Sandra. That horrible Schuster man, coming in and taking over George and Lavonne's old place is the worst thing that ever happened to our neighborhood. We were all so in sync and will desperately miss our Sandra. You are SO LUCKY to be getting her as a neighbor. You will absolutely LOVE what the place will look like when she is finished. Her taste in art is exquisite. We will definitely miss her."

While nice to hear such a great recommendation for a new neighbor, it almost had the feeling of a handwritten reference for a new job.

While this was going on, Stephen noticed Andrea seemed to have drifted off into that "distant space" he had encountered on more than one occasion. But he followed her gaze to the corner of the room where the twenty-somethings were loudly gathered. And now Stephen also noticed, no one in the room seemed particularly appreciative of the quite loud dance music apart from the young women. Giggling and hugging one another, it seemed to Stephen like they were a bit more handsy than you would expect to find at an upscale housewarming with a mixed group of unfamiliar people.

Still following Andrea's gaze, Sandra had gone over to the group to say something to the most boisterous woman. VERY blonde, VERY attractive, wearing a crop-top with very-low jeans displaying flashes of a hot-pink thong, the woman threw her arms around Sandra and attempted to give her a kiss. Sandra pulled sharply back and gave her a very stern look. Almost instantly, the woman looked like one of those flailing windsocks you see at a car dealership when they unplug it. She pulled back, and it almost seemed to Stephen she was about to cry.

Sandra strode away, and the rest of the twenty-somethings rallied around the woman, comforting her, and throwing murderous gazes Sandra's direction. While this was going on, Stephen turned to say something to Andrea, and he saw that Mona Lisa smile come over her face. Sensing there were undercurrents he didn't quite grasp, he turned and sought out Daniel.

While the young women were still pouting in the corner, very abruptly the loud dance music stopped. The silence caught everyone's attention. Sandra, now on the other side of the room, abruptly switched the music to Motown, and lowered the volume significantly. With this move, the group of young women gathered their things and quickly exited, most throwing angry glances Sandra's way, while the blonde looked over as if asking to be forgiven. Sandra ignored the group and (more forcefully than necessary) started an energetic conversation with another group of people.

With the change in music and atmosphere, the party seemed to rebound a bit, and conversations were more easily heard. Sandra was spending just the appropriate amount of time with each group, making sure glasses and plates were full, then moving on to the next group. One thing Stephen noticed was he never saw her with a glass or plate. Granted, hosting an event *is* time-consuming, but still, everyone needs a sip of something, even if it's just water.

Shortly before 9, the group of former neighbors said their goodbyes and exchanged promises to get together again once Sandra was finished with the remodel, as well as with Sandra's new neighbors. Once that group departed, there was a definite shift in the room's energy. Raising his eyebrows, a bit, Stephen signaled to Daniel it was time to go. Fighting the exiting throng, Stephen and Daniel made their way to Sandra to say their goodbyes.

Daniel said, "Thank you for having us. I cannot believe the amount of work you're doing. You have to have us over to see the finished product."

Sandra smiled and said, "I will certainly do that, but you don't have to leave yet."

Despite her wording, her body language and tone indicated it really **was** time to leave. Spotting Andrea now sitting on the floor by where the fireplace used to be, Stephen said they were leaving and asked if she wanted to leave with them.

Still with that faraway look on her face and the barest trace of a smile she said, "No. I think I'll stay a bit longer."

As they climbed the stairs, Stephen took one final look back, and could see Andrea staring intently at Sandra while Sandra was busy clearing glasses and plates.

Chapter 12 – Run Up to the Election

With the election results less than an hour away, Stephen found himself incredibly wound-up and nervous. Realizing that just a few weeks ago not only would he not have cared about any HOA election, but he wouldn't have known many of his neighbors or the dynamics now driving everyone to this point. Daniel, on the other hand, sitting in front of his computer didn't show the least bit of worry or – seemingly – interest in what was about to unfold shortly.

Stephen hadn't seen Andrea or heard from anyone else today. Pacing nervously and constantly looking over at the clock, he kept clearing his throat and making a bit more noise than usual, picking up his keys and jangling them before putting them into his pocket.

Daniel, a tad annoyed, looked at the clock and said, "They won't have the doors open for at least another thirty minutes. Chill."

Andrea fixed herself a large Dark 'n' Stormy: the dark rum, ginger beer, and lime slid down easily. Looking at herself in the mirrors over the wet bar in her den, she fluffed her hair a bit and grabbed a long silk scarf she had found in Sandra's belongings. She had also tried on a couple of Sandra's coats hanging in her closet, but Sandra was much more petite, so she made do with the scarf. Looking at the various cell phones on her kitchen counter next to her collection of binoculars, she double checked to see if she had missed any calls or texts. Stepping into the bathroom to brush her teeth, she gargled and set out for the clubhouse.

Jane was at the kitchen window washing up from dinner when she saw Stephen and Daniel head out. Catching Stephen's eye, she smiled and gave a big thumbs up. Stephen smiled and returned the gesture.

Thelma lit another cigarette and looked over at her husband asleep in front of the television set. He had dozed off during one of those police procedurals, but Thelma felt there might be more drama in the clubhouse tonight than on the TV screen. Category 3 Shitstorm incoming...

Audrey fished about wildly in her medicine cabinet looking for her anti-anxiety meds. Pulling out one bottle, then another, then yet another out of the medicine cabinet, she found a few prescriptions for sanding the edges off that would be fine any other night, but goddammit, where the fuck did the Xanax go?! Fishing about in her purse she thought she had fished a loose one out from towards the bottom. But it turned out to be a breath mint. Continuing to dig, she found a few more pills and although she had absolutely no idea what they did, she popped them in her mouth and washed them down with another airline-sized bottle of vodka. God, she loved having so many frequent flyer miles. When it was nearing time to leave, she finally spotted the hard-sought Xanax runner on the carpet in her bathroom and swallowed it dry. She revved her car a few times before opening the garage door.

Sarah went a bit heavier on the rouge tonight while thinking, "I KNOW Tom will be there. I just need to track him down before it gets too crowded."

Finishing off the glass of gin with the lipstick stains around the edge, she unbuttoned her blouse until it was practically hanging open.

Betty Jean yelled up at her husband, "Stan, are you going tonight?"

Noticing the binoculars were no longer on the dining room table, Betty Jean knew the answer.

Grabbing her keys, firmly turning the lights off downstairs, she yelled up, "For god's sake, keep the shades drawn tonight and the lights OFF in the kitchen. Okay?"

Christina pulled on her long sweater, grabbed her purse, and headed out for the clubhouse. As she was walking up her street, her nail snagged on her sweater. Cursing, she fished around in her purse for her nail file and trimmed the errant hangnail. As she stood there, nail file in hand, she spotted Melva's daughter's car parked in HER space. Again!

Starting to walk in the direction of the clubhouse, she stopped. Looking around, she realized the street was completely empty, the lights were off in most of the homes, as most everyone would probably be at the clubhouse this evening. Looking down at her nail file and looking over at the illegally parked car, Christina decided she could be a little bit late in arriving this evening…

Timothy's wife, Shayla, was yelling down the hall to her husband, "YOU SAW IT, DIDN'T YOU? An exterior air conditioner in their bedroom window directly across from our front door. Do we live in a trailer park? Correct me if I'm wrong, but isn't that EXPRESSLY FORBIDDEN in the by-laws? I know you're trying to mind your P's and Q's getting back on the Board, but for heaven's sake, grow a pair and go over there and tell them to remove it NOW!"

Timothy, smoothing over the longer flyway hair on top of his head, rolled his eyes, finished off the glass of vodka he had just poured, smiled tightly, and said, "Yes, dear," as they headed out for the meeting.

Before logging out of her work computer, Elena noticed a bunch of unread items in her inbox. Looking at the subject titles, "Increase your breast size," "I am a prince in Nigeria and need your help…," "You have inherited…," and a few more, she spent the next fifteen minutes opening and clicking on everything presented to her. Most seemed to go to unexpected places, a few asked for her banking information, and two needed her social security number. Clicking here, filling something out there, she looked at the clock and realized she needed to leave work if she was going to make it to the meeting on time.

As she got in the car, she thought to herself, "Ummm, I think I transposed my bank routing number in the last email…"

Alfred drove into his garage and opened the car door. To a casual observer it would appear Alfred's car interior was on fire. But it was the just the seriously dense cigarette smoke from the two packs of cigarettes he had smoked coming home on the short drive from his office in Berkeley. Stepping out into the clear air, he immediately lit another cigarette. Looking at the time, he weighed going in to say hello to his ever-complaining wife and her mother or head up to the meeting. Carefully considering how unpleasant their complaints and Board unpleasantness each presented, he opted to do neither and stepped out front to light another cigarette once the one he was currently smoking was finished.

Sandra looked at the flashing light on her answering machine. She knew it was Andrea wanting her to join her at the meeting tonight. Rolling the Scotch around in her glass, taking a sip, she pressed the delete button for the messages. Opting to stay in, she couldn't shake the feeling *something* had shifted in the office this week. As she started to refill her glass, the phone rang. Not even looking at the number, Sandra opened her laptop and started googling a few of the people in the office.

Chapter 13 – The Election

Approaching the clubhouse, Stephen and Daniel could feel the electricity in the air. If the rush of people at the previous meetings had caught people by surprise, tonight's attendance far exceeded even those gatherings. With absolutely no parking anywhere near the clubhouse, cars were circling, dropping people off, or just sitting in their running vehicles hoping a space would become vacant.

Stephen said to Daniel, "Is that Roger yanking flowers out of the landscape by the clubhouse door?"

Daniel looked over and said, "So it would appear."

Roger now had a large handful of daffodils in hand, as he brushed the excess dirt off his hands onto his pants.

Stephen just shook his head and said, "Odd."

As this moment of truth had approached, the expected reply, rebuke, or even retribution from the current Board had not materialized. Of course, this didn't stop people from warily expecting some type of hammer to drop before the evening was over. It was now open knowledge among most of the people present that the animosity on both sides was intense.

Stephen and Daniel made their way through the crowd and entered the clubhouse. While there were still many faces Stephen didn't recognize, there was now a mixture of many he did. Hands were waving from across the room, thumbs up were being given, and he could hear many of the comments swirling around him.

"What do you think is going to happen tonight?"

"I haven't a clue, but I don't trust Rebecca."

"Did you see the flyer? It helped me decide who to vote for."

"Has Rebecca ever lost an election?"

"These young interlopers think they can waltz in and just take everything over!"

And on and on and on...

Upon entering two large card tables were set up and on top of one sat a large locked wooden box. The sign said, "Ballots Here: For Those Who Missed the Mailing Deadline." Two women sat behind the tables: one the sad-sack management woman spotted at the previous meetings, and another woman with the air of upper management.

That woman was directing people as they came in, "If you brought your ballot tonight, put it in the box over here. If you wish to speak tonight, please use the sign-up sheet on the clipboard over there."

Stephen noticed Roger had made a beeline over to Rosemary, offering her the freshly picked daffodils. Although it was too far away to hear what was being said, the look on Rosemary's face was graphic with extreme displeasure as she waved the sad offering away.

Stephen found himself getting a bit overwhelmed by all the frantic activity around him. The chatter was unending, and tension in the room was palpable. Some people had their heads bent together whispering feverishly while looking about; others were laughing and joking; and a few others were scowling and grumbling. There were surprised looks of recognition, waves, and many people were trying to make their way through the throng to hug each other. While impossible to tell where the overall sentiment of the room truly lay, it appeared most people were here ready for a change.

Daniel had gone off to another area and was talking to people, and Stephen caught sight of Sarah as her head kept going back and forth saying, "Is Tom here? Has anyone seen Tom? If you see him, can you tell him I'm here looking for him?"

Trying to get his bearings, Stephen started to head into the main meeting room. Spotting Andrea he moved over to where she seemed to be holding a seat.

Smiling he asked, "Is anyone sitting there?"

Andrea's expression seemed to shift, and she cast a glance around the room. In only what could be described as disappointment, she motioned for Stephen to take the empty seat.

Stephen said, "Well, this is kind of exciting, isn't it?"

Andrea nodded but had a dejected look on her face. "Sandra said she would try to make it this evening, but obviously something came up."

While Stephen didn't know what to expect, he already had assumptions before arriving. As this was the annual election, Stephen assumed that after everyone had assembled, they would count the votes, let everyone know who won or lost, and then go home. As it turned out, he was mistaken and that was not the case.

Before they could say anything more, a hush came over the room. Looking towards the entrance, Stephen saw Rebecca enter. Her head held high and straight, looking at no one, she strode in and walked up the center aisle. Most definitely overdressed. While not that knowledgeable about couture, Stephen knew expensive when he saw it.

One of the two women he didn't know sitting behind Stephen sarcastically whispered, "It's the hyphen."

Turning to look, the other woman said, "More like the hymen! After all those years of Raul…" and now she held up her hands to do air quotes, "…doing her bush, I'm not sure what's left?"

A smattering of mean laughter echoed around them as Stephen just raised his eyebrows and looked at Andrea. Stephen leaned into Andrea and whispered, "Rough crowd!"

Before everything had settled, Durusha came in looking very worried. She made her way tentatively through the crowd. Thankfully, she wasn't as mismatched as at the previous meeting, but somehow, she still managed to look like she had dressed in the dark. Without any pleasantries, she went to her seat on the end of the dais and immediately opened her notebook but made no eye contact with anyone.

As Durusha was sitting down, Melva came striding in with Renaldo trailing behind her. With a theatrical flourish, she flung her paisley pashmina over her shoulder. But the woman near the front ducked this time and avoided any contact with the garment.

Someone said something to Melva that Stephen couldn't quite make out, but Melva smilingly replied loudly, "It is all in God's hands and will work out fine."

Renaldo, looking down, scurried to the opposite end of the dais, also not making eye contact.

Sylvia strode in briskly, making eye contact here and there, but to Stephen's surprise, she stopped at their row and leaned over him to hand Andrea a book, saying, "I thought you might enjoy this."

Stephen gave a questioning glance to Andrea, who only shrugged, not showing Stephen the book. Sylvia's hair looked redder than usual.

Stephen thought, "She went from Lucy to Bozo in three easy steps."

Eventually Roger made his way to Rebecca's side with noticeable dirt smeared on his slacks.

Everyone took their seats including the assistant from the management company, who still looked like she'd rather eat ground glass than be there.

Rebecca signaled for the meeting to begin. Banging her gavel, Rebecca announced "Roger will be stepping down from the Board and his position as Vice-President, effective tonight. We are all appreciative of his many years of dedication and service to the Association, and on the Association's behalf, I'd like to give Roger this inscribed Montblanc® pen as a thank-you."

While there was a smattering of applause, looks of confusion overtook most of the room. And a few people could be heard saying, "But I voted for him? What happens with my vote?"

Once the murmuring died down, the minutes from the previous meeting were read and entered into the official record. The first order of business was to get volunteers to count the votes. This somewhat surprised Stephen as he assumed things were already in place to deal with that aspect of the meeting and would have thought at least the mail-in ballots had already been counted.

After a call for volunteers only resulted in a lot of people looking around, Stephen raised his hand. Following his lead so did Andrea. Both were accepted, and then a couple more hands went up. A tad worried his affiliation with the flyer and campaign efforts might have had people questioning the truthfulness of his tally, he made his way back to the entry area.

The card tables from the entryway were now pushed together and further back in the room. Stephen and Andrea took their seats and said hello to Christina from the Communications Committee and another volunteer. They all made eye contact quizzically with each other.

The supervisor from the management company dryly explained each person would be given a stack of envelopes. It was imperative the envelopes be kept in good shape for the records as they had the names and addresses of whoever submitted the ballot.

With that, everyone dove in. Having had absolutely nothing to base his expectations on, Stephen had thought they'd be done in a short time. But an hour and a half later, with still more envelopes to open and count, he discovered that was not the case.

Starting out carefully, the pace started to pick up after the first twenty envelopes or so. Stephen was noticing a trend in his pile: Timothy was getting the most votes, followed by Carol, followed by Daniel. While there was a smattering of votes for Rebecca and the other incumbents here and there, it obviously wasn't coming out in their favor. At least not in Stephen's stack.

Not knowing if talking was okay, he glanced toward Andrea, and she looked up smiling, as did the other two. Once the last envelope had been opened and the tallies had been totaled on each of their clipboards, everything was turned over to the management company. Not having realized how exhausting this would be, the volunteers all exhaled loudly and made their way back to their seats.

Despite the fact Rebecca was reading from some report or paper, a hush came over the room as everyone's head turned to look as the volunteers entered the room. There were nods and raised eyebrows in anticipation of maybe getting an indication of who won. But Stephen and the others revealed nothing and sat down. No one would really know until the supervisor from the managing company read the official tallies.

After what felt like an eternity, the supervisor from the management company made her way to the front. Turning to face the anxious crowd she dryly said, "For the three open seats on the board the winners are in order of number of votes: Timothy Davis, Carol Lefler, and Daniel Monroe."

The room erupted. There were cheers; there were people hugging each other; there was laughter and shouts; there were high-fives; and there were a lot of thumbs up. Lurking in this outpouring of joy, though, there were some grumbles, dirty looks, and grousing. Several of the older residents who were quite clearly in favor of the old Board abruptly got up and stormed out as the rest of the people continued to celebrate.

Stephen noticed Audrey off to the other side of the room for the first time this evening. She was actually crying. Not just a tear or two, but openly sobbing and having trouble breathing. An elderly woman sitting near her, looking alarmed, took her by the hand and led her to the main exit. What Stephen didn't notice was Rosemary standing in the shadows of the entry, area clenching her jaw, and turning to leave abruptly.

In all the revelry, no one seemed to be paying attention to the current Board members. With stony looks on their faces, Rebecca called an end to the meeting and the Board got up and filed out the back door without making eye contact with anyone or showing any emotion whatsoever. People came over to congratulate Daniel, as well as over to Timothy and Carol, who seemed to be pinned to the other side of the room. It seemed like every holiday ever wrapped up in one jubilant moment. And Stephen realized for the first time in several hours, he could finally exhale and breathe normally.

While all this joviality was taking place, Stephen looked around and thought, "Ugh, now the REAL WORK begins."

Chapter 14 – Post-Election

With the election over and despite the big win, everyone still had an uneasy feeling something was going to happen. But so far, nothing had happened. So now the Communications Committee started meeting in earnest. What needed to be done first was to create a charter and have it approved. The first thing Daniel did was check with the management office to get a copy of any approved committee charters. As it turned out, the one-and-only committee to have had a charter approved was Landscape.

Since Andrea had expressed an interest and a desire to help with content creation, Daniel and Stephen sent the existing charter document over to her. After more than a week went by, Stephen touched base, and Andrea begged off, saying she was having an emergency with a client. So, Daniel deconstructed the charter, and he and Stephen rewrote it for the newly formed Communications Committee.

At the same time, Tom had rallied the people with construction experience and begun to pull together a Construction Review Committee as well. The intent of this committee being to review all work requests and orders, determine the most expedient and cost-efficient way to address the problems based on the Committee's experience, and submit their recommendations to the Board for approval. So, he modified the Communications Committee charter for use with the Construction Review Committee.

At the first post-election meeting the request for Communications and Construction Review to become official committees was submitted to be part of the meeting agenda. As the previous president had been voted out and the vice-president had stepped down, the first order of business at the meeting was to assign positions on the Board. And the new Board members noticed immediately while well attended, this meeting had nowhere near as many people as the previous ones and the "temperature" of the room was significantly less heated.

Much to Stephen's consternation, he spotted Audrey fidgeting and gazing about like a bird searching for crumbs to peck at. She was looking everywhere and anywhere, but steadfastly refused to look in Stephen's direction. Of course, that was absolutely fine with him. Just as the meeting was beginning, there was hushed gasp and Stephen turned, along with the rest of the room, to see Rebecca enter and sit towards the back. Audrey half-stood and waved frantically in her direction. Rebecca stared straight ahead, not acknowledging Audrey or anyone else.

As they began the meeting, Timothy stated, "The Board will need to vote among themselves on who will fill the open positions." Before he could continue, a woman in her late 40s or early 50s stood. Dark hair randomly piled atop her head with three conspicuously bright blue streaks, held in place by two yellow pencils, she had large, dark-framed designer glasses at an off angle on her face. She was wearing a bulky, stretched out sweater over baggy, paint-splattered jeans, and sandals.

Clearing her throat VERY LOUDLY, she said, "I'm Zelda Eventide. *Famed* interior designer."

Looking around and searching for nods of agreement but only receiving puzzled looks, she continued, "I've done a LOT of design work for Oracle. Oracle database software. You know? Oracle! Very well known for their design aesthetics."

At this, Stephen heard a woman whisper, "Oracle is known for their design aesthetics? Since when?"

Again, looking about and still receiving puzzled stares, she continued, "Well, I live on Hemlock Lane and I'm here to request the Board cut down all the trees around my home. I have two stalkers. You heard me! Two stalkers!"

Her head whipped around, murderously glaring at everyone around her, "They're using the trees to climb up on my roof and peer into my windows. I live in deadly fear of my life."

Now everyone in the room was murmuring, exchanging puzzled looks, and whispering.

Her voice going higher and louder, Zelda stated, "Oh, I know none of you believe this, but I was held hostage in my own home. Yes, he climbed the tree, entered my home, and held me against my will. He did..."

She sniffled a bit, but then, looking daggers at the two people who were starting to giggle, she continued, "I know a lot of you don't believe me. Well, trust me, I've been to the police many times. For whatever reason they can't do anything about Jam…, my stalker, umm, I mean, stalkers, but I have a note and they said you should just cut the trees down around my place."

With that, she sat down and stared intently at Timothy, who seemed to be running the meeting at this point.

Timothy, looking quite uncomfortable and just a bit surprised, cleared his throat and gathered his thoughts. He said, "Umm, well, uh, thank you Zelda. Did you submit this item to be on the agenda tonight? We can only address this if it's on the agenda."

At this point, Zelda stood up with her hand outstretched, with what appeared to be a piece of paper torn from a notebook limply hanging from her hand. More distraught than before with several tendrils of hair flailing about, she proclaimed, "I keep bringing this up and no one does anything. I have stalkers! Criminals! People! climbing up on my roof, entering my home, violating my space, this needs to be taken care of. I have a note from the Police Department!"

Timothy looked at the other Board members with a, "Do any of you want to take this?" look on his face and said, "Well, first up, the Board needs to select who will fill each position and then vote on it before we can proceed with any other Association business."

With that Zelda abruptly turned around and said loudly, "Well, this makes me very uncomfortable. I don't think any of us should be here for this. I think we should all leave. Now!"

With that, she proceeded to grab her bag and notebooks and stormed out towards the lobby. Shortly thereafter, everyone heard a very loud "BANG" as she slammed the front door shut!

As Stephen turned to look towards the lobby, an older woman sitting behind him whispered, "She lives up the street from me. She wants to sell her place, but the trees haven't been trimmed in years, so her view is the shits. She's pitching a Grade A hissy fit so she can sell her place as a *view home*. Oh, and her *design stuff*? She only does kitchens, and she doesn't remodel or redesign ANYTHING. She hangs garlic cloves from the ceiling, puts some terra-cotta pots with willows or branches sticking out of them around, places a few drip-candles around, and basically just loads up on whatever World Market has in stock! From the pictures on her website, she takes high-end kitchens and makes them look like a cheap Italian restaurant you'd find in a strip-mall."

(Months later Stephen heard that the "note" from the Police Department to the Association basically said, "This woman is three slices short of a sandwich and a pain in the ass. Cut her trees down so she'll stop bothering us and make her go away."

And after the Association had cut down ALL the trees around her unit as she had requested, within days the house was on the market, and she sold her view home for top dollar!)

As the meeting continued, the first question was who wanted the President's seat? Timothy and Carol's hands both went up. The Board voted, and Carol became President with Timothy as Vice-President. As Renaldo wasn't up for reelection, he continued in his role as Treasurer.

After dealing with a mind-numbingly long agenda of Association business, along with homeowner complaints and financial updates, they came around to committees. With almost no fanfare, both the Communications and Construction Review Committees were granted official status. As all committees had to have at least one affiliated Board member, Stephen was pleased they approved Daniel as the Board liaison for the Communications Committee. Carol said she planned to join as well. As no one volunteered for the Construction Review Committee, Daniel said he'd also be the Board liaison for them as well. The charters were finalized and approved.

Up next came the Landscape Committee. You could feel the tension in the room when this was announced. As Carol mentioned this, all eyes turned to Rebecca. No longer in the power suits, the meticulous make-up not in place, her hair looking less styled and more natural, she seemed more relaxed than Stephen had ever seen her.

Rebecca stood and said, "The Landscape Committee has a dedicated team who have worked long and hard to continually improve, upgrade, and maintain the vast acreage of our community. I, well, we on the committee feel it would be doing a grave disservice to everyone if the committee were not allowed to continue to provide the Association with its diligent work."

At this point Stephen noticed some familiar faces around Rebecca, but not sitting by her. Roger was there, and some other people he recognized, but did not know their names. And then Stephen noticed, standing in the back and almost in the shadows, was Rosemary.

Stephen and Andrea looked at each other. This seemed like a moment where the rubber would hit the road. Everyone knew the biggest expenditure of the Association was for landscape to the neglect of necessary and managed upkeep. Stephen was certain Carol and the Board would vote to disband this committee and start anew.

To his shock and dismay, without calling for a vote by the Board, Carol agreed to continue the committee with Sylvia as the Board liaison overseeing it. This seemed to surprise and even anger some in the room. To her credit, Rebecca politely thanked Carol and the Board and then left the meeting. A bit stunned, Stephen and Andrea left when the meeting shifted to the executive session.

Sighing Stephen said, "I don't know why Carol didn't just make a clean slate with everything. It was more than apparent what everyone wanted, and mostly got, was a reset with the Board and how things would be run."

Andrea, shaking her head, said, "Well, I'm sure she has her reasons, but still…."

When Stephen got home and turned on the light, instead of the buoyant feeling of a new beginning, he had a sinking feeling that a long-festering situation would probably get worse before it got better.

Chapter 15 – Committees

Since there were now three official committees and Daniel was on the Board, they had access to the clubhouse. Even after getting to know many of the people who had showed up for the various informal Communications Committee meetings, Stephen was a bit nervous going into the first *official* one.

When he and Daniel first got to the clubhouse, Stephen wanted to check if there were extra chairs in what appeared to be a storage room to the right of the main door. Opening the door, he found a room about the size of a large bathroom. In the back, were several tall stacks of unlabeled bankers record boxes. In the front, were various folding chairs, a vacuum, a broom, a dustpan, and some other cleaning items. Trying to recall how the smaller side space had been set up for other meetings he had attended, Stephen tried to mimic the placement of chairs and tried to ensure everyone would feel included.

Grabbing some of the folding chairs, Stephen and Daniel set up the meeting area. The usual group of people showed up, but there were a couple of new faces. Franny rushed over to introduce herself. A buxom petite woman in her late 50s, her chest seemed to arrive at least three minutes before the rest of her did.

She smiled widely and said, "Betty Jean lives across the street, and when I noticed she was heading out several nights over the past few weeks, I just HAD to find out what was going on. She told me about this committee, and I felt this was something I could really contribute to."

Betty Jean, sitting behind Franny, was rolling her eyes, and shaking her head.

Franny continued, "I work at Franklin-Templeton. I'm a senior accounts manager, and I LOVE my job. But what I really enjoy most is when a new project comes up, I make it a point to work directly with the designers to come up with fonts, colors and even paper stock for the various reports we do. They're not in my department, and it's not part of my job description but they LOVE working with me!"

Now, Stephen could clearly see Betty Jean as she used her hand to mimic a handgun and mimed blowing her brains out. Stephen smiled tentatively, hoping what he was seeing behind Franny wasn't showing up on his face.

Franny grabbed his hands, gripped them very tightly, and said, "You and I are going to get along famously," as she shook them up and down.

And with that, Franny turned to look at Andrea, and for just a moment a frown came over her face. She smiled again at Stephen, released his hands, and moved to the back to sit by Betty Jean. And Stephen couldn't help but notice how Betty Jean slide her chair just a bit away from Franny.

All the new people were introduced and in a surprisingly short period of time, the group had come together and agreed the new newsletter, while informative, should shy away from the scolding tone of past newsletters and also try to include one or more human interest or community-focused stories. Everyone also agreed this was a good way to introduce the community to the new Board members and set a tone of inclusiveness.

Everyone was now in complete agreement… until Franny raised her hand. "Well… that really does sound nice, but I have some thoughts…"

Stephen noticed Betty Jean now not only rolling her eyes, but shaking her head sadly, and if he had been a lip reader, he was pretty sure she was mouthing, "SHUT THE FUCK UP, BITCH!"

New Board members and an invigorated sense of turning things around sadly hadn't done much for the Association finances. Perilously close to insolvency, the two stewards, Renaldo and Sylvia, still maintained control of finances. One thing Stephen noticed immediately was the other official committees had posted meeting dates and set schedules on the management website. Granted dates could be moved depending on member availability or illness, once things were set it was publicly posted. Landscape met the first Tuesday of each month. Communications had chosen the second Thursday, Construction Review hadn't set a day yet, and the Board meetings were the last Thursday of the month.

But oddly, the Finance Committee had no set meeting time. Odder still, as far as anyone could tell, Renaldo and Sylvia were the only members. In fact, there didn't really seem to be a "committee" at all!

And at the most recent Board meeting, Sylvia had mentioned, almost as an afterthought, there would be a Finance Committee meeting the coming Saturday afternoon at 3 pm. Both the day and the time seemed to be very unlikely choices for HOA committee meeting. Most people had things to do or were away on Saturdays, so it almost seemed like they had picked the date to ensure no one else could or would attend. This pricked up Stephen's ears.

After the Communications Committee meeting, Stephen discussed this with Andrea and Daniel and they both agreed they probably should go. Promptly at 3 pm, the three of them showed up at the clubhouse, which was the emptiest any of them had ever seen it. In the same area the other committees had met, sat Renaldo and Sylvia. Both looked up, and both looked a little more than peeved to see Daniel, Andrea, and Stephen.

Smiling, Stephen went up to them saying, "Well, as Daniel is on the Board and Andrea and I are on the Communications Committee, we thought we'd sit in, see what you do here, and work out a way to include information in the newsletter to update everyone about what's up with the reserves and expenditures and what the plan is."

From the looks on their faces you would have thought a cow had just taken a dump on their feet. Frowning slightly, Renaldo and Sylvia looked at one another. It appeared both were recalibrating what they had wanted to say privately, as opposed to what would, or should, be said publicly. After a pause that was just a bit too long, both proceeded to talk a mile a minute. They put numbers up on the hastily set up whiteboard.

What fascinated Stephen was Sylvia would write a number, mention what it was for, then a few minutes later, mention the same line item, but this time with an entirely different number. Watching them put a number up, then another, then erase the first one, then put a different number up, only to be erased in a matter of minutes was mesmerizing. It reminded him of watching Stephen Colbert's comical use of an adding machine. It was like word soup with numbers. And some words.

One expectation Stephen had gone into the meeting with was everyone seemed to agree Renaldo was a decent guy and the only Board member speaking the truth. Despite hearing the dire news of the depleted funds, people respected Renaldo for boldly stating there were no funds remaining when everyone else was staying silent. On their way up to this meeting, Stephen had hoped to get some insight from Renaldo but was stopped cold with the way Renaldo glared at the three of them. He was obviously very peeved at their presence and appeared to resent having to explain anything on the list, regardless of how large or small.

Sylvia was more of a surprise. She was (surprisingly) civil and seemed to enjoy getting to extrapolate the numbers in front of them. Granted, she seemed to just spout off with random numbers the entire time and never once was able to tie any of it together in a way that made sense to the visitors. Two hours later, Daniel, Andrea, and Stephen left, feeling like they knew less about the funds or expenses of the Association than when they went in. All of them seemed to have a low-grade headache when they parted ways and headed home.

As time went on, the Landscape Committee continued to present items to the Board as if the election had never happened and nothing had changed. Some of it made sense, but the bulk of items seemed like a bunch of retired people with nothing else happening in their lives getting to play with someone else's money. While hoping to see some change there, Stephen, Andrea, and Daniel decided to do a field trip and attend the next Landscape Committee meeting.

Although after attending the meeting, it was somewhat funny in retrospect to recall that heading up to the meeting, the feeling of dread and apprehension Stephen had had was off the charts. Andrea was VERY quiet, and he sensed her unwillingness to go as well as her uncertainty. Daniel on the other hand seemed mildly annoyed at having to give up an evening at home to attend but was otherwise unfazed.

As they approached the clubhouse, Stephen noticed the building wasn't as illuminated as on their past visits. There was a barely visible glow from the windows by the side area where the Committees usually met, but it was much more subdued. It almost seemed like it was candle-lit. They turned to the left as they entered and saw a large group of people sitting in a circle. Immediately Stephen realized they hadn't turned on the overhead lights, as every other meeting seemed to do there. Instead, there was a dim glow cast by two very dated table lamps Stephen hadn't noticed before. Very old incandescent light bulbs beneath faded, old lampshades cast a muted orange glow over the room. As they entered, all the heads turned to look at them. Stephen shivered a bit and felt like they had walked into the coven from "Rosemary's Baby."

Stephen immediately saw Rebecca sitting in the center in front of the fireplace. Much like she was at the last Board meeting, Rebecca, was no longer attired in one of her power suits, with no conspicuous bling and seemed very relaxed and at ease. Since she was wearing all black, it added to the coven vibe. Around her, he saw Melva, who wore a loud purple pashmina with dark silks, seemingly in a trance, nodding, but not appearing to be looking at anything specific. On her other side sat Sylvia. Her bright henna hair was shining like a beacon and contrasted with the pale gray raw-silk suit and white blouse. Her hawk-like eyes bored into the interlopers with her lips tightly pursed.

Stephen wasn't quite sure, but he thought he detected the slightest nod of acknowledgement towards Andrea. Another surprise was seeing Renaldo sitting there. Inert, it was like seeing a full-grown garden gnome wearing dark slacks and a plaid shirt. And Roger was there as well. Still wearing his trademark slobbery smile, his pants now almost reached his collarbone. Stephen had assumed with Roger withdrawing from the Board, he wouldn't be involved in Association business any longer. Obviously, Stephen was wrong.

Audrey was there as well, looking as agitated and flustered as ever. Her hair askew, she had a fresh sheen of perspiration visible on her brow. She seemed like she wanted to say something, but kept darting glances back to Rebecca, who with a subtle hand gesture motioned her to stay seated and mum.

Surprisingly, or maybe not surprisingly, Zelda, the seemingly crazed design maven, was there as well. Still as frazzled and frayed as she was at the last open meeting. Her hair was not as wild as it had been at the Board meeting with the two chopsticks now holding her hair into a tight bun. A dark blouse and pants that weren't paint splattered gave her a slightly more credible appearance this evening. But her presence puzzled Stephen as he was sure she had already sold her place.

To Zelda's right was an older man who, despite it being a very warm night and even warmer in the enclosed clubhouse was wearing a full winter coat, buttoned all the way up. Very elderly, a bit stooped over, he was glaring at the newcomers, and although his lips were moving, nothing audible could be heard. Clutching a cane, his bloodshot eyes peered over his thick glasses. Stephen had the distinct feeling the old man was either summoning a demon from another universe to smite them or he was witnessing an extreme case of senility in action. After the fact, Stephen found out this was Theodore Chapman, a retired judge of some renown.

While he was taking this all in, Stephen was startled to realize Rosemary was sitting very quietly in the far corner. With the shadows the table lamps created, she was almost invisible. He could *just* see the reflection of the lamps in her glasses as she silently stared directly at the visitors. This grim appearance was more than a bit unnerving and for some reason brought The Godfather to mind.

Yet another couple caught Stephen's eye. The man looked… the only word Stephen could conjure up, was diminished. He appeared to be in his 40s but had a bowl haircut. All the way around. Nothing below the ears, but long and dark on top. Coupled with the unfortunate haircut was an incredibly blank expression. His gaze was fixed solely on Rosemary.

To the man's right was a woman of about the same age and coloring, and while not a bowl haircut, it reminded Stephen of the old Flowbee hair-cutting attachment for cutting hair that used to be advertised on minor TV stations. She also had the same blank look on her face and her gaze never seemed to leave Rosemary's face. Stephen assumed they were probably not only brother-and-sister, but quite possibly twins.

To Theodore's left was a fidgety, overweight man who was sweating profusely. Despite his weight, he had a pinched face, a 70s porn-star mustache, and thick Coke-bottle glasses.

Before anything else happened, he jumped up, running over to the newcomers, getting well into their personal space, almost shouting, "I'm Terrance. Terrance Birkhead. We've been a part of this committee for many years, and there is nothing you can do about it! Don't even think about trying to disband us or impede our efforts!"

Terrance's face was flushed with spittle flying out and his eyes were bulging and crazed. He was also breathing very heavily.

Stephen and Andrea took a step back, involuntarily. But Daniel stayed put, smiled, and said, "Hello, Terrance. We're not here to disband, change, disrupt, or do much of anything else. We've heard about this committee, I'm new to the Board, and we wanted to come observe the work that you're doing and how the committee functions."

Having worked himself up into a near stupor, Daniel's words seemed to have knocked the wind out of Terrance's sails. Stepping forward, his mouth open, ready to speak, he stopped, blinked a couple of times, and took a step back.

Still spoiling for a fight, but with a bit of the bluster gone, he muttered, "Well, uh, we were in the middle of discussing replacing some of the trees on Oleander Place. Nigel from Tree-Trimming-For-You is here to present options."

With much less bravado, Terrance sat down again facing Rebecca. This didn't stop him from suddenly jerking around, looking behind himself at Daniel and the group over and over again as if he was expecting a sneak attack.

Interestingly enough, Rebecca, completely and totally unfazed, carried on as if the observers weren't even there. A massive binder in front of her that looked like three New York City phone books from the 70s combined, she rattled off addresses, plants, problems, and some high-level botany jargon. All the while, the very smarmy man in glasses, with a Tree-Trimming-For-You logo embroidered on his polo shirt, stood somewhat behind

Rebecca. As the meeting progressed, Rebecca finally turned the meeting over to the man.

Nigel stood, cleared his throat, looked about, smiled broadly, looked a bit dubiously at the three visitors, and introduced himself as a long-time vendor for the Association and Landscape Committee. He then proceeded to go into painstaking and exhaustive detail over plans to plant two dozen crape myrtles as well as showing a diagram of areas where older trees needed to be removed. As he methodically explained the plans, what he didn't discuss was costs. Or what had come to bedevil the Association even more: the cost of irrigation and water as well as the cost of replacing or resurfacing the sidewalks, walkways, and streets where the root systems of previously planted trees had ruined them in the older subdivisions.

Stephen was furrowing his brow and wondering if Andrea or Daniel were thinking the same things. Throwing Andrea, a quick glance, she didn't notice Stephen, but was staring straight ahead and had a rather glazed and distant look on her face as she stared intently at Rebecca. Daniel on the other hand seemed to be the most relaxed person in the room, arms crossed, listening to what everyone had to say.

Once all the proposals were gone through, a vote was held, and to no one's surprise, every hand in the room went up in support. Stephen thought he spotted Nigel's hand starting to rise as well. A low level of conversation began with people congratulating themselves on another successful meeting.

As it appeared the meeting was over, Daniel spoke up and thanked the committee for allowing them to attend. To no one's surprise, there wasn't really any response from the committee members, as Stephen, Andrea and Daniel made their way out onto the street.

Walking quietly away, no one speaking for a while, Stephen finally said, "What the hell was that? And where did they find those people?"

Andrea kind of chuckled but at the same time pulled her sweater a bit tighter, throwing a worrying glance back over her shoulder.

Daniel, on the other hand, just kept going, not giving the meeting or the people a second thought.

Once they had parted ways with Andrea and were at the front door, they both said, "Wine?"

Chapter 16 – Sandra Moves In

Now sitting in on two committees as well as the Board meetings, it soon became common knowledge Stephen worked from home. So, if something came up and someone needed access to the clubhouse, they'd call or stop by. While this might have made other people feel put upon, it actually made Stephen feel more connected with the community, so he didn't mind the interruptions.

In the meantime, his friendship with Andrea became closer and stronger with the HOA being the glue holding things together. While they were definitely now interacting more socially than in an HOA manner, Stephen did notice the subject of Rebecca came up. A lot. Still. In the early days, this made a certain amount of sense but as time moved on, there seemed to be less of a need to discuss her versus more. And while Stephen and Andrea certainly joked and kidded a lot, sometimes things would seem to him to be a bit… juvenile?

Once, while standing out front talking to Jane, Andrea, walking by, joined in the conversation. Stephen mentioned an upcoming trip out of state and mentioned his friend Candice would be stopping by the house to water the indoor plants and check for packages.

Andrea responded, "If you gave us a key, we could do that. And you know what else would be fun? We could go in and completely rearrange the furniture and go through everything!"

Stephen smiled thinly, but a part of him actually believed she would do it given the opportunity.

Another time, while over at her place for a glass of wine, the conversation was about Andrea's lovely patio area. But then she said, "I can hear the two guys living next door. It used to be I heard them making out loudly, which was annoying, but now I overhear their arguments like, 'Carlos, can't you at least ACT like we're a couple when we're out?', and other very personal conversations."

Andrea seemed to really enjoy having this type of insider information. And sharing it. Which is why Stephen, while open and honest to a point, purposely never shared anything truly personal or troubling with Andrea.

And then while she was airing the dirty laundry of her next-door neighbors, she took a very sudden conversational U-turn, and said, "You know what would be a lot of fun? We should go out one night after dark and climb that tree by Rebecca's. I have a few pairs of binoculars. We could look in and see what really goes on there. She never closes her drapes. I know as I've walked through that section at night many times before."

Not really sure if she was kidding or not, Stephen smiled tightly and said, "Maybe some other time."

The number of stories Andrea had about Rebecca was staggering. From the story of her buying all three units in her building to make them into one mansion, to the one about her getting some type of financial kick-back for using Landscape Dreams, or even weirder, about her being the silent owner of Landscape Dreams, to yet another about her having some kind of illicit relationship with Raul the gardener from Landscape Dreams. And then there was the one about at least seven other residences being owned by Rebecca's family or children. The focus on Rebecca was disquieting at best, and Stephen started to change the conversation whenever Andrea brought her up.

As these changes were taking place, a moving truck pulled up to Sandra's and an army of movers worked diligently for the better part of a day. Stephen noticed he wasn't hearing from Andrea as much at this point but chalked it up to work involvements (she did seem to have a lot of work emergencies to deal with), as well as the new Association involvements. About four weeks after the moving truck left, Andrea let Stephen and Daniel know Sandra's place was settled and she was having an informal housewarming with just the four of them.

Andrea knew Daniel and Stephen loved sushi and went out for it every Saturday. Andrea had relayed that information to Sandra, and when Stephen asked if there was anything they could bring, Andrea said, "Sandra suggested you bring some of the sushi you two like."

That seemed a bit specific for an informal gathering, but Daniel, not wanting to do something poorly, went to the Asian market their favorite sushi place sourced their fish from. Ordering a large platter with a wide variety of sushi and sashimi, he also purchased special saucers for soy sauce and wasabi, along with very nice chopsticks. And he grabbed a very good bottle of sake. Meanwhile, Stephen asked Andrea if they wanted to meet and go together, but Andrea said she'd meet them there.

As the HOA owned the exteriors, there was nothing Sandra should have done to alter the exterior appearance. But in going up the walkway towards her door, visible changes met them. While everyone in their area had natural wood decks that were pressure treated. Sandra had painted hers a very bright orange. She also had installed a fair amount of outdoor artwork hanging on the wood-paneled walls along the walkway. In front of the door was an oriental carpet. It didn't look like an indoor-outdoor imitation oriental carpet, but an actual oriental carpet. Looking at the surroundings and at each other they knocked.

A voice from inside said, "Come on in."

The entryway now had Pietra Firma LuxTouch tile! The 1,000 diamonds version! The walls were ever-so-slightly off white, with an asymmetrical, but obviously expensive, light fixture hanging above. Turning left to go down to the great room, an entirely different interior greeted them. Now with the drywall up and the ceiling finished, the room felt much larger than it actually was. The same off-white walls now had select, but dramatic pieces of artwork, each with its own individual spotlight. But what struck Stephen was, the artwork all involved battle of some sort. There were also what appeared to be, antique weapons displayed along with a shield dramatically taking up the center space on the wall where the fireplace used to be. Much to Stephen's surprise, she had actually moved the fireplace over and into the corner. How she was able to do that structurally was beyond him.

The kitchen, now part of the great room, had cabinets extending sixteen feet into the air, not quite touching the now twenty-foot ceiling. The cabinets were the same off-white, along with two large islands with butcher block tops. Both islands also had large wine refrigerators built in. On top of the luxurious flooring were several plush and expensive looking oriental carpets underneath large, but again expensive-looking furniture. The sparseness and angularity of the obviously expensive furniture was less than inviting and seemed more staged for an upscale sale. Sitting on the floor, in almost the same place Stephen had left Andrea during the original party, sat Andrea. A large glass of wine in hand, she again had that distant look on her face.

Sandra stepped around from behind the kitchen island, took the sushi platter and accoutrements and welcomed Stephen and Daniel. She offered them both drinks, but Daniel asked if they could have the "cook's tour" of the place first. Sandra readily complied. Both of them were absolutely stunned at the transformation as Sandra showed them the kitchen area in more detail. She explained why she removed so much of the unused space with the drop ceiling and a storage area behind the old closet, which was now also gone.

Going back up the main landing, she showed them the half-bath, now redone with a pedestal sink, and if Stephen weren't mistaken, she had moved the toilet from one side of the room to the other. Less combative artwork adorned the bathroom along with just a bit of tasteful wallpaper. Across from that was the utility room. Stephen and Daniel's model had their washer dryer in the garage, but in this model, there was a designated laundry room with a sink. Again, beautifully done, with custom cabinets over new appliances and a singular piece of artwork adorning one wall. Enquiring about the artwork, it would never have occurred to Stephen to commission art for a laundry room.

They continued up the stairs to the second floor. Another custom light fixture illuminated the staircase along with more distinct, but less combative, artwork. Arriving at the narrow walkway that led to the bedrooms, there was now a very narrow desk underneath the windows with a small workstation and computer chair. Stephen was a bit surprised to see her putting her computer in the middle of a narrow passageway, instead of setting up a home office in one of the other bedrooms or in the den. Turning right to head towards the master bedroom, Stephen was again surprised. The bedroom fireplace was gone. This was the feature most people actually sought out in this model. In its place was now a very large walk-in closet. It seemed like she had also raised the drop ceiling a few feet.

The master bathroom was yet another surprise. She had removed the bathtub and put in a very large, black-tiled shower. In fact, what area wasn't tiled was painted black. Stephen noticed she had walled over the existing small window, so the bathroom was completely enclosed. Along with the black tiles, was a black toilet, a bidet, and a floating sink of frosted glass. The room felt *very* claustrophobic. Noticing more nozzles than he had ever seen in a shower, it looked more like a carwash than a shower. They left the bathroom and went on to the next room.

For most people with that model, they either used that room as a home office or a small guest room with a daybed. This is where Stephen would have installed the computer work area. Instead, Sandra had created what looked like a man-cave on steroids. An oversized, curved, black-leather couch took up most of the space, and faced what Stephen thought was one of the largest flat-screen TVs he had ever seen. A small black refrigerator sat in the corner, and a small black coffee table took up the remaining space. A series of speakers and a massive subwoofer were barely visible in the all-black room.

Going down the narrow walkway to the guest bath and bedroom, Stephen noticed Sandra had removed the bathtub here as well and had made a white version of the all-black bathroom in her bedroom. Smaller but almost identical. But the stark whiteness didn't have the same claustrophobic feeling as the blackness of master bath had. But the biggest surprise was the guest bedroom: it had a Pottery Barn Farmhouse Bedroom feel. Sandra had removed the closet, painted the room white with blue trim, added a flowery wallpaper border, and put in a white-washed armoire with a matching single bed,. Although the rest of the house had austere automatic blinds that were invisible when open, this room had puffy white drapes. Cornflower blue was the main accent in the bedspread and throw pillows, making the guest bedroom the coziest and warmest in the house. But even so, it still felt like a display in an upscale furniture store.

Going back to the great room, Sandra pulled out plates and let everyone help themselves to sushi. She poured everyone a glass of sake, and Stephen noticed she had two small pieces of sashimi on her plate, nothing else, while everyone else had selected six or eight pieces along with some edamame and some California rolls. The conversation was rather general with both Andrea and Stephen updating Sandra about the wacky and weird neighbors they had been encountering. While polite, there was a certain reserve with Sandra Stephen couldn't quite get past.

The topic came up of how long Stephen and Daniel had been together, and then some general chit-chat about relationships and couples. Sandra said, "Well, when I was married…"

Andrea's eyes got big, and she looked at Stephen. Sandra noticing the shift and let the sentence trail off, so Stephen, caught off guard as well, said, "Oh, when was that?"

Sandra looked into the distance, seemingly lost in thought for a second or two, then said, "Oh, this was ten, maybe fifteen years ago. I think I liked the idea of being married more than actually being married."

And with that, Andrea blurted out, "To a man??"

They all looked at Andrea, and she flushed, realizing the faux pas.

Sandra's brows furrowed a bit and she said tersely, "Of course to a man."

Daniel shifted the conversation to his travels around the world and his time in Japan. This brought everyone back to the sushi and sashimi and more sake. Everyone seemed to relax finally until about half-past 9, when Sandra suddenly got up and started purposely putting everything away.

Stephen shot Daniel a look and tilted his head towards the door. Clearing his throat Daniel said, "Well, it's getting late, and we should get going."

Sandra, still clearing things without looking up, said mechanically, "No, you don't need to leave yet," but still kept noisily returning things to the refrigerator, putting glasses and plates into the dishwasher, and clearing countertops.

Stephen piped in with, "Thank you, but we should get going. You have a lovely home and have done some amazing things with the place."

Looking over at Andrea to see if she would be joining them, she again had that far-off look. Stephen finally made eye contact, and without asking Andrea said, "I'll stay a little while longer and help Sandra clear up."

As she made this statement, she was making no move to get up from her place on the floor.

Leaving, Stephen and Daniel raised their eyebrows and called it a night.

Chapter 17 – New Neighbors

Then there were changes closer to home. The elderly woman next door, whose name they never had learned, was suddenly gone. Stephen and Daniel were coming home one Saturday afternoon to see "Roseanne" driving the elderly woman away. While driving by, the elderly woman didn't look particularly well. Not having been friends or close in any way, they heard no news immediately or received any updates.

Things were blissfully quiet until Stephen encountered Thelma a few weeks later getting her mail. She informed Stephen the old woman had passed away. It turned out she was the mother of the morbidly obese man. It also turned out the obese man was a world-renowned heart specialist.

Stephen said, "No! Really?"

And it turned out "Roseanne" was his wife and possibly in the medical profession as well. When the doctor and his wife lived there, Thelma said she had come home many a time to see the good doctor parked two to three blocks away from their street scarfing down McDonald's or some other fast food and then just flinging the trash from his car into the vacant lot near the entrance to Thornwillow Heights where he was parked. Thelma suspected he was trying to keep his dietary choices secret from his wife. Stephen relayed this story to Daniel who just shook his head. While Stephen said he was worried about what it would mean to the unit next to them, Daniel shrugged it off.

Then the noises started. For a few weeks it had been blissfully quiet. But it didn't take long to realize contractors were coming in at all hours of the day and night beyond the times allowed by the Association. It was also apparent they were doing structural work that was NOT generally allowed by the Association. Jack hammering for hours on end, crashes, and bangs that shook the entire building, it now felt like a war zone. Aware that Sandra had made many major structural changes, Stephen assumed the current contracts had pulled the appropriate permits and were adhering to the rules.

The contractors looked more like extras from a movie about gang warfare with manners and demeanor to go with the looks. They'd show up well before 7 am and start blasting their radios, usually to some very lame hair-metal station. They'd block driveways and leave debris and junk about. Seeing evidence of subpar work and the disregard for the basic construction rules, Stephen began to suspect they were not doing permitted work.

One day Stephen had had enough listening to the metal music blaring away and marched over. When Stephen entered the open garage, he encountered the main contractor; a massive slab of muscle, every inch of visible skin tattooed, including his face. The music was cranked far beyond the pain threshold. Stephen eventually got the thug's attention, and he demanded in no uncertain terms that the music be turned down. Staring up at this massive man, who was so incensed and obviously not used to anyone telling him what to do, they stared at each other murderously. In different circumstances Stephen might actually have feared for his life, but by this point he was ready to bring it. After staring each other down for a few minutes, the ruffian muttered under his breath and turned the music down. A bit. Still, a win was a win, and Stephen was glad he had finally said something.

A couple of inquiries were sent to the management company, but no reply was forthcoming, and no apparent action was taken, as the work and annoyance continued. Despite Daniel being on the Board, and Stephen's involvement in the various committee work, they didn't want to abuse their new positions, their involvement with the HOA, or seek any favoritism.

And then one day, it was quiet. Stephen went out front. No contractor trucks, the front relatively tidy. No obvious construction debris was visible. It was like he could exhale for the first time in weeks. But he also knew that either meant "Roseanne" and the dogs would be moving back, or they'd be getting new neighbors. A new cloud of pressure started to accumulate over Stephen.

A few days later, after Stephen had been lulled into a false sense of security, the nightmare with the new neighbors began…

Sitting at his computer in their office area, a low rumble started and began to get louder and louder. For a moment, Stephen thought it might be an earthquake. The rumble kept getting louder, and he could actually feel the house shaking. Realizing the sound and vibrations were coming from the front area he stepped outside and looked over at the previously quiet home. Sitting in the adjacent driveway was one of the most massive muscle cars Stephen had ever seen. Or heard. And then the second rumble started. Looking further up the street Stephen could see a smaller, but equally loud, sports car roar up and pull in behind the first sports car. With the shock of the sound and size of the cars, Stephen didn't notice "Roseanne" was parked on the other side of the driveway.

Standing by the idling sports cars were a couple. One was an attractive young woman with long red hair, dressed in kind of a rave-goth hybrid outfit. Standing next to her was someone of indeterminate gender wearing baggy shorts and a baggy football jersey with a bit of dark hair peeking out from a baseball cap worn backwards. "Roseanne" now stepped over to them and after some back and forth – it was impossible to hear what was being said over the rumbling motors – she handed what looked like keys and an envelope. Stephen's heart sank, but he stood by the garage and busied himself trimming some dead leaves off the camellia bush. Eventually "Roseanne" said her goodbyes and drove off. At this point, the young woman went over and turned her car off. The other person did the same and they vanished into the open garage.

Not wanting to be neighbors like "Roseanne" had been, Stephen stepped over and introduced himself to the young woman. The young woman smiled and said her name was Ashlee and that they were renting the place. The other person by this time was in the garage fiddling around with something and making no effort to come out. Ashlee smiled, stepped into the garage and the door quickly shut behind her.

In no time flat, Stephen and Daniel's small part of the neighborhood became massively unpleasant and over populated. The walls had already been much too thin back when they moved in, but the new residents had obviously installed a state-of-the-art surround sound system with a massive sub-woofer and indulged in playing video games and listening to music at earsplitting levels. And even worse, they didn't seem to have jobs, were always home, and the gaming and music would go on long past 2 am.

Again, trying to be good neighbors, they held back on going over to say anything. After several days of the constant noise, one evening, well after 10 pm one evening as they wanted to go to bed, Daniel and Stephen had had enough and went over to request they turn things down. They could hear the deafening sound cascading from the unit outside well before they got to the front door. They rang the bell. No response. They rang again. Still no response.

Finally, in anger, Daniel banged furiously on the door. The person who answered appeared to be the previously unidentified "partner," though with a baseball cap pulled down and bulky sweatshirt, there was no real way to tell for sure.

This person opened the door, looked at Stephen and Daniel and said "Huh?"

Daniel very politely, but firmly said, "We are your next-door neighbors. We are attempting to go to sleep. We would greatly appreciate it if you could turn the sound down."

Getting more of a grunt than a reply, the door shut in their faces. The sound went down. Somewhat. But was still going strong and continued each and every day and night.

After three or four more attempts at getting them to be less noisy failed, Stephen and Daniel adapted their sleeping routine to now include a loud fan, a white-noise machine, and earplugs. Even so, the thuds, bangs, and explosions would still come through sometimes.

While attempting to ignore the noises from next door, a former neighbor brought some of the realities to light. Stephen had gone out to water the front area one morning to see an envelope wedged into the screen door. Opening it, it was an invite from Brenda, Michael's wife. Stephen had run into her occasionally at the grocery store, and she had said she'd be sending out invites for a housewarming once their new place was settled.

On the day of the housewarming, Stephen and Daniel congratulated Brenda and Michael on their new place. Brenda beamed with pride, but then her brows furrowed, and she asked Stephen if she could speak to him away from the others.

Once they were away from the throng, she said, "You know, I work mostly nights at the university? I was coming home fairly late the other night and realized I had the invites sitting on my car seat. I figured rather than mail them and have them delayed, I'd just swing by the old neighborhood and drop the envelopes off on my way home. Well, I had left my glasses in the office, so things were probably a bit fuzzier than they should have, driving home and all. But when I got to your street there were all these people in your driveway and around. I thought maybe you were having a party or something. As I got nearer, I realized everyone was considerably younger than most of the people in the neighborhood, but I asked one of them if you or Daniel were around. To my surprise, without a word they all scurried into the open garage next to you and quickly shut the door."

She looked around, lowering her voice, "And frankly the place smelled, not only of weed, but there was a very pungent odor that I believe was someone smoking crack. I didn't know if you were aware of any of this, but I thought you should know."

Stephen's heart sank, but now many things started to make sense as all his worst fears seem to have been confirmed. Early on, Stephen had often noticed Ashlee on some evenings placing very small paper packages behind the wheel of the sports car they couldn't fit into the garage. If she caught Stephen looking over, she'd smile, but it wasn't a friendly smile. It felt more like a warning. And in the mornings when Stephen went out to water, the packages were never there. Plus, he had also noticed some pungent odors but had never been able to put his finger on where they came from.

But with Brenda's revelation, the blinders were off, and Stephen realized they were now most likely living next to drug dealers. Or at least, drug users. The day they moved in, instead of the closed wireless network he and Stephen had, and the ones for their other two nearby neighbors, suddenly ten new closed networks appeared, all with the same name, but a different number after each network identifier. Stephen and Daniel's first thought was they might be web developers, but in light of the incredibly late hours, packages placed and then vanishing, smells and late-night visitors, it seemed to indicate more nefarious work at play.

Along with this realization was fear. Although everything pointed to some type of criminal activity, it was all circumstantial. If they called the police, the most the police could do would be to "have a chat." Sharing his worries and concerns with Andrea, she just nodded sadly and really didn't comment.

Knowing a former neighbor's husband had just retired from the police force, Stephen went over and shared his concerns. The retired officer said there was little they could do with what they had. If anything, he thought if the police were to contact the neighbors, they would probably immediately assume it was Stephen and Daniel who had pointed their behavior out. And the consequences could be anything from very uncomfortable to, well, they didn't want to know.

So, moving forward, Stephen, and to a lesser degree, Daniel, tried to ignore their neighbors. But one Saturday night, as Stephen and Daniel had just finished dinner and were settling in to watch something, the wall started vibrating and they heard a very loud rumble. Their first thought was that it was a tremor, but the vibrations and rumbling noise kept going and were steady. After exchanging puzzled glances between them, Stephen put his shoes on and stepped out front.

To his immediate right were his other two neighbors. Both also in their pajamas, necks craned towards what was now referred to as "the drug dealers' den." Across the way Stephen saw a few others also looking over. Stepping further out into the driveway, he saw the garage door was up next door with the incredibly loud sports car up on a rack in the garage while its owner tinkered with the motor. For the first time, Stephen could see into the brightly lit garage and was stunned at what the new tenants had done to it.

They had placed high-quality indoor flooring down on the garage floor, they had put up drywall all around, and the room was flooded in light from several vintage pinball machines, neon liquor lights, and several vintage video games, like Ms. Pac Man.

Also, Stephen smelled *that* acrid odor. Along with the noise of the car, a stereo was blasting rap music at a deafening volume. Stephen hoped one of the other neighbors would be sufficiently annoyed to call the authorities. But it appeared everyone else was living in the same abject fear as Stephen, and the car tuning went on almost to midnight.

There were a *few* bright moments during this time when Stephen was able to smile. One day he heard a lot of mechanical noise out front. Sticking his head out, he saw a massive tow truck attempting to lift the loudest of the sports cars from where it sat in the middle of the street and had apparently died. The high-end towing service would be there a lot over the coming months.

At about the same time the "drug dealers" moved in, the owners of the unit next to Sandra had obviously had enough of *her* continual construction. (Stephen could SO sympathize with them now!) Even though the construction was pretty much over, days and weeks of daily noise and the unending commotion finally drove the current owners to leave, and the unit went onto the rental market. Stephen dryly commented to Andrea maybe she and Sandra would luck out and they would get some nice drug dealing neighbors of their own as well.

In very short order, a U-Haul truck pulled up with a small family. A young couple with a small boy... Things seemed promising... until they weren't....

Something was most definitely off with these people. In short order, they learned the new neighbors' names were Brad and Melissa Samuels and their son's name was Tony. Their move-in seemed to go on forever.

What Stephen observed when he went to get mail or came home was a sizeable U-Haul truck parked as far into the street as possible., When the woman opened it, there would be a single basket full of dried flowers, or a single small box of towels. The U-Haul would vanish only to return later the same day and inside again there would only be a small chair or maybe a garden hose.

Stephen figured there had to be a reason the new neighbor was driving somewhere reasonably close by, only loading small, light items, driving back to unload, and then going through the same motions over and over again. As this was practically in Andrea's front yard, Andrea was now suddenly writing, calling, or coming over quite frequently to complain about these new neighbors. Stephen dryly thought, "Welcome to MY world."

Melissa's behavior was, well, no getting past it, odd. While Melissa would only put one or two items in the truck when she drove it, when her husband showed up with the truck, it was actually full of things filling the cargo area. When a full truck arrived, an older woman, whom everyone assumed was the mother of one of the parents, would show up with other friends or relatives. While everyone else unloaded things, Melissa sat on the lawn LOUDLY talking on her cell-phone non-stop, complaining about her husband, the move, their new home, and essentially just everything.

Andrea had taken an instant and intense dislike for this family. While incensed at Melissa loudly yammering away almost outside her kitchen window, Andrea took a modicum of satisfaction in knowing Melissa was sitting on the small patch of lawn most of the dogs in the neighborhood favored for relieving themselves.

And it was very clear Melissa did not like being in her new home as she was never actually in it. She was ALWAYS sitting in the spot where the dogs did their business, narrating a continual soliloquy to whomever she had just dialed. At that point, there was some sympathy for her husband Brad and their small son, Tony. Until there wasn't…

Very early on, it appeared there was something wrong with Brad. From a quick glance at a distance, he seemed like a nice, pleasant enough looking guy. The presumption of someone moving into Thornwillow Heights during an overheated realty market was it would be someone who either came from money or was most certainly making it. No one could quite figure out what Brad did or why they had chosen to move here. It was obvious Melissa couldn't stand Brad, didn't seem to have a lot of affection for her child (which everyone assumed was hers, but who really knew?), and obviously did not like their new home.

Another strange thing was Brad never seemed to go to work. Or if he did, it was very late in the morning, although he was always home playing with Tony out front by early afternoon. This was another bone of contention with Andrea and several others. Despite having a clubhouse, a short walk away, along with several park areas, Brad and Tony would literally play in traffic. And in observing them play, Brad was the one who looked like the child while Tony would throw the ball back to him with a cold, focused glint in his eye. And frankly, while the unit they moved into was very nice, it was not what anyone would deem "kid friendly." The back of the unit had a lovely view of the open greenspace, but there was a perilous drop from the deck so there was no real backyard to speak of other than the private deck. And while they had a two-car garage, there was barely a driveway to speak of. Not idyllic or even very safe for small children who like to play outside.

Another behavior rankled almost everyone, although no one wanted to come right out and say it: they were white trash. Despite the lovely individual deck behind their place, every weekend Brad would pull out a giant cooler of beer, a rickety BBQ, and some folding chairs that had seen better days to set up shop, not so much in their abbreviated driveway, but right in the street.

This forced everyone to drive VERY carefully – and sometimes creatively – around them. Despite the dirty looks, the occasional horn honk, Brad would sit there with a dim smile on his face. While this was going on, Melissa, well settled down amid the neighborhood dog piss, would ignore everything and everyone while droning on in her dramatically loud voice on her cellphone. No one could really make out what all the drama was about.

But Tony was completely different. For such a small child, there was a cunning coldness about him that was unnerving. He actually brought Damian from *The Omen* to mind.

Much to Andrea's consternation, Tony seemed to be fixated on her. At least she said he was. He always played as close as possible to her place. And Melissa, probably having discovered she'd been sitting in dog piss for weeks, had taken her sad folding chair and set it up almost underneath Andrea's kitchen window. Now Andrea was coming over to Stephen and complaining almost daily about the Samuels.

One story Andrea had shared with Stephen was she had come out one morning to find Tony's skateboard in the middle of her walkway. She knew it was Tony's as she had seen him riding it the day before. She picked it up and deposited it at the bottom of her trashcan. Just to make sure it couldn't be discovered; she placed several full trash bags on top of it. She told Stephen two days later Brad and Tony showed up at her front door. They asked if she had or had seen Tony's skateboard.

Andrea looked them in the eye and said, "No, I don't have your skateboard."

It was then that Brad said, "We asked at the unit next to you and the guy who answered the door said you skateboarded in your house all the time and might very well have the skateboard."

And with that, Andrea said both Brad AND Tony were craning their necks trying to peer into Andrea's living room to see if it was set up to skateboard in. Still denying she had the board or had seen it, Brad had a look on his face like someone told him there was no Santa Claus. Tony on the other hand, glared up at her with a look of grim determination. She knew Tony didn't believe her. Andrea smiled while retelling this story and seemed actually to be proud of herself.

The next Sunday morning Stephen heard a "thud, thud, thud" coming from the front of their house. He stepped out to find Brad and Tony playing catch directly in front of Daniel and Stephen's garage door. The "thud" was their softball striking the garage door, as neither were very good at catch.

Stephen was furious and said, "Excuse me, but this is not a public play area. We homeowners are responsible for our garage doors, which we just replaced a couple of years ago. Please take this up to the clubhouse or park. This is not your play area."

What stunned Stephen was, Tony just glared at him and stayed firmly in place, but Brad stared at him in this curious way, as if he had never seen another human being, let alone had one speak to him. He just stood there with this glassy look and then mumbled, "Thank you" and started to walk away.

Tony was still glaring up at Stephen, but eventually followed his father into the street, where they kept up their feeble game of catch in the middle of the street. But Tony kept glaring at Stephen.

And a curious event happened not a week later. Stephen had to run down to the local grocery store around 10 am. Although the parking lot was very empty, he saw a man dribbling a basketball among the more closely parked cars, throwing the ball up high into the air, then dribbling, and then throwing it again. The man seemed vaguely familiar, and it was certainly an odd place to be doing this, but Stephen dismissed it and ran into the store. As he was checking out, a sweaty man in cutoffs and a tank top came into the store dribbling the ball. The man looked at Stephen with a big dumb smile, and Stephen recognized Brad.

Seconds later realization seemed to come over Brad and recognizing the man who had chastised him and his son, his smile abruptly faded and he darted further into the store.

But Stephen could still hear the noise of Brad dribbling the basketball down an aisle and shouts of, "HEY, watch it, you almost knocked me over!"

As Stephen went back to his car, he thought, "Wait until Andrea hears THIS!"

Chapter 18 – A Newsletter

Now that the committees were approved and actually up and running, real work began on the first newsletter. Everyone agreed there should be a section on the HOA finances and where the reserves stood and where current expenditures were going. But the Committee also wanted to be as positive as possible to foster inclusiveness and a stronger sense of community. For that, human interest stories were also proposed and included whenever possible. Stephen also felt it was important to break away from the mimeograph-look most HOA newsletters seemed to have by default.

THE STORY about finances needed to be first and foremost. Everyone knew where the money was going, but at this point, it was still only a vague conjecture. Andrea, with Daniel's assistance, finalized the numbers to show where the monthly dues had been going. To no one's surprise, the biggest chunk was still going into landscaping.

Stephen and Andrea thought a visual chart would show where funds were currently being directed in a better way. At first, they created an Excel pie chart. While it was efficient enough, Stephen had the idea to take a hundred-dollar bill and divvy it up into sections, each with a different color to correspond to the specific expense. When he had come up with a comp, the Committee agreed this was an even more effective way of illustrating where all the money was going.

Once the Committee members signed off the newsletter, it was sent to the Board and immediately received approval with no editorial requests made. Stephen sent it to Sandra requesting the amount needed for the entire Association.

He didn't receive a reply, but as this was most definitely a "gift horse," instead of pestering her, he decided to wait a day or two. That night, the doorbell rang. Standing there was Sandra, who seemed a bit harried. She simply said, "Here," as the loud thud of the newsletters hit the ground and you could hear her very high heels fading into the distance.

Stephen alerted Mathilda the debut newsletter was ready to be distributed to the street ambassadors, and he sent a PDF version to the management company to upload to the Association website. By the end of the week, a copy of the newsletter had gone out to each and every unit in the Association. While there were no misgivings about publishing the article, Stephen sensed this might stir up a bit of a hornet's nest. At their next meeting, the Board addressed it with Rebecca in attendance. At the appropriate moment, Rebecca was recognized by the Board and voiced her disapproval of the article.

Rebecca said, "The amount shown in the newsletter going towards landscape is inaccurate and *not* the incredibly large percentage presented in the illustration. I feel a retraction should be published post-haste."

This created a bit of a murmur amongst those in attendance. It took a couple of minutes for the meeting to come to order.

Daniel thanked Rebecca for her time and opinion and then proceeded to explain, "Yes, on the surface the number might seem inflated or incorrect with only a cursory review of the budget. However, after we dug deeper into the budget and the numbers, there were many line items that while not specifically labeled as Landscape but were in fact directly going to Landscape. Our in-depth examination eventually revealed the mislabeled expenditures. So, the number presented in the chart is indeed accurate."

With this Rebecca got up abruptly and stormed out the front door.

At the next Communications Committee meeting, everyone was in a jubilant mood, happy to know they had been able to get the appropriate information out to the community. Everyone also felt this set the stage for more awareness of the expenditures as the Association was going to enter into new agreements with several vendors. While still congratulating themselves, everyone turned to the entry area where there was a very loud bang of the front door.

Almost flying into the room was Gabrielle Gilbert. Gabby was a neighbor and close friend of Rebecca's and Stephen recalled her face from the ill-fated landscape meeting he attended. Gabby's face was flushed with anger, her nostrils flaring. Possibly in her late 50s but more probably in her mid-60s, her hair looked like she had stuck her finger in a light socket. A very wide face and a broad nose gave her tiny eyes a cartoonish feel and were made even more cartoonish by the incredibly thick and large lenses of her glasses that filled her face completely. Stephen knew of her but had never met or dealt directly with her before. Since his natural inclination was to avoid conflict, he went on a charm offensive.

While everyone was taken aback by this sudden and unexpected visitor, Stephen stood smiling, and said, "Welcome Gabrielle! We are SO HAPPY you could join us. We can use all the help we can get around here."

This was so obviously NOT what Gabby was expecting, and a bit stunned, she tentatively mumbled, "Uh, thank you."

And as she sat towards the back, the negative energy emanating from her started to recede a bit.

Not feeling the need to edit or change the agreed upon agenda, Stephen then laid out what was ahead for the Board in terms of getting vendors, quotes, and presentations so they could better work on a long-term overall plan to meet the maintenance needs of the Association now and moving forward.

Once the shock of Gabby's presence had worn off, the meeting flowed with lively conversations, suggestions, with everyone contributing. That is everyone except Gabrielle.

As the meeting wound down and everyone was saying their goodbyes, Stephen went up to Gabrielle and said, "Again, it was so nice of you to attend this evening. Hopefully this means we can look forward to your regular attendance? We noticed your street doesn't have an ambassador to distribute newsletters and help keep everyone informed. Maybe that's something you'd be interested in doing? Also, word has it you were once on the City Planning Commission. If that's so, you would be a real asset to the Construction Review Committee with recommendations for vendors. We'd love to see you there as well."

Gabrielle, all her bluster now completely evaporated, looked around tentatively, as many of the committee members were scrutinizing her intently as she said, "Uh, well, ummm, I don't think I could assist with vendors as that might be a conflict of interest with the City, but you know… umm, we'll see."

Gabrielle was never seen at another committee meeting or Board meeting after that.

Much later down the road, she threw her hat into the ring for some role on the City Council. The day after the city-wide election was the Board meeting. Stephen had gone up early to help set it up, and Timothy was at the door holding a piece of paper and chuckling.

Stephen said, "What's so amusing?"

Still chuckling, Timothy showed him the City Council voting results for their district:

"Gabrielle Gilbert – Votes: 1"

Smiling broadly, he said, "That means none of her friends voted for her, and as I suspect she voted for herself, not even her husband cast a vote for her."

Stephen had to laugh at that.

Chapter 19 – The Firebreak

Around this time, Stephen and Andrea had the idea to (perhaps) dig into the archives to see if they could (maybe) create a history and timeline for the Association since it was now over thirty years old. That could provide a background for the current residents most of whom came in long after the HOA was initially established. What was interesting was when they asked the current management company people about this, they had *no* archive documents predating their being engaged. Thinking back to that first committee meeting and remembering the bankers boxes in the supply closet, Stephen made a mental note to check them out the next time they had a meeting at the clubhouse. Someone had mentioned these might have been the historical documents that survived. Was it Thelma?

At the next meeting at the clubhouse, when Stephen and Daniel looked in the supply closet, all the bankers boxes were now gone. No one admitted to taking or moving the boxes, though Andrea voiced suspicion that Rebecca and her followers removed the documents for nefarious reasons, not articulated. A few emails were sent out to longer-term residents inquiring if anyone had any historical and/or original materials from the inception of the HOA.

One day Daniel received an email from Rosemary, "Daniel, I am in possession of many of the original documents from the incorporation of the original HOA. This includes the original sales brochures and marketing materials. If you would like to stop by this weekend, I can lend these to you if you like."

Daniel replied, "I'll come by later on Saturday, if that's okay with you."

Rosemary agreed, so that Saturday Daniel knocked on her door. Answering with a big smile until she caught sight of Stephen coming up the walkway. Then her entire face closed like a bank vault. Stephen caught her gaze and could feel the animosity as he walked up to the door. Turning to face Daniel, a forced smile reappeared as she welcomed them into her house. It was pretty much what Stephen suspected it would be like, dark colors, older style furniture, oil paintings of landscapes that could very easily been acquired at a motel-art auction, doilies (lots and lots of doilies), and a very large collection of ceramic cats. Rosemary indicated the box was on the landing and asked Daniel if he could retrieve it for her.

As he went up the steps, Rosemary turned to Stephen and with a tight smile said, "It really would be a shame if *some people* had a grudge and were using a newsletter as a way to settle a score."

Before Stephen could respond, Daniel had returned down the half-flight of stairs with a medium-size bankers box in hand and Rosemary turned to smile as she thanked Daniel for getting the box for her.

Thanking Rosemary for the materials, she gaily said "Please, keep them as long as you need them. Just return them when you're done with them" and then shut the door behind them.

As they walked up the street Stephen said, "Do you know what she said to me?"

Something had been nagging at Stephen for quite a while: the terrain around their community. With acres of dense brush, just looking out of their living room windows they could see five-foot high weeds, pampas grass, dead or dying oaks, and a lot of pine trees surrounded by acres of dried pine needles. All the previous HOAs and apartments he had lived in had been very urban, either downtown or downtown-adjacent locations. Thornwillow Heights had a vast green space (that wasn't all that green most of the time) and it had obviously not been trimmed or suffered a fire in decades. All this dry and highly flammable material made Stephen uneasy.

With so many items in front of the new Board, front and center being the budget, Stephen brought it up casually with Andrea.

Not recalling where Andrea cited as her source, she did say, "Rebecca is apparently friends with the local fire chief and has relayed that the Association is in full compliance with any and all fire regulations. They apparently hang out at swanky cocktail parties."

For a moment Stephen thought, "Regardless of what the situation or question might be, if it regards Rebecca, Andrea ALWAYS knows the backstory or has the answer."

While this might in fact be true, Stephen was still uneasy with what he saw all around him. At the next Communications meeting, he raised the subject as a possible article to bring to the Association's attention.

One of the women present, Estelle, said, "I've noticed the same thing. I'm going to call the Fire Department and see if they could send someone out to walk the grounds and review our readiness."

Everyone was in complete agreement. A few days later Stephen got a call from Estelle saying, "Deputy fire-chief Tory Mayberry is coming Tuesday morning at 10 to walk the grounds. Would you like to join us?"

Stephen readily agreed.

A very small group made up mostly of volunteers from the Communications Committee greeted Tory when she arrived. Medium build, possibly in her mid-30s, Tory was in uniform and had a no-nonsense demeanor. She had allocated about two hours to walk the grounds. They started out around the clubhouse and the nearby buildings.

Tory was nodding, making small notes, and commenting here and there:

"You might want to remove those trees. They're a bit too close to the roofs"

"That area should be cleared. Should a fire break out, that would go up instantly and endanger those buildings over there."

And so on…

A bit over an hour in, Stephen suggested they drive over to the area behind where his home was. The caravan of cars parked, and they walked back behind his building.

Tory dropped any pretense at cool and said, "Holy Shit! Clear this out IMMEDIATELY! This area is a massive fire danger. It looks as if it hasn't been trimmed or cleared in years. Between all the dried material that would go up instantly and the angle of the hill, this entire area is a VERY HIGH RISK!"

One of the women said, "Well, I think that's county or city land just beyond that group of bushes. Will they take care of that?"

Tory said, "ABSOLUTELY NOT. It's a green space. However, if your group were to clean it up you would have no complaints or worries from the city or county."

Everyone looked around at each other, eyes wide, just a bit sobered. They all thanked Tory for her time and said they'd touch base with her once the area was remediated.

Andrea and Stephen wrote up Tory's findings and recommendations, and it was submitted for the Board agenda. The subtext being the Landscape Committee's mania for aesthetics had been to the detriment of the overall safety and well-being of the community. While the new Board had been very reluctant to address the old guard's Landscape Committee, this was yet another reason to finally disband the committee!

Chapter 20 – Trouble in Paradise

The anxiety and pressure on Stephen and Daniel's end of the street just kept building. The "drug dealers" behavior seemed to be on an upswing. On the rare occasions Stephen saw Ashlee out during daylight hours, she'd smile and wave, but it had a decidedly "ironic" feel to it. Stephen wasn't sure which was worse: the actual disruptions that started daily around 11 am and went on long past midnight, or what he imagined behind the noise and activity?

Stephen and Daniel had an elliptical trainer set up in the garage, with a small TV and headphones so they could watch DVDs while working out. Daniel usually watched Teaching Company lessons, while Stephen ended up watching episodic TV. Just when the "drug dealers" moved in, Stephen was about a season and a half into *Breaking Bad*. Between the actual disruptions and what his imagination was laying out, he found he had to find something safe like *Friends*, or even *Burn Notice*. *Breaking Bad* felt a bit too close to home… almost literally.

Stephen and Andrea still messaged back and forth throughout the day, worked together on getting the newsletter ready, and dropped in on one another for tea or wine. While over at Andrea's one afternoon, Stephen noticed she now had five cell phones spread out on her kitchen counter. Stephen had a couple of phone numbers for Andrea but had assumed one was the home number and other her cell, but on the few occasions he had tried to call her, all of his calls went unanswered. Now he wondered why she needed so many phones. But he didn't ask. It was also then when Stephen noticed several pair of binoculars of varying sizes and magnification and a telescope in the corner. And today Andrea seemed a bit more stressed than usual.

She had confided to him earlier about her intense dislike for her workmate Luke and their fraught dynamics. Apparently despite her very best efforts at appearing friendly, Luke had apparently complained to their supervisor. Andrea found out Luke felt she had had too many "work emergencies" and wasn't really doing the work required for the project. Andrea was worried she'd lose the gig. Stephen tried to talk through the worst-case scenarios and help Andrea try to salvage the strained relationship.

He suggested Andrea make more of an effort to actually be there (she always did seem to have a lot of work emergencies), and maybe lean in and at least *pretend* to have some more interest in Luke and the project. She seemed to be taking the suggestions seriously, and after talking over a few other items, she said she was going to head into the office and see if she could put any of this to use.

So Stephen was pleased to receive an email that evening saying her efforts at befriending Luke and trying to make him an ally seemed to have worked. She said once she showed concern for him and his issues, his rancor melted away and when she expressed her own worries about Suzanne, Luke said, "Not to worry. I've worked with Suzy for years, and I'll put in a good word for you."

Andrea was VERY relieved and felt her continuation was on firmer ground now.

A few days later, Andrea sent one of her daily missives and mentioned the large estate adjacent to Thornwillow Heights. Andrea was apparently friends with the woman who owned the property and she just found out that after thirty-three years, this woman planned to sell. This didn't really matter to Stephen, but it seemed important to Andrea. The estate's driveway and about twenty feet of the woman's property overlapped onto the HOA property, but for all intents and purposes, it was a separate world. The woman said she had an easement.

What Stephen was now hearing was there was bad blood between the Landscape Committee and the estate owner. They had almost come to blows a few times in years past. It seemed to be about the two largish trees near the estate's driveway. Stephen couldn't see why it mattered to either party, but for whatever reason, it did. And even more puzzling to Stephen was why Andrea was so caught up in it.

But Stephen realized, if it had to do with Rebecca, then Andrea was interested. Suddenly now, out of the blue, Andrea was now voicing concerns of legal retaliation from Rebecca.

"Retaliation for what?" asked Stephen.

Andrea got all quiet and looked around like her place was bugged. Stephen thought she was being funny. Except she wasn't trying to be.

And that's when Andrea said, in all seriousness, "She might subpoena my emails to you."

Again, dubiously, Stephen said, "Why?"

Andrea ignored that question, but now said, "I read there is this thing spies do that I think we should utilize."

Stephen looked at her with an "Are you shitting me?" expression.

Andrea went on, "I'll create an email account at Hotmail, and we'll both have the log-in and password. But instead of sending and replying to emails, one person will log in and create a draft, then sign out. Then the other person logs in, reads the draft, then deletes it and leaves a new draft. This way there won't be an email chain to follow."

There was a VERY LONG silence as Stephen looked at Andrea. He knew she had a dry sense of humor and liked taking the piss out of people. But he couldn't read if this was one of those occasions. Stephen had witnessed her when she encountered someone from the Landscape Committee. She'd smile warmly and give them a friendly, "Hello, how are you doing?" only to mumble underneath her breath, "Asshole!" after they left. Stephen was wondering if he was now on the receiving end of one of these moments.

Still not sure how serious she was, Stephen asked, "For real?"

Andrea laughed, but a laugh Stephen couldn't really read, and said, "It will be fun!"

So, with that, Andrea grabbed a piece of paper and wrote down, "Anastasia1918 at Hotmail" and jotted down an arcane password down.

Heading home, Stephen wasn't completely sure if he was just made a fool of or if this was a middle-aged woman reliving (or possibly living) some type of high-school fantasy game like passing notes in the hall. When he got home, he let out a long sigh, logged into the Hotmail account, and there was a draft waiting, "Let's not use real names. We know who we're talking about. This will be fun. Bye."

Still unsure about the whole thing, Stephen erased the draft and typed, "So, is the person selling the big place (at a loss as to how to mention the estate going on sale) really going through with the sale?"

He logged out and worked on some other things. Just before bedtime he logged back and found, "Yes, it is going on the market soon. You should go up there with me and meet her tomorrow."

Stephen erased the draft, and replaced it with, "See you at 11" and went to bed.

The next morning Stephen went through his "usual" email and completely forgot about the sign-in, sign-out account. He knocked on Andrea's door and she led him up the street and then up a steep driveway towards the neighboring estate. She was bubbling over talking about how palatial the place was, having existed many years before the HOA, and as a result of selling land to the HOA, they had an easement.

As they made their way up, Stephen was even less impressed with the small easement space and two trees than he had been. Sycamores were never a favorite of his and he couldn't see much difference between them being trimmed down or left to grow to their full size. Greeting them at the top of the driveway was Lily. Probably late 50s, five foot four or so, and a bit on the sturdy side, she was quite friendly and welcoming.

She led them to the front door and gave Stephen and Andrea a full tour. It was somewhat of an odd layout. It appeared there might have been a single-story ranch home originally, but over time they had added rooms on either side, and eventually even a second story. Lily loved the place, but her kids had moved out, and it just felt too big for her to be alone in.

As Lily was pointing out this or that, Andrea brought up the subject of Rebecca. Lily, her friendly demeanor vanished as she stopped dead and said, "THAT CUNT! I do not know who-the-fuck she thinks she is, but she has been a pain-in-my-ass since she ascended to the throne of the HOA. You've seen the easement area? It is nothing. Literally nothing. You would think doing the slightest bit of trimming or change was equivalent to painting a mustache on the Mona Lisa! To be honest, more than anything else, that's why I want to get out of here. It's just bullshit!"

Stephen found himself looking down the driveway at the incredibly small area and was at a loss for words why anyone on either side of this divide would care what happens there at all. It simply didn't look like a make-or-break type of thing. Calming down, Lily, regaining her joviality, invited them to have some tea and they spent a very pleasant couple of hours together.

A few days later Stephen's phone was going crazy. Going over to look at the phone, there was a message from Andrea, "GET OUT HERE NOW!"

Not quite sure what was so urgent, Stephen threw his shoes on, dashed out the door, and ran up to Andrea's. Andrea was standing in the street pointing up at Lily's driveway.

Standing in the street was Rebecca wearing a jogging suit, sweatband around her head, with a water bottle and small towel in her hands. Standing just up the driveway was Lily wearing red shorts and a white short-sleeved blouse. Both of them were clearly screaming at each other and were furious. Andrea was thoroughly enthralled and clearly excited by the battle up the street. Stephen tentatively moved forward behind Andrea, who was now charging up the street.

As they got nearer, the words were becoming clearer, "You fat cow, who the fuck do you think you are telling me what I can or cannot do on my own property?"

Rebecca, almost rabid, responded with, "You think you're so fucking great! The queen of the walk? That Little Miss Butter-wouldn't-melt-in my-mouth, you just love to screw with me. YOU KNOW that isn't your property. You're just giving one final finger to me before you blow out of Dodge on your high-and-mighty horse! I'll see your fat ass in court before I let you touch those trees!"

Lily, now looking like she could murder Rebecca, shrieked back, "You nasty bitch. Where's your pool boy, I mean, Raphael, or whatever the fuck his name is? Has he run out of bushes to trim at your house? Maybe he's not here with you because he's in the hospital with a sprained dick! I will see

YOU in court if you so much as LOOK AT ME DO YOU UNDERSTAND, BITCH??"

And with that both started to walk towards each other, and violence was clearly in the air. Had this been a movie, the music from *The Good, the Bad, and the Ugly* would be playing.

Andrea seemed to be in a trance, unblinking as she watched the two gladiators meeting in the ring. And it was at that very moment a very loud and long horn honked as a car came rolling down the driveway directly behind Lily. Everyone had been so caught up in the brewing battle, no one had noticed the vehicle.

The driver, a college-aged woman, was now leaning on the horn, her head outside the window yelling, "MOM. STOP! DO NOT LET THIS WOMAN GET TO YOU. GET IN THIS CAR RIGHT NOW!"

Lily stopped, turned to look at her daughter, and then turned to look at Rebecca, who had stopped in her tracks. You could almost hear the internal dialog, "I should just haul off and deck the bitch!" but at the same time you could see the conflict.

Taking a deep breath and throwing another murderous glance over her shoulder, Lily turned and got into her daughter's car. Rebecca, breathing heavily, glared at the car as it almost ran her over speeding out of the driveway and up the street. Seemingly unaware of Andrea or Stephen's presence, Rebecca stood there a moment longer, toweled down her face, turned and took off running in the opposite direction.

Seeming to not want to leave whatever space she was in, Andrea turned to Stephen grinning from ear to year and said, "Wasn't that WONDERFUL?"

Having a flash-back to Christine at their old condo, again, Stephen found he had absolutely no words. None. He turned and started walking back home. He thought Andrea would do the same, but she just stood there looking at the site of the fierce spat, as if it were to rematerialize again at any moment.

That evening Stephen recounted the whole incident to Daniel, who seemed annoyed at just having to listen to it. He really didn't like a lot of these people and hearing the bad behavior just reinforced his negative impressions.

Turning back to his computer Daniel stopped and said, "Well, this is interesting. I'm assuming this has to do with the incident you witnessed earlier today. It seems the owner of that property, whatever her name is, has requested an in-person meeting with the Board this weekend to discuss what happened."

Stephen kind of raised his eyebrows and logged into the shared email with Andrea. To his surprise, instead of a new draft or the old draft being there unread, there were now TWO drafts, one in Chinese and one in Russian. Alarmed and more than a bit rattled, Stephen logged out and made up his mind he was not going to log back into that email ever again.

As it turned out there were a lot of different things going on at the moment, so Stephen not only didn't run into Andrea, but at that point, he also had no reason to communicate with her immediately. He soon forgot about the whole email subterfuge until many months later and he realized Andrea never asked why he wasn't using it.

That Saturday, Daniel headed out for the impromptu Board meeting. He was back within an hour and smirking. As Daniel had never met Lily, he was going in with a relatively unbiased opinion, minus Stephen's retelling of the incident.

When he got back, he said, "She was SO demure, and was going on and on with 'I was in fear for my life. This woman just came out of nowhere threatening me, calling me vile names. I've never felt so scared in my entire life. She said 'F-you', I mean language I've NEVER USED IN MY LIFE, and much worse.'"

The upshot was, the Board agreed with her standing on the easement, told her to do whatever she wanted to do to sell the property and not to give Rebecca or the Landscape Committee another thought. And that was the nail in the coffin of the Landscape Committee.

Chapter 21 – The End of a Committee

The next Board meeting had more people in attendance than usual. And once again it had a crackling energy. In attendance were all the Landscape Committee members. Possibly signaling battle was imminent, Rebecca, once again, was decked out in her designer suit, power red lipstick in place, hair styled, and conspicuous bling on display. Sylvia, her hair just that much redder than usual, sat by Rebecca glaring. Melva for once wasn't wearing her trademark pashmina but was attired in a simple pantsuit. Sitting to Melva's right was Audrey. Visibly shaking, she was glaring murderously at Stephen. Terrance was also moving about with nervous energy, as were the rest of the committee members, who all seemed to be having a difficult time staying still.

While there were Landscape supporters present, they were far outnumbered by those who were more than ready to finally see an end to this wasteful committee. The meeting began as usual, taking care of old business before addressing new items. When the agenda item for the Landscape Committee came up, several people tried to talk over each other, and it was a bit of a challenge to bring order to things. Despite some impassioned pleas from long-term residents aligned with the Committee, what had previously felt like a bully pulpit with the old Board and Committee was now reduced to begging and pleas to allow things to continue unabated.

Rebecca asked to speak and restated everything she had put forward when the new Board had taken over. However, this time, she was thanked without a reassurance the Committee could continue.

With this Audrey jumped up to the annoyance of just about everyone in the room and shouted, "I HOPE YOU ARE ALL HAPPY. WE, REBECCA, ALL OF US, HAVE GIVEN SO MUCH AND YOU'RE NOT LISTENING TO WHAT WE'VE BEEN SAYING!"

Catching her breath, Audrey continued, with a bit less volume, "And that is why me and my husband Dolph have put our home on the market and will be moving to a friendlier and more agreeable community!"

Stephen was fairly certain Audrey was looking for people to protest and ask her not to move, but there was a collective sigh of relief and a couple of people actually clapped.

NOT getting the response she thought she would, she gathered her things and stormed out shrieking "FUCK ALL OF YOU!" and banged the front door shut on her way out.

At that point, everyone could hear a car revving over and over again until it finally peeled out loudly, tires screeching. And just like at that first Communications Meeting, there were horns honking, sounds of yelling, and finally the sound of a car screeching off into the distance.

After all that had settled down Terrance Birkhead rose to speak without being recognized. The agitation rising in his voice, he not so much asked, but DEMANDED, the Board allow things to continue as they had, going as far as to threaten lawsuits claiming, "The ONLY THING keeping our property values up is the AMAZING JOB OUR LANDSCAPE COMMITTEE has done!"

Daniel, unruffled, let Terrance continue speaking until the point when Terrance seemed to have exhausted himself.

Then Daniel calmly said, "Thank you very much for expressing your opinion and showing up this evening. We will be taking everything that is presented here this evening into consideration."

This seemed to catch Terrance by surprise, and you could now see confusion overtaking the extreme anger he had displayed.

Daniel, receiving a nod from Carol and Timothy, went on quietly to say, "We've heard from a lot of people this evening, but in light of the recommendations from the Deputy Fire Chief, the budgetary concerns of the organization, and opinions expressed, both pro and con, regarding the current Landscape Committee, I propose we disband the current Committee and begin again from scratch."

And with that the motion passed to disband the committee with a notice to go out when a new Committee would convene.

When he arrived at the meeting to establish a new Landscape Committee, Stephen noticed it was not nearly as packed as some had suspected or worried it would be. There were quite a few people Stephen had never seen before and more surprisingly, not as many from the old Landscape group as he was anticipating. Most of the Board was there. While awkward, clumsy, and possibly not as defined and focused as it might be, the nay-sayers were sorted out much sooner than anyone thought.

The biggest nay-sayer, Terrance Birkhead, was one of the first to argue they couldn't disband the previous committee. Again. Threatening legal action, restating his claims that the *ONLY* thing keeping property values up was the landscaping, he blathered on for well over ten minutes, more-or-less replaying his "greatest-hits" of as to why they could not disband the Landscape Committee.

But they could, they did, and after letting him rant for far too long, Daniel said, "We're really glad you showed up and expressed how you feel about this. We will certainly take your comments and thoughts into consideration as we move forward."

Terrance couldn't quite grasp whether he had been dismissed or if he had possibly won his point. Obviously confused, he stepped back and sat down. As the meeting progressed it finally dawned on him that, indeed, he had been dismissed, even if it was in a polite manner, and he stormed out.

As the door banged behind him, one of the older women whispered, a tad loudly, "Good old Dickhead finally figured one out!" and there was a round of terse laughter as everyone glanced about wondering if there was still anyone present who might report the laughter back to Terrance.

Another thorny subject was soon to arise as well. Landscape Dreams. They had been the main vendor for landscaping for as long as anyone could remember. And there were a lot of whispers, rumors, and wild theories about their participation with the Association.

One woman in the back said, "I heard Rebecca is an investor, so the Association has been paying HER company to do the work around here. Which, frankly, isn't that great. That's unless you live on HER street."

This resulted in murmurs of "I didn't know that?" … "That's horseshit, Rebecca is far too smart to invest in that outfit" … "What is everyone mumbling about?" …

It was then that Stephen noticed Sarah Smith to the left of the main group. Of course, he should have known she was there earlier as the strong scent of gin had been wafting through the room for a while now.

Sarah stood up, slurring ever so slightly, "It's the main guy, Raul. What a stud. He's doing half the women up here. Don't know if Rebecca is one of the lucky ones, but let's say I've seen him coming out of more front doors, than I have seen him doing any yardwork in front of the doors."

Sarah added, somewhat wistfully, "Raul NEVER attends to my shrubs."

And with that, she sat down with an unceremonious plunk. This reduced the chatter in the room to deafening silence, as everyone looked at each other and then over at Sarah, who it appeared might be taking a nap now.

Waving away the gossip, Carol opened the discussion so people "with an actual opinion about Landscape Dreams" could speak up.

This resulted in a solid half hour of mixed reviews and opinions. A tad more than a simple majority all had complaints of inattention on their particular streets. Water had been turned off or was malfunctioning or was flooding. Plants were struggling, and in many cases had died.

There were some, though, who felt Landscape Dreams were doing an admirable job and defended the areas that were flourishing due to the vast size of the property and funding limitations the previous Committee had put in place. This was said with a wary glance about, fearing pushback or reprisals from the former Committee members.

Thankfully, all the conversations stayed civil. After two hours of discussions, it was suggested the Board allow other vendors to come in to present and offer quotes and also see if there might some fresh eyes and thoughts on how to combat the worsening drought situation.

Leaving the meeting Timothy said, "It felt like we had some adult and respectful conversations tonight, minus, ahem, SOME members speaking up in less-than-respectful ways."

At the next Board meeting, the main agenda item was to hear from prospective landscape vendors. It had turned out due to the size of the complex and the terrain, there were only a few companies with the scale needed to take on the task. After several phone calls they found an engaging young man, whose company currently took care of three HOAs of the same approximate size and terrain in the area. Lawrence was incredibly personable and also exceptionally well prepared. Showing before and after pictures of the work they had done elsewhere, he also came prepared with Thornwillow specifics and showed diagrams and pictures of the areas where he felt immediate work was needed. In addition, he even had a proposal for a long-term plan. As an added bonus, he said he could supplement their workforce to take on the very challenging and large firebreak work that was pending.

His presentation was met with nods of approval and energized whispers. While the overall mood of the room was positive, in the corner a few of the old Landscape Committee members sat, glowering, and whispering tersely to one another. To many people's dismay, Landscape Dreams was allowed to also make a presentation. Raul was there, but the main person speaking was the actual owner of the company. Cheery and having the same level of smarmy the tree trimming firm had had, the two of them presented lovely pictures (probably taken on Rebecca's Street), charts, graphs, numbers, facts, and figures. But although there were a lot of words and numbers, their main take-away was, "Yes, we can reduce costs, but this will come at a reduction of services and coverage."

With this pronouncement, eyes were wide, and there were more whispered murmurs.

"Reduce it more? Wouldn't that make us an actual desert? "

"So, that's Raul. I've heard of him, but never seen him on our street."

"I've seen their trucks parked in other parts of the city, but never once have I actually seen their people out on our street doing anything."

Their presentation ended with the Board promising to review it along with the other proposal.

As everyone exited, Stephen felt like a very good first step had been made.

That weekend Andrea showed up at Stephen and Daniel's front door first thing. Since Sandra had moved in, this wasn't a common occurrence.

She seemed very upset and said, "Timothy and Carol have received a firmly worded request, which frankly, is more of a demand, to meet with the former Landscape Committee at Rosemary's house this afternoon."

Andrea seemed very distraught over this. She went on to say, "Timothy is unavailable, and Carol is traveling, and they asked if you (Daniel) and I could go in their place?"

Daniel looked peeved but not the least bit ruffled. He looked at Stephen, and then back to Andrea and said, "I guess I can go. I mean, what the hell do they want or think they're going to get? Fine. What time?"

Andrea looked relieved, but still tense. She said, "I believe they requested one this afternoon."

Daniel rolling his eyes and said, "Fine" and then went back downstairs to what he was doing.

Stephen stayed at the door chatting a bit longer with Andrea. Stephen, his brow furrowed, asked, "Why are you so concerned? What do you think they're going to do that has you so worried?"

Andrea, looking over her shoulder, said, "They're capable of anything. I have this feeling Rebecca has it in for me."

Stephen, the expression on his face showing incredulity said, "I'm not sure she even knows who you are. I have doubts they can say or do anything. Daniel is very unflappable, so just let them have their say, and life will move on."

Andrea, still not looking convinced, said, "Good. I couldn't face that group alone."

With that she left, and Stephen went down and asked Daniel, "What do you think this is about?"

Daniel, looking annoyed that another moment of his weekend was being consumed by nonsense said, "Who cares? They have no power or influence. There goes an hour of my day I'll never get back."

After getting back from errands, Daniel went by Andrea's to pick her up and they headed towards Rosemary's place. Stephen, not being on the Board, wasn't invited and was relieved he wasn't. Less than an hour later Daniel returned home with Andrea in tow. Both were chuckling, and Andrea seemed relieved and almost light-hearted.

Stephen said, "So? How did it go?"

Chuckling a bit, Daniel said, "It was *really sad*. Like, nine out of ten on a Richter Scale of sad. The entire former committee was there along with a few others."

Andrea, standing there, was nodding along.

Daniel continued, "Well, right off the bat Rebecca said, 'We want Landscape Dreams back as our contractor' and I said, that is absolutely not going to happen under any circumstances. It is not going to happen. Ever!"

Daniel said, "With that, everyone started talking amongst themselves, mumbling stuff about this not being right or fair."

Daniel continued, "Rosemary then spoke up and asked, 'Well, can Landscape Dreams do the firebreak work? Or could they be an adjunct to the new vendor?', to which I replied, no. Just no."

Andrea now piped in with, "And what about Rebecca? DID YOU SEE HOW SHE LOOKED? OMG. It was like she was unwell. No make-up, her hair just kind of limp and hanging there. Wearing a blouse that looked like she got it from the clearance rack at Target."

As she said this, there was unrestrained glee in her voice and a big smile on her face.

Daniel kind of dismissed that part of Andrea's narrative and continued, "And of course Terrance had to pipe in. All red-in-the-face, voice pitching higher-and-higher, cracking just a bit. Geez, when he said, 'Well no one better touch *my trees*. They're mine and they CANNOT BE TOUCHED OR TRIMMED without my express approval!', and the group kind of applauded and made noises of agreement. It was really sad and pathetic."

Andrea seemed to have completely moved on from her fearful mood this morning. She was now giggling and even gloating a bit over the perceived impotence of the former group.

Stephen, while he had been curious about the requested meeting, had more-or-less assumed what they had just told him was what pretty much what he expected to happen.

With that, Andrea said they should have a bottle of wine to celebrate.

Daniel looked at Stephen with a "What the hell?" look.

As Andrea said, "I'll be right back. Oh, I'll stop by and see if Sandra wants to join us."

Stephen made a bit of a face behind Andrea's back, but also shrugged. A few minutes later, a less buoyant Andrea returned.

Bottle of wine in hand, she said, "Well, I knocked on Sandra's door, and when she answered she looked like she had been crying. I asked her if everything was ok, and she said 'Fine', despite not appearing fine in the least. I invited her over and told her about the meeting, but she just said she wasn't in the mood and shut the door on me. I wonder what that was all about?"

Chapter 22 – Changes

Shortly after the formal dissolution of the Landscape Committee, more surprises came. Sylvia and Durusha tendered their resignations. Around the same time, Renaldo just quit showing up. No official notice. When Carol eventually reached out to Renaldo, she was notified that he was done. Shortly after these updates, Andrea reached out to Stephen asking him to stop by. He wondered what could be happening now and she quietly informed Stephen she had met with Carol and Timothy and had agreed to fill a seat on the Board until the next election.

While this was good news, it confused Stephen since Andrea had been vehement about having absolutely no desire to *ever* be on the Board. And even more confusing was the fact they seemed to talk about everything and get each other's opinions on things of much lesser importance. Not hearing about this until after the fact was a bit off-putting to him. Regardless, Stephen was happy and felt the hard work and agendas everyone had worked towards would be continued.

A few days later, when Stephen had gone over to Andrea's to drop off some materials for the Communications Committee, she invited him in. Offering him a glass of wine, they sat down in her living room.

Turning to Stephen she said, "I'm not sure stepping into the Board position is the right thing to do."

Stephen paused and said, "Well, maybe this is one of those lessons life can present. Maybe you'll discover aspects of yourself you weren't aware of?"

Andrea, with that half-smile of hers, took a sip of wine, nodded, and said, "You might be right. Cheers to a learning experience!"

But then the old saying about "when something is going right, something needs to go wrong" kicked in. Andrea showed up at Stephen's door almost in tears a couple of days later. He invited her in and asked what was wrong.

She sat down at the dining room table, took a deep breath, and said, "So, Thursday I was in the office. Luke was being… well, Luke, annoying the living shit out of me. He completely dropped the ball on his part of this current project, doing lord-knows-what on that screen he always keeps hidden. Well, the fetid turd doesn't say boo until 4:55, and as he got to the door, he casually dropped, 'Oh, I didn't get to the product specs, the write-up, or start the summation. I know it's due tomorrow, but hey, if we show up first thing tomorrow, we can pull something out our ass (or asses)' and then left!"

"Firstly, it wasn't as dire as he thought. I had eighty percent of it already done. The remaining twenty percent really is a cakewalk, and his participation was not only not needed, but it's also frankly unwanted. *BUT* the fact he didn't know I had really pissed me off, and I immediately started to write a BLISTERING email to Suzanne going back to day one, listing Luke's faults, each and every single one I could think of. Then I proceeded to lay out my case as to why they should just terminate him on the spot and bring me in full-time. The remainder of the email was extolling my expertise, experience, and reliability. And then I did something so incredibly stupid! Before I sent it, I went to grab a bite. I received a couple of phone calls and got distracted, and when I finally looked at the time it was after seven. They shut and lock the doors at 6 pm. So, I headed home. THAT EMAIL IS OPEN ON MY COMPUTER. ANYONE COULD SEE IT! WHAT DO I DO?"

Stephen was dumbfounded. In his many years in large and small organizations, while there had been conflicts and flare ups, it never once occurred to Stephen to mount a behind-the-scenes coup and try to remove someone in such a passive-aggressive manner. Thinking hard he queried, "Did you actually send the email, or is it still unfinished?"

Andrea dryly replied, "It's unfinished."

Stephen then said, "Can you run down there tonight, maybe have the security person let you in and either delete it, or send it?"

She replied quietly, "No. I'm a contractor and once they lock up at 6 pm for the night I cannot get back in until the front desk opens tomorrow morning."

Stephen then said, hopefully, "Does a screen saver kick in? Maybe that will happen, and no one will even look at your screen?"

Andrea looked even worse and said, "I found the screen saver annoying, I disabled it a few weeks ago."

The very last thing Stephen could think to say was, "You need to head down *very early* and be the first person in and either delete it or finish it and send it."

Andrea looked shaken, but thanked him, giving him a tentative hug, and went home. Stephen found the whole backstabbing thing distasteful but felt nothing would probably come of it. He suspected she'd get down there first thing, probably err on the side of deleting the email, and they'd get back to where they were.

Around eleven the next morning Stephen got a text asking if Andrea could come over. Sensing this wasn't going to be good news, he put some water on, and Andrea was standing at the door when he opened it a minute later.

She sat down and said, "I went down there first thing in the morning like you suggested. However, there were already five or six cars there. I saw Luke's car was one of them. As an employee he has a key card. Deciding he wouldn't bother with my computer, I went in, only to find my workstation gone, and a note to see Suzanne. I went in ready to state my case, but Luke was sitting in her office. He was smirking and Suzanne looked very grim. Rather than say anything, I just handed them my company belongings, signed some paperwork, and came home. What am I going to do?"

Stephen felt terrible for Andrea and brushed aside the negative misgivings he had about her behavior. She stayed for quite a while and discussed various options she thought would be viable. While hardly buoyant, by the time she left, Stephen felt she was doing a bit better. He was stunned but pleased when he found a couple of days later Andrea had already landed a full-time gig at a social media marketing company in Berkeley. Stephen was happy for Andrea but a bit surprised.

He googled the company. It appeared to be mostly twenty-somethings with the company leaning more hipster than traditional. Not to say Andrea didn't have her talents, but she wasn't going to see that side of young again, and the materials she had produced so far for the HOA were serviceable at best, but nothing stellar. Still, he felt relieved for her. With Andrea focused on the new job, she had even less time for the Communications Committee and the newsletter. Still chiming in and providing an article if time allowed, she definitely wasn't as all-in as she had been.

Another surprise was Sandra was now part of the Communications Committee. She wasn't consistent with her attendance, and for the most part, she just sat and listened. If she had an opinion about something that came up, she voiced it, but otherwise she seemed more of an observer than anything else. One thing Stephen noticed, though, was aside from Andrea, the other women on the Committee and the one older man didn't seem to warm to Sandra.

While no one said anything directly, Stephen sensed a modicum of relief whenever Andrea said, "Oh, Sandra won't be making it tonight. They're got a big project at work she needs to oversee."

Still, things seemed fairly congenial in the neighborhood, but Andrea didn't seem to come over as often, and most of Stephen's communications with her were now via email.

Around this time, Stephen sensed something was up with the "drug dealers" next door. There seemed to be a flurry of activity of a different nature. Dreading whatever change might be in the offing, Stephen was overjoyed to see someone dropping off moving boxes one day!

Over the next couple of weeks, the noise and activity next door were amplified tenfold. Stephen found himself grinding his teeth from time to time when there would be incredibly loud crashes and booms, and it seemed the street and driveway were always jammed with vehicles now, even though the street was clearly designated as no parking and no stopping. The last four days seemed to be the worst. The noise and activity were non-stop, with them dragging out their last day well into sunset. As the moving van pulled away and the roar of the two incredibly loud sports cars started to fade, suddenly ten wi-fi hotspots vanished from Stephen's phone, hopefully never to return.

At this point, it seemed like the only time Stephen heard from Andrea was after she started painting a much darker picture of Brad, Melissa, and their son Tony. She stated she had definitively heard fights at Brad and Melissa's and some had even escalated to a physical level. Andrea claimed Brad was no longer living there.

She also claimed the new neighbor next to Melissa and Tony had told Andrea she had looked out her living room window one afternoon to see Tony exposing himself to her. Stephen asked Andrea if it had been reported, and Andrea said the neighbor hadn't wanted to do that to the boy. Even so, Andrea seemed very focused on this.

She invited Stephen and Daniel over to Sandra's for wine shortly after all this came up. Andrea was going on and on, saying Tony was doing the same thing to her, exposing himself, and how the Association needed to step in and do something about it. Not saying anything, Stephen was a tad annoyed since (as far as anyone knew) drug dealers had been living in their midst, and no one had offered an ounce of support. But now Andrea was asking them to take care of this problem. If the accusations were true, yes, something *should* be done for the child's sake. But it was nagging at Stephen perhaps this could be an exaggeration or worse, a fabrication to set things in motion to drive the unwanted people away.

Mimicking the words, he had received when talking about the drug dealers, Stephen felt the people who had direct knowledge of this were the ones who needed to report it, if indeed it had happened. Much to Stephen's surprise, Daniel said Andrea not only brought the subject up in the next Executive Board session but had even persuaded the Board to send a notice of appearance to the owners of the unit to appear so they could hear the claims against their renters, Brad and Melissa.

From what Daniel later shared, the owners had shown up, ready to push back at the Board, but were silenced when Andrea now expanded upon her accusations and concerns. Very shortly after that meeting, the infamous U-Haul® trailer showed up again at Melissa's, with her once again taking her place amid the dog piss, while family and friends carried one item after another into the truck and drove off with the truck ninety percent empty, only to return and do the same light run over and over again. With the end clearly in sight, Melissa glared murderously at everyone and anyone who passed by her sitting on the grass.

Stephen also noticed Andrea seemed to be MIA, no longer out walking her dog, watering, or even sitting out in her back patio. Keeping her drapes drawn, he thought she was staying firmly out of the line of potential fire from Melissa. Stephen didn't know what the owners had relayed from their meeting with the Board, but he suspected Andrea might have been identified as the main driving force in their expulsion from the street.

Still, once their final trip with the U-Haul had pulled away, there was almost a palpable sense of relief in this part of the neighborhood.

Chapter 23 – Life Goes On

Now they were several months into this new world of Association and neighborhood involvement, Stephen was starting to notice his neighbors more. Gone were the days of not knowing (or really caring) who the neighbors were or if they were home or away. Stephen found himself getting in tune with the rhythm of the community.

The person who seemed to know what *everyone* was going to do, even before they did it, was Thelma. Always at the ready with a sharp tongue, Stephen was able to share some chuckles with her acerbic asides, but secretly wondered what she was saying about him and Daniel when they parted company.

Thelma was the one to point out the people adjacent to Andrea. Stephen had never actually seen anyone enter or leave that particular unit in all their time there. In fact, he had never really noticed the place. But Thelma assured him a most dysfunctional family were indeed living there. Along with the raccoons…

Stephen thought he had misheard and asked Thelma to repeat that part. Thelma, fishing out a new cigarette, pointed to the property in question and explained it was a single mom, her daughter, and a boyfriend who had moved into the place when her mother had become ill.

Once her mother had passed, they all stayed. And so did everything in the house. The woman really didn't care for her mother's taste in furniture or decor, but she also feared there might something of value amid the clutter. So, their answer had been to banish each and every item from her mother's home into the garage. And the reason Stephen never saw the garage door open or close was that, through very careful placement, the garage was 100 percent full, front-to-back, floor-to-ceiling.

Thelma, living closer to them and within eyesight, said she had observed a very healthy family of raccoons entering and exiting the torn vent near ground level by the garage door. As the family never went into the garage, Thelma was waiting for the day they discovered they had pets!

As Thelma was going on and on about the tumultuous dynamics at "the raccoon house," a loud slam and shouting diverted their attention. Across the way an older man (who usually just meandered around the neighborhood) was running down the walkway of his house as objects went flying by him. A wooden spoon, followed by a book, followed by a glass vase that shattered when it made impact with the ground. Behind this physical onslaught, a very petite middle-aged woman was screaming at the top of her lungs.

The man, Kevin, was frantically fishing for the keys to his car. After three failed attempts, he got the car door open, and jumping inside, he gunned the engine, backed out with a sudden burst of speed, and then with tires screeching, floored it as he left the street. Standing in the driveway among the dissipating exhaust of their decades-old car and shards of broken glass, the woman was muttering, glaring in the direction of the rapidly vanishing taillights.

Thelma and Stephen just froze, staring at the spectacle. The woman stopped, glared briefly at them, then turned and tromped back into the house.

Thelma, with her cigarette now smoked down to the filter, laughed heartily, and said, "I have no idea what her name is. Kevin I've met when taking the trash out. I don't know what their deal is, married, living together, whatever. He's kind of clueless, but a tad on the creepy side. He chats me up and starts these mind-numbingly boring conversations where he'll ask for an opinion on something, and then proceed to S-L-O-W-L-Y negate and disqualify whatever I've said. I also get a definite flirting vibe when we talk. While I think he's blowing smoke, I do it literally and leave. She on the other hand seldom comes out, but when she does, it's generally one of these displays. Again, no idea what their situation is, but the further away I can get from it the better."

And in another literal puff of smoke, Thelma turned tail and was back in her house. Stephen looked up and down the street and wondered what other stories were hidden behind the mandated white window coverings?

Now the election and committee issues were over, Carol reached out to Daniel and Stephen and suggested they attend a "get-to-know-each-other"

tea which would also include Timothy and his wife as well as Andrea. It turned out Andrea had invited Sandra as well. At this point, there was a conflicted sense about the inclusion of Sandra, but no one objected openly.

On the appointed day, Stephen and Daniel met Andrea and Sandra and they headed up to Carol's. Andrea was already well acquainted with Timothy and his wife, Shayla, who arrived at the same time. Bottles of wine in hand, everyone made their way to Carol's.

Carol welcomed everyone into her home, which was one of the largest models. Once inside, they saw a tasteful arrangement of older, but high-quality furniture. The dining area had a large dark-maple dining table with fruit, bread, cheeses, meats, and drinks on display. What surprised Stephen was seeing there among the Bernardaud China, some incredibly cheap snap together plastic champagne glasses in bright neon colors. This clashed with the more traditional taste displayed elsewhere.

Looking further into the living room was a VERY plump couch with massive throw-pillows matched by the very cushioned chairs around a low coffee table. Carol didn't offer a tour, and no one seemed anxious to ask for one. Telling everyone to grab a drink, everyone quickly discovered the tops of the plastic glasses didn't match (or at least didn't fit) the bottom part. Once they had filled their glasses, it became clear no one could put them down again. Carol motioned everyone to sit in the living area, so everyone took a seat.

Stephen asked when Sam would be joining the group.

Looking a tad surprised Carol said, "Sam? Oh, you know, he said he had a couple of errands to run. I'm sure he'll be back shortly."

As she was speaking, Timothy, his wife Shayla, and Daniel sank deep into the exceedingly large couch cushions. Andrea, Sandra, Carol, and Stephen took single chairs opposite the couch.

Small talk ensued with everyone clearly excited by the election results and the renewed energy and interest in the Association. There was a buoyant optimism evident in the positive conversations. While people were talking, Andrea went over to look over the food on the dining room table and glanced into the kitchen. Up on the counter a large black and white cat was up on the counter, licking a small carved turkey.

Andrea's eyes grew large with alarm and she cleared her throat loudly, then said, "Uh, Carol? Should the cat be up on the counter?"

Carol, in mid-sentence, stopped speaking, got up, and yelled, "GET DOWN FROM THERE. YOU KNOW WE'VE TALKED ABOUT THIS BEFORE. SCOOT!"

The cat, a very dismissive look on its face, kept licking the turkey, ignoring Carol. Carol went in and everyone heard "Shoo, now go on, get" as the cat hissed loudly.

Everyone looked around at each another, and the conversation stumbled awkwardly on. The three people on the couch were so deep into the cushions they didn't notice the errant cat come into the room and jump up on the back of the couch. Carol was sitting off to the side engaged with Timothy and Daniel about some upcoming HOA issues she felt they should start to focus on. Shayla, not a large person, seemed to be vanishing bit by bit over time into the massive cushions.

As the conversations got more intense, Stephen looked up to see the cat start to move directly behind Timothy. While not bald, his hair was definitely on the thinning and wispy side. With it being a somewhat breezy day, he had several longer fly-away strands sticking out. For whatever reason, the cat became transfixed by the flyaway hair and started batting the ends of it. Back and forth, just missing Timothy's scalp by the thinnest margin. Stephen had to bite his lip to keep from laughing, and Andrea looked over, obviously trying to contain herself as well. Carol paid the cat no mind, and Sandra seemed… completely bored just having to be there and seemed to have zoned off into another space.

The batting and near misses continued until Stephen couldn't take it any longer and excused himself to check out the food and drinks in the dining area. Andrea got up and joined him. The two of them holding each other's glasses as they tried to refill the flimsy plastic cups seemed to attract the cat's attention. Before anyone could say a word, in a lightning fast move, the cat darted off the top of the couch and was on top of the dining table, licking the food, and dragging her long hair through the dips and the cheese plate, coughing all the while.

Stephen, a bit alarmed said, "Carol, uh your cat is up here on the food…"

Carol stopped in mid-sentence, turned, and shouted, "You know better. Down! Down!"

The unfazed cat simply stretched, extending her fur into more food, hissed, jumped down, and proceeded to work very hard and loudly at dislodging a furball.

Stephen whispered to Andrea "Uh, doesn't that cat look like Michael and Brenda's cat?"

Andrea really looked at the cat for the first time, shrugged, and said, "All black and white cats look alike to me."

Timothy valiantly made a concerted effort to restart the previous conversation and ignore the cat's antics.

As the afternoon wore on people started making noises saying that it was time to leave.

Carol, looking at the untouched food on the dining room table said, "Oh, it doesn't look like anyone ate much. Can I get some of this together so you can take some home?"

Everyone looked at each other, hoping someone else would say something. Stephen finally said, "Oh, thank you very much, but we have dinner plans, and need to get going."

Everyone seemed relieved and started heading towards the door. As Stephen turned to say goodbye, looking into the kitchen he could see the cat up on the counter touching and licking everything and anything.

Stopping for a second, Stephen said, "We're sorry we didn't get to meet Sam."

With that Carol turned around and shouted out, "Sam, did you return from your errands? SAM. Are you here?"

Receiving no response, Carol shrugged, looking at her cat as she closed the door muttering, "I should give you a bath today. You've been prowling around for a couple of weeks now."

Franny was re-reading the email on her computer before hitting send.

> *I am at a loss as to why the Management company or Board has yet to respond to my VERY REAL and VERY SERIOUS complaints. That feral cat kept us prisoners in our home for well over a week.*
>
> *My husband is not in the best of health. What if I had needed to get medicine? What if there had been an emergency?*
>
> *Opening our front door to be confronted by a large, hissing feline, that very likely had rabies, is NOT acceptable. While I was doing the dishes, I was terrified to find a hissing cat at the window which almost gave me a heart attack.*
>
> *Frankly, we did not appreciate the sarcastic reply from the previous Board instructing us to chase it away with a broom. That was just insulting. Thank goodness, the cat, for reasons unknown, has obviously found another home to terrorize.*
>
> *I look forward to your reply and an apology,*
> *Franny and Robert Worthington*

Hitting the "Send" key, Franny peered out her guest room window that served as an office. She saw Betty Jean's headlights coming up the street. Grabbing a sweater, she dashed down the stairs to her front door. As it turned out, Franny's guest room was at the *perfect angle* to view Betty Jean's place. Armed with her small telescope, and provided Betty Jean's husband left the shades up, she could look right into most of their home. The view Franny enjoyed *the most* was the unobstructed view into the bedroom. Franny hadn't minded one bit that Betty Jean's husband Stan slept in the nude and rarely thought to close the blinds.

Betty Jean pulled into the driveway a bit after six o'clock. Looking around, specifically at Franny's place, she quickly pulled into the garage and shut the door.

She thought, "Shit. The light was on in her office."

Quickly turning her car off, she quietly got out of the car and stopped for a second to listen. She exhaled, thinking, perhaps, she had escaped Franny's eagle-eyed watch on her home. Grabbing a couple of bags of groceries and her computer bag, she opened the door into the kitchen. Immediately she panicked! WHY her husband had not only not closed the blinds but left the lights on was beyond her. She quickly drew the blinds shut, dimmed the lights, and scurried to the window by the front door. Just as she was about to close the blinds, there was Franny, peering in waving at her.

"Jesus Christ" Betty Jean muttered underneath her breath.

Putting on a very forced smile, she opened the door saying, "Franny! What a surprise. I just got in, but this isn't a good time…"

But before she could continue, Franny had already put one foot into the entryway and said, "I know, I just saw you pull in, and I thought this would be a good time chat about some of the issues here on the street. I know you're involved with the new Board and are on at least two committees. *Anyway*, did you see what those horrid renters are doing to the front area? It's CRIMINAL. It's looking like a frat-house. I really think YOU need to bring this up. Also…"

Before she could continue, Betty Jean's smile, now completely gone, firmly said, "Franny, I have a HORRIBLE HEADACHE. I mean, I may throw up at ANY SECOND!!"

Franny started to speak, then you could see her eyebrows knit together as she scrutinized Betty Jean's face. This was not the first time this *"migraine"* plea had come up, and Franny had spotted Betty Jean going about her business just fine after such a claim several times before.

Unconvinced and undeterred, Franny continued, "And I just dropped ANOTHER note to the management company. They NEVER sent anyone out to deal with that horrid feral cat that kept us prisoners in our home for far too long, I mean…"

Betty Jean's smile tightened as she forcefully kicked Franny's foot out of the doorway. "We'll touch base later in the week. Bye."

Leaning against the door, and with just a hint of an actual headache now coming on, Betty Jean called out to her husband, "Why did you leave the blinds up and the lights on again?"

Not hearing an answer, Betty Jean listened, but couldn't figure out where in the house Stan might be lurking. When her eyes caught the time on the clock, she KNEW where he was. She charged upstairs, pulling the blinds firmly shut as she went along, until she saw Stan at the bedroom window, binoculars in hand.

Betty Jean clearly annoyed said, "Franny was at the door *again*, blathering on about being held hostage by that goddamned cat..."

Stan looked over, smiling lasciviously, "She's at it again!"

Pointing across to the other development across the greenspace. "And tonight, she has co-stars!"

Betty Jean marched over and snatched the binoculars out of his hand and squinted. "Geez... she actually has a cameraman and what looks like professional lighting tonight! For God's sake, she COULD pull the drapes, but I swear she KNOWS everyone on this side of the green space is watching. Are those three men AND a cameraman?"

Stan grabbed at the binoculars, and Betty Jean muttered, "She has to have carpal-tunnel pussy by this point in time."

As she headed back down to the kitchen, she thought she heard Stan mutter, "I hope not..."

Stephen had volunteered to take a stack of newsletters to some of the streets a couple of blocks away. The Street Ambassador he was going to visit wouldn't be home until after five. He encountered Carol, who was out for a walk. They chatted amicably about the way everyone was pulling together and how things really seemed to be turning around in the community. Stephen asked about her husband Sam.

Carol, looking a bit confused, saying, "He's fine. I mean I guess he's fine. I haven't seen him for a couple of days. Our schedules and all."

At that moment, Stephen audibly gasped and stopped in his tracks. On the deck facing the busy street they were walking up, above them stood Sarah Smith, arms outstretched wearing a kimono that was open wide without a stitch of clothes on underneath.

Carol stopped and looked up. Rolling her eyes, she said, "Welcome to the Thornwillow Heights Center for the Performing Arts. She puts on this little show in the morning first thing, and an encore around this time every evening. And on some days, she'll do a matinee or two."

Carol also said, "She definitely put the *social* in her time as a *social worker.*"

Stephen started to open his mouth to reply while trying not to look at the 80+ year-old skin on display but couldn't really respond.

Carol went on, "I ran into Sarah one day and said, 'Sarah, old skin just doesn't look good. Give it a rest.'"

Sarah had apparently replied, "It is for my health."

Carol said, "That was the end of the story, but the start of her unbroken record for most performances without missing a day due to illness or needing an understudy."

They kept walking, but Stephen, despite himself, kept looking back over his shoulder, not really believing what he was seeing. Did she really have a piercing *THERE?*

While Stephen was out delivering the newsletters, Daniel had gotten into his pajamas and was catching up on email and social media. Unbeknownst to him, he was being observed.

Crouching in the tall grass directly behind their unit, peering up with her eyes just above the floor of the deck, Andrea watching him unobserved.

Daniel and Stephen never shut the blinds on their windows to obstruct the view. They never really worried about anyone peering in, as it was an incredibly steep angle and drop-off to the walking path fifty feet below. Daniel kept scrolling and sending a few emails until Stephen got back. Once Stephen changed and was in his pajamas, they both settled in to watch *The Daily Show.* It was already dark without much moonlight, but for just a second Stephen thought he caught some movement down the hill out of the corner of his eye.

Classical music was turned up very loudly on the newly installed Dynamiks Ultima sound system recently installed in Sandra's home. Swaying to the music, a glass of Suntory Hibiki 21 whisky went smoothly down her throat. Not a bottle she ever broke out with friends *or* acquaintances. But tonight, she needed it.

Sandra thought, "THAT BITCH!"

She wondered how long she had been at that biotech firm now? Sixteen years? Seventeen?

"That place was barely an office with a high-school equipped lab when I started. And now? Stock options, offices around the world…"

It was only because she was a woman that she wasn't CEO. She had MADE THAT PLACE. She was platinum. And then that hussy. A project manager. A PROJECT MANAGER! Not even a good one. But suddenly there she was at all the high-level meetings, meetings that previously had only been for SVPs and above."

Sandra recalled being surprised at seeing Tiffany sitting there, in HER seat, next to the CEO. Feeling Tiffany had possibly overstayed a status update briefing, Sandra walked over to her chair, a fierce smile on her face, quietly saying, "Excuse me, but you seem to be in my chair and the meeting is about begin."

Tiffany, not budging, looked up at her, but remained mute.

And then the CEO, James, said, "Uh, hey Sandy, do you mind finding another seat? Tiff and I were going over some items and I thought it might be beneficial if she sat in on a few meetings. She has all her notes here, and it would be easier if you sat… there's an open spot over there by Sean."

Something like this had NEVER HAPPENED, the worst part being the knowing and very smug smile Tiffany had shot her as they exited the meeting. Not once in her many years with the company had Sandra ever had a single hint of a hostile work environment, or even a subtle suggestion of anything beyond a professional relationship with ANYONE in the company.

Well, that didn't strictly apply to Barbara the admin. Sandra, Barb, and a few of her friends had drifted beyond being strictly professional a few times. And it was most definitely a mistake to invite them to her housewarming. But still…

At her housewarming Barb had clearly overstepped, and it became painfully clear to Sandra THAT could never happen again or go beyond what it had been. She felt everyone admired her, and yes, probably even feared her a bit. And she liked it that way. But there was something very different about Tiffany. While she had never picked up that James was a philanderer and had seemed very happily married to his wife, what was her name? But obviously something had changed. And she did not like it ONE BIT!

Refilling her glass, she pulled out her laptop and began googling this woman. She was far more accomplished than she ever would have suspected, but worse, there were page after page of her sunning herself on yachts and vacationing in France with a string of VERY influential and important people. Many Sandra not only recognized, but wished she had their names and numbers in her own phone. As Sandra drained her glass, she looked over at the deck through the open sliding glass door. For a moment she thought there might have been an animal or bird there. She detected the slightest bit of movement. Turning back to the pictures on her laptop, she thought, "Tiffany keeps it pretty tight…"

Chapter 24 – Neighbor Nonsense

Stephen hadn't been hearing as much from Andrea recently, so he was surprised when she called one afternoon. Andrea explained she was still at work but had convinced another neighbor close by – Debbie Brown – to join the Board on an interim basis.

Debbie Brown was someone Stephen had seen out and about walking her dogs, but they had never actually spoken. Stephen assumed this was how, or where, Andrea and Debbie had become acquainted but now Andrea was all in a dither worried about Debbie.

Stephen thought, "Ugh! Shades of Sandra…"

It turned out one of the very large eucalyptus trees was slated for removal because it was perilously close to two homes. Naturally, both of the owners had been notified in advance of when the trees were to be removed.

One of the owners was an older woman who had been there so long, people had a theory that instead of moving into Thornwillow Heights, she had always been there, and they had built the place around her. It quickly became very clear she was violently opposed to the removal of the tree. In fact, she had been so loud and abusive to the people from the tree trimming company, they had just left.

Debbie, in her new role as a Board member, had gone down there to see if she could smooth the situation over. According to Andrea, Debbie was now being verbally abused, so she asked if Stephen could go up and help diffuse the situation.

Getting in his car and driving up to the site, Stephen began to question what he had actually gotten himself into with all this HOA nonsense. Pulling up, he saw Debbie standing there, with an older woman screaming and gesturing wildly.

Stephen hurried over and said, "Hello. Can I be of any assistance?"

The older woman, turned, narrowed her eyes, and said, "Who the fuck are you? Get out of here."

Stephen smiled uncomfortably and said, "Well, I'm part of the new Landscape Committee as well as other HOA committees and I heard there was some issue up here. I'm sure Debbie explained to you the HOA would be replacing the tree in question, but with something that is less of a fire hazard and more appropriate size-wise for the narrow space between the two buildings."

The woman's lip curled as she spat out, "Fuck you and fuck the HOA. That tree was why I bought this place. I don't want to look at the assholes living across from me. Hell, I don't want to look at you either. Don't lay a finger on the fucking tree or I'll see you in court," and with that she turned and tromped into her house.

Stephen exhaled deeply and turned to Debbie, "Are you ok?"

Debbie smiled and said, "It looked worse than it was, but it was nice to see a knight in shining armor pull up. I'm not sure how much more of that I could have taken. As you can see, the tree people had it with her and took off. All of this is way below our pay grade."

With that they both chuckled, she said, "Nice meeting you," and they both took off.

Stephen sent a text to Andrea telling her that it was fine, but there would be some kerfuffle to deal with at the next Board or Landscape Committee meeting.

Andrea then replied with, "Did you see her rack? Her husband is a VERY LUCKY MAN."

Stephen just replied with a smile emoji and went home, thinking to himself, "Yes… it's Sandra Mach II."

Not a week later, Stephen received another panicked call from Andrea. She said Debbie was being harassed by the same neighbor, but a different situation had arisen. She asked if Stephen could check it out and assist.

Expecting the same foul-mouthed woman and a repeat of the previous visit, Stephen was stunned to see Theodore Chapman hugging the tree. Even though it was an incredibly warm summer day, he still had on his overcoat, gloves, and a hat, just like he had worn at that first Landscape Committee meeting. And as he got closer, he realized Theodore wasn't "hugging" the tree, he was chained to it.

There was a small group of people and a lot of discussion going on. As Stephen got closer, he spotted Debbie, looking very confused, the foul-mouthed woman telling everyone to fuck off, and a bunch of tree trimmers looking very nervous, and Terence Birkhead shrilly telling everyone he was calling CNN and would shame them all on national TV if they didn't back down.

Stephen signaled to Debbie, and she said, "We have the permits, the Board approvals, everything ready to go, when that harpy walked over and chained that old coot to the tree. And the old coot is droning on about legalities and lawsuits and how he'd rather die than let that precious tree be removed. Then this shrill man with the porn-star moustache starts in. I swear, I did NOT sign up for any of this."

At that moment, Timothy pulled up and walked over to the owner of the building where the tree was. He huddled with the woman for a few minutes, then Timothy waved the tree trimmers off.

He came over and told Stephen and Debbie, "We've been doing this the right way, which was wrong. I told her she could have her tree. Once she goes in and all the hubbub has died down, we'll just come back and take it down."

Looking over at the tree, everyone had left the area, but Theodore was still tethered to the tree. Stephen was going to mention maybe they should release him, but when he saw everyone else turn to leave, he shrugged and joined them. As he was driving away, he could still see Theodore chained to the tree all by himself.

Despite the volatility of some of the inhabitants of Thornwillow Heights, the good had so far outweighed the bad. One evening while making spaghetti for dinner, Stephen realized they had way too much sauce again. So, he texted Andrea to see if she'd like to join them for an impromptu dinner.

Andrea replied in the affirmative but then threw in, "Oh, I'll ask Sandra to join us."

Not overly pleased, Stephen didn't want to say no and told her there was plenty to go 'round. Very shortly thereafter Andrea showed up as they opened a bottle of wine. They were discussing the latest hubbub around the HOA, laughing about Theodore, and enjoying themselves. Then the doorbell rang. Andrea jumped up almost knocking her chair over. As it wasn't her home, Stephen and Daniel found it a bit odd, not to mention off-putting, for her to answer their door.

Andrea welcomed Sandra in, and Sandra said, "Oh, I'm not really hungry, I'll have a glass of wine, but you don't need to fix a plate for me."

Stephen, who was very proud of the recipe that Daniel and he had come up with together over several years, was now rather put out to hear this after having Sandra shoehorned into their gathering.

He said, "No, I insist you have some. This is a recipe we've been working on for years and I think you'll enjoy it."

Sandra, with a look on her face like someone just offered roadkill on a fork, said, "Well, ok … but a small plate. A VERY SMALL plate."

Daniel, Stephen, and Andrea all had nice sized portions in front of them and the evening was pleasant enough. After being there for about an hour, again, Stephen noticed a rather sudden shift in Sandra. The look in her eyes, her demeanor, it was like someone pulled the plug somewhere.

Rather abruptly she said, "Well, this was lovely of you for having me over. Dinner was wonderful, but I have a big day tomorrow and I should take care of some things before then. Goodnight."

And with that she was off.

Not commenting on Sandra's abrupt departure, watching Andrea looking at the door, Stephen wondered what else was going on with Andrea. Andrea's mood instantly dropped. She stayed for another half hour and finally said her goodbyes.

Later that week, a small incident happened on the street. A neighbor of Thelma's who was on the elderly side must have had some type of medical incident. Stephen, still on alert from all the firebreak awareness, heard a siren blaring down their street. His first instinct was the worst had happened, so he grabbed some important papers and his laptop and threw them into his car. As he opened the garage door, there was a fire engine making its way down what now felt like an impossibly narrow road. It had never been a wide street, but with the strict no parking at any time policy, it had never seemed all that narrow.

Now seeing the large hook & ladder vehicle make its way down, Stephen had a newfound appreciation for the no parking rules. A bit after the paramedics rushed in, it turned out the elderly neighbor had fainted. It was attributed to her not taking her morning medicine as well as forgetting to have lunch. She was fine but watching the hook & ladder truck try to turn around to exit the street was sobering.

About three weeks after this minor medical incident, Stephen and Daniel were coming back from doing errands on a Saturday. What they saw coming down the street were cars parked on both sides of the street, end to end, completely filling and semi-blocking the street. From the signs on the garage door and streamers, it would appear the daughter of the neighbor Andrea had more-or-less kept to herself was having a graduation party. On the very few occasions Stephen had seen the woman out and about, she would at most wave, but she never made a move toward any other interactions.

With the memory of the tight turn with the hook & ladder truck, Stephen was beside himself.

He said to Daniel, "OMG… what would happen if there were a fire or medical emergency right now? We have some *very elderly* people down here, not to mention the high fire risk! There is no way a full-sized fire truck could get in and out of here."

Daniel was furious. Pulling into their driveway Daniel took off and headed up to the house where the party was taking place. Stephen started to put away the groceries, when a few moments later Daniel came into the house, upset.

He said, "It was her daughter's graduation party. I told them there was absolutely no parking allowed at any time and she said, 'It's just a few of her friends. It's her graduation party!', to which I replied, 'If everyone doesn't move their car in the next ten minutes, I'm calling the towing service.' Sadly, her daughter broke into tears and ran upstairs sobbing loudly, and her mother just glared at me."

Sticking his head out fifteen minutes later, all but one car was now gone. Before Stephen got back into the house, Andrea was on the phone.

She said, "Daniel upset Abagail. He ruined her party. Everyone is VERY upset. I know it's not as safe as it should be, but couldn't he have let this one ride?"

It was all Stephen could do to reign in his anger, but talking slowly and quietly he said, "You were not here when that hook & ladder was trying to get in here. With no vehicles on the street, it was a challenge for it to get in and out again. If there had been *any sort* of emergency, they wouldn't have been able to get in at all, and with all those cars on the street, no one would have gotten out either."

For a moment Stephen wondered if Andrea was still on the line.

Finally, she said rather coldly, "Daniel needs to apologize to them. It absolutely ruined their special day."

And with that, Andrea hung up. Despite not being in the wrong whatsoever, Daniel and Stephen picked out a nice orchid the following day and Daniel took it over and apologized. But he didn't go into any detail about how it was received.

Another change that taken place was with the care of Andrea's dog. Previously Andrea had shown Stephen where she hid a spare key and when she knew she'd have a long day in the office she'd have Stephen go over and take her dog for a walk, maybe give her a treat and let her do her business. So, Stephen was somewhat surprised when he was chatting with Betty Jean about some committee work. Betty Jean casually let it slip that Andrea's dog had nipped her husband. Stephen assumed that it took place out on a walk, but Betty Jean went on to say Andrea was away for the weekend and they were coming over to make sure there was food out and walk the dog. As Betty Jean lived several blocks away, Stephen was a bit surprised he wasn't asked, but didn't question it.

Around this time Stephen also noticed Sandra's car was in the driveway most of the time. Since she had made it known when she moved in that a twelve- to fourteen-hour day in the office was the norm for her rather than the exception, he found her car being there so much now to be rather surprising. He never saw Sandra, but it made him wonder. Not too long after noticing the car in the driveway, Stephen read an article about Sandra's company in the business section. There was some kind of managerial shake-up and Stephen wondered if it affected Sandra?

Chapter 25 – Dumb (and Dumber)

It was also becoming apparent to Stephen and Daniel that some of the people at Thornwillow Heights didn't have two IQ points to rub together. Stephen had just figured with the realty prices being as high as they were anyone living there would have to have been accomplished enough in life to be able to afford living there. He suspected a few of the residents might have, or have come from, money, but overall, he assumed (and he knew very well what you get when you assume) most of them had achieved a certain level of success in life along with the accompanying financial rewards.

Aaron was the first example to hit him in the face. An older man, Aaron had worked in local media and had written two very well-received books. He and his wife had lived on Foxglove Place for ages. Aaron had expressed some interest in joining the reconstituted Landscape Committee and was initially warmly welcomed. But right after joining, he requested the Committee and HOA pay for and replace a rather large Japanese maple that had died about three feet from his front door.

When asked what happened, Aaron explained, "Well, the irrigation stopped working. I requested it be looked at and repaired many times, but no one came out. *Yes*, I could have very easily just filled a pot with some water and kept the lovely tree alive until a time when someone came out to address the situation, but frankly, I didn't feel it was *my job* or responsibility. It looks horrible now with the dead tree staring at me and my guests when they come to visit. I request this be addressed immediately."

Everyone just stared at the man. Members of the new Committee made a field trip to his house to see what the situation was. What made his statements all the more infuriating was he had a large selection of potted plants not two feet away from the now-dead Japanese maple and he readily admitted that he went out to hand water them on a daily basis.

One of the new committee members hissed, "What an asshole and what an idiot! I say we go put a big ugly cactus in its place."

Another example was Hal. A regular at each and every Board meeting, Hal always had something to say. For the longest time he complained about the streetlight on the main road by his place.

"It's been out for months. It's a HAZARD. That turn in the road is pitch dark. I swear someone is going to get killed if that isn't fixed."

The reply was always the same, "Hal, that road is a public street. Have you contacted the city? The city is responsible for the streetlights there."

And Hal always responded with, "Well, they never respond to me, and no one ever fixes it. I think you should do something about it."

And he made this same request many, many times.

Hal also claimed the speed limit and traffic were a hazard. He often complained, "Why I've almost been hit, seven, maybe eight times out on that stretch of street. It's a hazard the way people drive. You need to do something. Speed bumps, or reduce the speed, or more lights."

Again, the response was for him to contact the city.

Shortly after the last meeting, coming back home one evening, just as Stephen rounded the corner near the spot Hal was always complaining about, out of nowhere, Hal jumped out of the bushes and looking surprised, he scurried across the wide road as fast as his elderly legs would carry him with a bunch of dried rushes in his hand.

At a later Board meeting, running into Hal before things started, Stephen asked about the rushes in his hand. Hal said, "Oh, my wife has this thing for terracotta pots, and I run over from time to time to get some rushes, or willows, or whatever is growing in the greenspace."

But the thing that got everyone's eyes rolling was when Hal stood up, very agitated and indignant, saying, "Those damned hyaenas in the greenspace across the street are keeping me up at night. Someone needs to do something about them, IMMEDIATELY!"

Everyone looked back and forth and one of the women in the audience tentatively said, "Uh, Hal, don't you mean the coyotes?"

To which Hal snapped, "I most certainly DO NOT! I can hear those hyaenas laughing in the dark, and it unnerves me. I believe the HOA should step in and do something."

Fighting hard to control their laughter, Timothy said, "Thank you Hal. We'll have someone to look into the hyaena problem as soon as possible."

Hal sat down with a very self-satisfied smile and looked all around, so everyone would know he had been right, and it would be properly addressed!

At the same meeting, Stephen noticed Rosemary was present. He hadn't seen her at any meeting since the landscape vote. Sitting next to her were the couple Stephen had assumed were siblings, if not twins. The bowl-haircut on the man was the same style as Stephen observed at the one Landscape Committee meeting, and the woman seemed to be wearing a dress that she possibly made herself with a "I cut my bangs with children's safety scissors" haircut. They were on the agenda this evening. When they were called upon, the man was quite upset and not incredibly articulate.

After struggling to explain himself, Rosemary patted his hand, and said, "Phil and Margery have lived next to me for ages. They have been a godsend and are an incredibly nice couple."

Stephen's eyebrows rose hearing this.

Rosemary went on, "I know this is a landscape issue, but apparently the *new* Landscape Committee" and with this, Rosemary cast her gaze about reproachfully, "has decreed the large tree growing in their front area is to be severely trimmed. They love this tree, but it also serves a function for their household. Their pet cat climbs the tree and enters through the open bedroom window when they are at work. Without this mode of entrance or exit, this would severely limit their beloved cat's access to their home. Also, they love the tree, which provides a modicum of shade and privacy for them."

For Stephen this created more questions than answers. Firstly, they were adjacent to a large greenspace and there was a very active rat population that was a very serious problem for many of the buildings. Stephen thought, "If their cat can get in and out, heaven knows what else is going in and out of their place?"

There was a lot of mumbling, and Stephen could tell he wasn't the only one in the room looking at the couple in a quizzical manner. The Board discussed pros and cons, with more cons, but Rosemary was relentless in her defense of the couple's request. Either worn down (or just tired), the Board agreed to postpone the tree trimming. The couple was jubilant, leaning over and hugging Rosemary.

After the meeting eventually adjourned Stephen headed home. Just outside of the main doors, someone rushed by him, brushing his shoulder firmly. Stephen noticed it was Phil from the meeting. He was actually skipping down the center of the street, zig zagging back and forth and was now howling like a coyote at the top of his lungs. Skipping wildly, arms outstretched as if mimicking Julie Andrews from *The Sound of Music*, he kept howling at the top of his lungs. Stephen shook his head a bit wondering if he truly witnessed the man's unconventional exit from the meeting. Behind him, he saw Rosemary slowly making her way out, with Margery taking her arm protectively. Stephen also wondered if Phil might be the *hyaena* that Hal had been complaining about?

To Stephen's shock and surprise, he later found out Phil and Margery were both teachers at the local community college!

Stephen hadn't heard much from Andrea for a while and chalked it up to time spent at her new job where there couldn't be any client emergencies to address now she was a full-time employee. He also suspected Sandra was taking up more time, as her car hadn't left the driveway in several days.

Upon getting back late one afternoon Stephen saw an email from Andrea; "Will you be around tonight? You are NOT going to believe what happened to Sandra."

His curiosity piqued, he responded he would be home for the rest of the day. Within minutes there was a knock at the door.

Not having really interacted with Andrea for a while, he noticed she seemed a bit worse for the wear than the last time they got together. Her flannel shirt was untucked and was quite wrinkled, the distressed jeans seemed to be on the verge of total surrender to the many rips and holes covering them, and she just seemed disheveled. Breathing heavily, her eyes ablaze, she suggested they bypass tea and have some wine.

Pulling two glasses and a bottle out, before he could sit down, Andrea breathlessly started in, "Sandra wasn't clear on what exactly happened at first, but there is a shitstorm of lawsuits engulfing the company at a very crucial time when they are seeking a partner for a new cancer drug. Again, not sure who, what, or when, but she's been demoted and placed on a sort of administrative leave. She was technically working from home, but she wasn't given anything to do. And then the real kick in the balls happened. She was told she was far too toxic to be allowed back into the office, but because she's been so integral to things, they can't let her go. So, GET THIS! Now she's basically the house manager for the CEO's estate in Atherton. She runs the household, whatever the fuck that means."

What was interesting was Andrea had that same glint in her eye that she had when Rebecca and Lily had thrown down that one time.

Stephen was dumbstruck. Letting this info sink in, he immediately thought of all the *stories* Andrea had relayed about Rebecca, and once again, wondered if she was pulling his leg and making fun of *him*. But she had a very earnest look on her face and was obviously expecting some type of reply.

Stephen furrowed his brow, took a second and said, "So, she, uh, like stocks the toilet paper and has to make sure the maids have turned down the beds and stuff like that?"

Andrea now really surprised Stephen when she let out a very hearty and dirty laugh, and in a mocking tone, "OH SANDRA... PLEASE MAKE SURE TO ORDER THE CHARMIN NEXT TIME. THE SINGLE-PLY THAT ARRIVED TUESDAY WAS COMPLETELY UNSUITABLE FOR THE MRS."

Stephen DID find this funny, but again, he was rather conflicted, as he was under the impression Andrea had some type of feelings for Sandra. But also recalling Sandra's tightly coiled persona, the idea of her doing a Costco run for the estate was kind of humorous.

Again, having absolutely no way of knowing if this was true or not, the rational part of Stephen's brain said it just seemed so demeaning that he couldn't envision a CEO actually doing something like that to someone regardless of what they may or may not have done to incur corporate wrath. Eventually Andrea seemed to tire of finding the humor in Sandra's misfortune and went home. Stephen could hear her chuckling as she walked out the door.

As he shut the door Stephen thought, "Gee, I thought they were *good* friends."

When Daniel got home, Stephen recounted the conversation.

Daniel, not looking up from the mail he was opening said, "It couldn't happen to a nicer person."

And then at the next Board meeting came the next surprise. Carol announced that Sandra would be joining the Board to fill the last vacant seat until the next election cycle. Seeing Sandra sitting on the end of the dais next to Andrea seemed a bit surreal. And Stephen also thought he noticed a shift in Andrea. She was no longer staying meekly quiet, buried in meeting minutes. She seemed to be exerting herself more forcefully. It was Sandra now who looked like a waxwork version of herself, sitting mute, staring straight ahead.

Chapter 26 – Firestorm over a Firebreak

In the meantime, the new landscape vendor who had been selected hit the ground running. Lawrence and his teams were out investigating the irrigation, the condition of the existing landscaping, and the vegetation. Most importantly, he had brought an expanded team out to begin creating meaningful firebreaks. There had been discussion about using one of the services that sent herds of goats out as a more environmentally friendly manner of doing firebreaks, but it turned out the areas had been neglected for so long, the goats couldn't get access until more substantial manual clearing had been done. While this was met mostly with enthusiasm, it soon became clear there were more than just a few people who not only did not want the firebreak work done, but staunchly resisted it.

Sadly, Stephen was the first to feel the ramifications of this up close and personal. One Wednesday neither Daniel nor Stephen had anywhere to be and were both feeling a tad under the weather. They had opted to stay in their pajamas. It was nearing noon, and Stephen had started some soup for lunch. While it was warming, both were down in their office area working on their computers, when the doorbell rang.

Daniel didn't look up, and said, "Can you can get that?" and continued typing.

Thinking it might be a delivery, Stephen tied his robe a bit tighter and opened the door. Standing there was Dora, a neighbor from a few doors down. On the rare occasions they saw each other, when one or the other was going or coming, they'd wave, but up until this moment, there had never been any direct social interaction. Stephen mostly saw her husband, Alfred, smoking out front or when he attended the Architectural Review Committee. Standing now on his front step, Dora's face was red and blotchy, and she was sobbing into a thoroughly soaked scarf. Her hair was unbrushed and askew, and Stephen noticed the large gray sweater she was wearing wasn't buttoned correctly, so it hung on her at a peculiar angle.

Surprised and a tad alarmed by this crying woman standing at the door, Stephen inquired, "What's wrong?"

And with that, Dora started crying and sobbing hysterically and said, "All this firebreak activity is DESTROYING MY PRIVACY. I FEEL PERSECUTED. EVERYONE CAN LOOK UP THE HILL INTO MY HOME. EVERYONE CAN SEE ME AND SEE EVERYTHING I DO. ALL. THE. TIME!"

This was followed by more sobs and attempts to catch her breath. Stephen, stunned and utterly surprised at such an extreme reaction to something so rational and prudent, furrowed his brow, saying, "Uh, Dora. You DO KNOW that should all that dry brush on the hill were to catch fire, this entire place would go up in a matter of minutes? And you do know, the nearest walking path is well over sixty feet below your home, so no one is looking directly in your windows?"

Dora exploded with more tears and said, "Well, if there's a fire, I'll turn on the garden hoses. We have two. One in the front and one in the back!"

Dora seemed to think this was a completely rational and reasonable answer to this crisis. Except it wasn't. And it was with increasing horror Stephen stood at the open doorway and listened to Dora cry, whine, complain, and carry on for FORTY-FIVE MINUTES… NON-STOP.

Trying to explain the importance and severity of the situation should a fire break out, Stephen referenced the massive fire that had taken place in Arizona a few years earlier. Stephen explained when you have a wall of fire coming at you a garden hose won't do a thing.

Dora stunned him by saying, "Oh, we were living in Arizona when that happened. We saw it up close."

Stephen was speechless when she shared this. He realized Dora had probably latched onto the idea he had been the one involved in bringing the Fire Department up there and was one of the drivers for getting the firebreak done. He listened as patiently as possible, interjecting with sane and balanced reasons as to why this HAD to be done, while Dora continued to sob and cry. At one point he stopped listening and wondered at what point a human body would just run out of fluids to expel? He then realized sadly he might be the first one to be able to observe that statistic.

What had started as a semi-assault, the complaint session had now devolved into a completely circular monologue that kept coming back into itself. After forty-five minutes or so, Stephen LOUDLY coughed, motioned to his robe and pajamas, and informed Dora he wasn't the least bit well and needed to go take something.

Dora, momentarily surprised, seemed to notice he was in a robe for the first time during the entire barrage, but then her expression hardened as she suspected that Stephen was saying this to simply get rid of her. This was true, but at that point, she had nothing more to work with, and left in a massive huff. Stephen noted the tears had stopped as if on cue.

Stephen stepped downstairs and said, "You're not going to believe what I just had to endure."

Daniel, not looking up from his computer said, "I heard. Better you than me. I suspect the soup is shot. Do we have anything else?"

A few days later, there was a knock on the door. Post-Dora, Stephen had now come to dread noises at the door. He very quietly walked to the blinds in the kitchen, which for now were ALWAYS kept firmly shut. Trying to peer through the small holes the rope ran through, he could see it was Sandra.

Relieved it wasn't Dora or someone trying to "spread the good word," he opened the door and gave a friendly greeting to Sandra. Not completely surprised after Andrea had commented that she thought Sandra had been going through, Sandra stood at the door looking a bit worse for the wear.

While no evidence of tears, there was a definite shift in her demeanor. Wearing a simple short-sleeved blouse over dark slacks, she looked Stephen in the eye and said, "I'm very displeased with the firebreak work. The rational part of my brain knows it should be done and needs to be done, but I was unprepared for the ramifications. Before the trimming there was enough growth that if you are down on the walking path, which I know is a fair distance away, you couldn't see into any of the buildings. Now, the neighborhood and specifically my place are on full display. I don't feel like I have any sense of privacy and I'm feeling very vulnerable."

Stephen started having Dora flashbacks and not really knowing what to do with this said, "Umm, you know this has been mandated and we can't just stop the work, or undo what has been done? From what the Fire Chief said, this was beyond serious. This was a deadly incident waiting to happen."

Sandra, staring straight ahead, unblinking said, "Yes, I know. But I wanted to let you know."

Stephen, not being able to read what exactly what was going on, asked, "Are you okay? Is there anything else going on?"

Sandra blinked a few times and as if a light-switch had come on, her steely facade was now firmly in place as she said, "Everything is fine."

With that, she turned tail and walked away.

While he wasn't quite sure where he got the information, Stephen knew Andrea's birthday was coming up. After running it by Daniel, they offered to take her to dinner. Zagging off a note, she replied almost instantly that while it was a lovely thought, she already had plans. Neither Stephen nor Daniel gave it a second thought.

Then, late in the afternoon of Andrea's birthday, Stephen got a text saying, "My plans changed. Can I take you up on your offer?"

Stephen replied that would be fine and they made reservations at their favorite restaurant down the hill. Dinner was pleasant and (for once) the conversations didn't include Sandra or the HOA. They had a very enjoyable time sitting outside, and it solidified the feeling that they were indeed living in an actual community with friends.

However, what did bother Stephen a couple of months later was when his own birthday was coming up. Daniel had extended an invite to Andrea asking if she'd like to join them for dinner. She said she'd pass, but when the day came and went, not even simple birthday wishes were extended. But what surprised Stephen even more was some of the women from the Communications Committee actually baked him a cake and brought it over.

A few weeks after that it was Daniel's birthday. Stephen reached out asking if Andrea would like to join them for dinner. Again, without explanation, a simple "I'll pass."

And as far as Stephen knew, she never offered birthday wishes to Daniel either. While not a major issue, for whatever reason, the lack of reciprocal birthday wishes from Andrea bothered Stephen on a certain level.

One warm Saturday afternoon, Stephen and Daniel were going to sit out and make the signature cocktail they had discovered at a bar in the Mission District of San Francisco, a "Lady Guadalupe": Tequila, Rinquinquin, passion fruit syrup, lime juice, grapefruit bitters, and a muddled habanero pepper. They had made it quite a few times and had had Andrea over for it on a couple of occasions.

Stephen sent Andrea a text asking if she'd like to come over and join them. She texted back, "Oh, my friend Tamara is visiting. I've been telling her about you both, and I even mentioned the drink. Maybe you could bring the drinks over here?"

Daniel and Stephen gathered all the ingredients, the pitcher they made it in, the special glasses they bought for the drink and carted everything over to Andrea's. Her friend Tamara was sitting on the couch and introductions were made. While Stephen and Tamara talked, Daniel went into the kitchen and made drinks for everyone. While he was doing this, he noticed smoke coming from the back patio. Andrea obviously had something on the BBQ.

They sat and drank, and had a seemingly enjoyable time, when a timer went off.

Andrea stood up and said, "Oh, our steaks are ready. Thank you for coming over and bringing the drinks. We'll talk later."

Daniel and Stephen gathered everything they had brought over and headed home. Nothing was said for a few minutes when they both said simultaneously, "Was that weird that she didn't even ask if we wanted to join them?"

They both kind of shook their heads and when they got in the door Stephen said, "Wine?"

Chapter 27 – New(er) Neighbors

With the "drug dealers" now gone, a For Sale sign was up next door. Stephen caught sight of "Roseanne" a few times, but she charged into the house and quickly left the few times he saw her.

Thelma was out front one day and Stephen went over to say hello.

He pointed at the sign and said, "I wonder how much they'll get for it. I'm not sure why they rented it to those horrible 'drug dealers' and are now selling?"

Exhaling a massive puff of smoke, Thelma said, "Oh, I guess you didn't hear. The good doctor passed away shortly after his mother, the paper thief, passed away. *SHE* (meaning "Roseanne") is living in Marin now, and I think they might have wanted to sell it back when the mother passed, but with everything going on it was easier to rent, so she's unloading it now."

Thelma went on with, "She'll do quite well. They bought in early on and the market is red-hot, so no worries for her."

Stephen looked over at the For Sale sign with a bit of trepidation.

Very quickly there were several open houses slated. When the first one was scheduled, Stephen dropped Andrea a note asking if she'd like to peek inside with them. He did not receive an answer, so he and Daniel went over to check it out. It had turned out "Roseanne" *had* made some structural changes, removing the entire wall between the kitchen and living room. Not dissimilar to what Sandra had done, but very much on the cheap. Also, either the "drug dealers" or the same people that had removed the wall had painted most of the place with very dark but gaudy colors, and most surprisingly, used the type of glossy paint you'd reserve for a bathroom.

Later that afternoon, as Stephen was putting something away in the hall closet, he looked out the upstairs window to see Andrea with Sandra in tow heading into the open house. He was fine with them going together and passing on joining him and Daniel. He figured whatever was going on between the two of them had progressed, but he was still annoyed Andrea couldn't be bothered to simply state she was going to view the place later with Sandra. Whatever…

The open houses, though, turned into their own form of torture. Despite being clearly marked "No street parking at any time," this did not stop hordes of people from doing just that. Also, there were some cavalier types parking directly in Stephen and Daniel's driveway as they sauntered about. Coming out to put their trashcans out Stephen saw a car illegally parked blocking both Stephen's driveway and the area the trash cans needed to go.

A man was slowly heading towards his car as Stephen, smiling said, "This isn't a parking area."

The man assertively leaning on his car, smiled, and said, "When I live here it will be."

Stephen, summoning an equally insincere smile said, "You're going to *love* our towing company!"

The man's smile dropped like a rock, and he angrily revved his engine as he pulled away.

To everyone's surprise, the unit did not fly off the market. Granted, the colors were hideous and the work had obviously been done on the cheap, but in a red-hot market, neither would normally be a deterrent. There were three subsequent open houses each weekend after the charming interaction with a potential buyer. But after the fourth weekend of open houses, a "Sale Pending" sign went up.

At this point, not being completely sure how he felt about new neighbors after everything that had been going on thus far, Stephen braced himself and was praying someone decent would move in. In short order, the realty gods let Stephen know who that would be. The day after the sign went up there was a knock at the door. When Stephen answered, there stood an older man who was shaped like a beachball with a walrus moustache and a big smile. He introduced himself as Carl and said he and his wife Stella were going to be the new neighbors. Stephen felt a sigh of relief wash over himself, feeling they finally had some mature neighbors. That feeling was to be VERY short-lived.

In an effort at being good neighbors, Daniel and Stephen invited both Carl and Stella, along with Andrea and Sandra, over for a "Welcome to the Neighborhood" party.

Carl was very impressed by the fact both Daniel and Andrea were on the Board and joked, "Maybe I'll be asking for some special favors once we're here!" followed by hearty laughter.

Gazing about, Stella, on the other hand, had a look on her face like someone was offering a tour of a crack-house to a junior-league member. Polite, but there was zero friendliness or warmth on display. Also, much to Stephen's dismay, they had two very small and potentially yappy dogs. Stephen did note that on their first day after closing on the new property, Stella walked her two dogs over to relieve themselves on the patch of grass closest to *his* front door.

Almost immediately the dreaded construction vehicles were back. But this time, they were from a much more inept, rude, and frankly inconsiderate and sloppy construction company. Which Stephen hadn't thought was possible. Not only would they block the driveway, but they'd also park directly on the already struggling patch of grass that lay between the two units. And again, their hours were well beyond the ones allowed by the HOA, with them showing up sometimes as early as six am and staying well past seven and even pushing it until 9 some nights. And they were there EVERY weekend as well. At first Stephen thought "Roseanne" had already done so much structural work everything else would have to be cosmetic."

WRONG. Apparently, Stella felt the garage was too narrow for her to comfortably park her car, so they went about removing the single center wood beam that was the main support for the second story, with a plan to place a steel I-Beam in its place. If Stephen had thought the previous construction was loud and the "drug dealers" were disruptive, the new company far exceeded their noise and annoyance factors by a massive amount. It sounded and felt like they were living in a war zone. To make matters worse, Carl was often there, puffing away on an endless supply of cigars, not only acting all buddy-buddy, but more than implying when they moved in, they'd be seeing *a lot* of each other.

Stella on the other hand was like a walking iceberg. The disdain on her face and her frigid greetings spoke volumes. Stephen did get a small chuckle one time when he stepped out front. Seeing Carl and Stella, he stepped back quickly, hoping they hadn't seen him. But before he did, he saw Stella starting to say something to Carl and he blew a huge smoke ring directly into her face.

Through a friend who knew one of the building inspectors with the city, Stephen learned the company Carl and Stella had engaged had never done a project of this magnitude before. Looking at the incredibly long hours, the massive mess, and the frayed nerves on display, Stephen thought it was obvious they were completely out of their depth with this project. Stephen also had a suspicion Carl, and especially Stella, were being absolute pills about what was being done and pushing them to complete things by a set date. And probably complaining about the costs, trying to get things below market value.

Another "bonus" of Carl moving in, was, when he was there, he ALWAYS came over to talk. Most of it was good-old-boy puffery, but sometimes little tidbits of truth crept in.

Stephen asked, "So why are you moving up here?"

To which Carl replied, "Well, we've been at the old place for, ummm, what is it now? Thirty, thirty-five years? Some of the neighbors were not the most congenial, and Stella was having some… some issues. It felt like a good time to switch things up."

Stephen could certainly envision Stella being a world-class bitch and could very easily see neighbors near and far harboring animosity. Sadly, he felt the animosity was just changing zip codes.

Another "perk" of Carl and Stella was their son. He apparently lived more than a few miles away, but when he visited, he would pull in and block the shared driveway. There was *zero consideration*. But Stephen continued to try to talk himself into believing this was an upgrade from the "drug dealers" and whatever else might be lurking out there in terms of neighbor potential.

After months, which frankly now felt like years, Carl proudly announced the end date for the construction was fast approaching. With that, it felt like there were two weeks of 24-hour, round-the-clock activity. As the last day and hour were fast approaching, Stephen heard the contractor himself had had a nervous breakdown of sorts and would not be present when the actual day occurred. Still, Stephen had become very adversarial and was over more and more requesting they park in the visitor spot, turn the goddamn music down, and clean up after themselves. He was sick to death of finding screws, nails, and small bits of wood strewn across his driveway and even in the street!

With great fanfare when they officially left, Stephen thought he could exhale. He was wrong. Now began the laborious, and sadly, still loud efforts of repainting, redoing the floors (not that he blamed them for not wanting the cheap-ass peel-and-stick linoleum tiles "Roseanne" had put in), and everything else to make their home "perfect." With nerves shot and frayed, one evening well past 8 pm, there was noise coming from next door. Stephen, exhausted, went over and found a young Hispanic man loudly playing music while he painted.

Stephen said, calmly, "This is well past the hours the HOA allows contractors and vendors to be doing work. You need to wrap up and come back tomorrow."

To his surprise, the man kept painting, and then said, "I'm her cousin. I can do whatever I want, as long as I want, so piss off."

Stephen looked at the man and thought about the lily-white faces of Carl and Stella, and really couldn't imagine that being remotely true. Also, with their money, there's no way that "if" this were a relative, they'd have him up painting their place late at night alone.

Two days later, Stella was out leading her dogs over to relieve themselves in front of Stephen's area, and Stephen said, with a bit of an edge to his voice, "Oh, I met your *cousin* a few nights ago. He was painting well past the time anyone should be making that type of noise. He said he could do whatever he wanted to do."

Stella seemed to tense up, and it would appear she was now weighing the options and ramifications of what to say. She eventually said, "Oh, I… ummm… well, that's strange. He is *most certainly not* my cousin or any relation. How peculiar he would be saying that to you."

Stephen noticed she didn't apologize for the noise or the late hours. Actually, he now suspected she had instructed the contractor to give that story out if anyone questioned his presence beyond normal hours, but with systemic racism being what it was, Stella couldn't own her part of that narrative. Stephen also saw there was no love lost between Stella and Carl.

Carl looked like he was only a cheese puff away from a massive heart attack and Stephen suspected if Carl dropped dead in the driveway, Stella would let her small dogs relieve themselves on him. Provided Carl dropped dead on Stephen's side of the driveway...

But things eventually seemed to level out with the new neighbors once they finished moving in. Despite the vast amount of money they had obviously spent on their new place, Stephen smirked a bit when Stella proudly hung a basket of obviously fake plastic flowers outside of their garage. Even though Stephen and Daniel were loath to have much to do with Carl and Stella, they were both a bit surprised to find out Carl and Stella had invited Andrea and Sandra over for dinner to see the newly remodeled house, while no such invitation had been extended to them. Stephen quietly hoped they would both choke to death on the olives in their martinis.

Chapter 28 – "THE INCIDENT"

Tom Fields had slowly been backing away from the Construction Review Committee and he finally announced he and his family were moving. Thornwillow Heights was never meant to be their "forever home," and they had finally found the perfect place closer to Tom's work. At first everyone felt the Construction Review Committee would suffer as a result, but Tom had been able to pull together a surprisingly talented group of people from within the community. Alfred, an architect, took the lead initially on many items. His biggest liability being the amount of cigarettes he consumed; the entire clubhouse reeked for hours after he had been there. Another member, a woman who was a civil engineer, had been very subdued when Tom ran the committee, but once he left, she really stepped up and brought a lot of focus and great ideas to the table. But this was yet another committee that Daniel was the liaison for, and that Stephen sat in on as well.

With diligence and the assistance of the community, in a little over a year, the HOA had been able to rebound from having next to nothing in the reserves to having over a million dollars. Along with having reserves now, they also had roadmaps for construction and repairs, as well as for roof and street maintenance. Combined with a workable budget, they had thus far avoided a monthly dues increase or special assessment.

Andrea wasn't really checking in much with Stephen these days, but Stephen chalked it up to her new job and whatever might, or might not, be going on with Sandra. The next Landscape Committee meeting was coming up, and Stephen wanted to run some things by Andrea beforehand. Among the many issues still bedeviling the HOA were rodents. They seemed to be spending more and more on pest control and laying poison out, but still having serious issues. An item Stephen noticed online was the Hungry Owl Project, where they used the raptors for natural pest control as opposed to putting poison out that would then end up back out in the ecosystem.

Thinking Andrea would be a bit excited by the possibility of reducing the amount of poison out and about in the community, Stephen was a bit surprised at how muted she was when he brought it up. He asked how things were going, and she was rather noncommittal with her reply. For the first time that he could recall, the conversation felt a bit strained. Stephen mentioned that this coming Friday was his and Daniel's sixteenth anniversary.

He expected some kind of congratulations, Andrea only said, "That's nice. I'll see you at the meeting."

This meeting had a few more people attending than usual. Along with some new faces expressing interest in joining the committee, almost the entire Board was in attendance, along with their new landscape vendor, Lawrence. Lawrence had quite a few promising updates along with some presentations on proposed future projects. When the Hungry Owl Project was brought up everyone in the room seemed very interested. This meeting felt different to Stephen than ones in the past. Everyone was participating and there was an overwhelming feeling of positivity and engagement.

At one point Stephen experienced something he had never felt before; It almost felt like time had frozen for a few moments and he could see and feel the end result of the days and months of work and effort to make their community a better place. Despite the trials and tribulations of life on their street and the weird and wacky neighbors they had gotten to know, Stephen felt like they were making significant contributions to their community and that the efforts were appreciated. This was a very unusual feeling for Stephen as he was generally focused on the next project, task, or destination ahead. For the briefest moment, he was able to take everything in and appreciate the journey as well as the destination.

The meeting felt like a massive success. Everyone was all hugs and smiles at the end of the night as Stephen and Daniel started putting the chairs and tables back into place and cleaned up.

As people were leaving Andrea and Sandra stepped over and Andrea said, "When you're done, can we have a word over there?" indicating the smaller area by the fireplace.

Stephen smiled and said, "Sure."

As it was just the four of them now in the clubhouse, he momentarily wondered why they didn't just offer to go to one of their homes and have a glass of wine like they had done so many nights before. Daniel and Stephen kept working until the room was set up for the next Board meeting the following week. Finally, the last table was back in place and all the chairs were properly aligned they looked around to see if there was anything else they might have missed. Daniel and Stephen brushed their hands off and headed over to the more intimate area by the fireplace.

Sitting in a chair by the fireplace was Sandra, and on the couch facing the fireplace was Andrea. Daniel took the chair on the other side of the fireplace, angling it somewhat so he could face both the women and Stephen pulled a chair out between Sandra and Andrea.

Once seated Stephen cheerily said, "What's up?"

Sandra sat there for a moment, then straightened herself in her chair a bit, clearing her throat and said, "We've been asked to speak to you on behalf of several neighbors. There have been a lot of complaints about your behavior."

Stephen wasn't sure what to expect when they asked to talk, but this most certainly was not it. Absolutely stunned and VERY confused, the words just hung there, suspended in time. Finally breaking out of his shock, he looked over at Daniel who looked equally perplexed.

Sandra continued, "People feel you've been abusing your Board and committee status and have become bullies."

Absolutely stunned beyond belief now, Stephen felt the pit of his stomach drop. Again, he looked at Daniel, who was also at a loss for words. It was then that Stephen looked over at Andrea, who had so far not said a thing. Staring straight ahead at the fireplace, she wasn't making eye contact with anyone in the room. Stephen couldn't put his finger on it, but this wasn't the gauzy dreamy space he had seen her inhabit before. This was tension. Tightly coiled tension.

Daniel, now showing signs of anger, said, "What people? What have we done?"

Sandra paused, taking her time, and said, "Some people. Some people feel you're overstepping your place and you are being bullies. We just want things to go back to the way they were."

Stephen, silent, was looking intently at Sandra, who was not making direct eye contact.

Daniel, now VERY ANGRY, again said, "WHAT PEOPLE? What specifically are you talking about? When did whatever allegedly happen, happen?"

The room, feeling very large and empty, was punishingly quiet.

Sandra, pausing longer than necessary said, "It was some people. You've been pushing people around, bullying, and we are asking you to just let things get back to the way they were."

Stephen was now himself furious but held his tongue. Looking from Sandra over to Andrea, Andrea made the briefest of eye contact and then resumed staring straight ahead, and then momentarily met Sandra's gaze.

Daniel, now beyond furious, roared, "AGAIN! WHO ARE THESE PEOPLE? WHAT SPECIFICALLY ARE THEY, OR YOU, TALKING ABOUT?"

Sandra, keeping a calm unmodulated tone repeated, "People have complained about you. You are bullies, you're abusing your standing and power with the HOA, and it has been requested that things just go back to the way they used to be."

Completely incensed Daniel said, "AGAIN, I DO NOT KNOW WHAT OR WHO YOU ARE REFERENCING OR WHAT OR WHEN SOMETHING HAPPENED! I…"

And before he could continue, Stephen raised his hand for him to stop and said, "We've been going round and round now for far too long. She can't or won't tell us who, what, where, or when this alleged thing or things happened. This is going absolutely nowhere. WE ARE OUT OF HERE!"

And with that Stephen grabbed his messenger bag, and strode to the exit, with Daniel by his side. In his fury, without thinking, he hit the light switch, leaving the entire clubhouse in complete darkness. Realizing what he'd done, Stephen turned back and flipped the light switch back on. With a very loud bang they left the building and walked back home at a furious pace. Neither of them said a word.

Getting in the door, Daniel and Stephen just looked at each other. Neither of them had any words for what had just happened. And worse, there had been no advance warning or indication of who was complaining, what specifically had happened, when whatever happened took place, or anything else. Stephen started wracking his mind over what could have happened. And when. Absolutely nothing came to mind.

And Andrea! Just sitting there while Sandra kept recycling the same charges over and over again. Stephen was now even more furious than he was when they were first confronted. Daniel was breathing heavily as Stephen went and poured two very large glasses of wine as they sat down at their computers. Both of them opened their emails thinking, or hoping there might be some clue there that would shed more light on what had just happened. Or at least give it a frame of reference. But there was nothing there.

Stephen was blindsided beyond belief by Andrea. He thought they were friends. For the life of him *if* something hideously egregious had transpired, and in thinking a bit more about it, Stephen sincerely doubted that anything had, he could not understand *why* Andrea wouldn't have just pulled him aside or had him over to discuss it? Daniel was very quiet as he went through his email.

Finally, breaking the silence, Daniel asked, "Do we need to move?"

Sadly, Stephen had been thinking the same thing but had tamped it down feeling he was being too knee-jerk.

Taking a deep breath he said, "It's a possibility, but I think we need to think about it a bit and mull things over."

Neither of them talked about it any further that night. They went into the living room and caught up on a bit of TV, but they were both so deep in thought, neither of them could tell anyone later what it was they watched that evening. Sleeping very poorly, Stephen tossed and turned all night. When sunlight was coming through the window, Stephen got up and checked his email and phone. Absolutely nothing from Andrea.

After making some coffee, when Daniel came down, Stephen said, "I'm going to withdraw from the Communications Committee and all committee work."

Daniel said, "That's fine."

Stephen thought long and hard about how to do this, and what specifically he wanted to say. He didn't feel it was right to replay the previous evening's events and air dirty laundry, so to speak, so after workshopping the note and running it by Daniel he typed: "After careful consideration, effective today, I am stepping down from my position as chairman of the Communications Committee and withdrawing from all other committee or Board activities. I know the committee will be on good hands with Andrea and Sandra."

With that, he pressed send.

Almost immediately his in-box was full of replies from committee members, aghast, asking him to please reconsider.

One of the older gentlemen in the group wrote, "DID someone say or do something to you? I swear, I'll take them out back if they did."

Stephen smiled at that. Missing in the replies was anything from Andrea or Sandra. Over time word got out to the other committees and Board members, all of them asking him to rethink his resignation. Appreciative of all the kind words, Stephen felt like something had died in the clubhouse that couldn't be brought back to life. Stephen thanked everyone for their kind words of support, but he said he was standing firm on his decision to step aside.

Still unsure if he and Daniel had indeed crossed a line, Stephen walked over to their next-door neighbor Jane to apologize. Jane was stunned.

She said, "What are you talking about? You and Daniel have done SO MUCH for the community. We're all grateful for your efforts. What on earth happened?"

Stephen replayed "the incident," as it would be referred to ever after, and Jane just shook her head, casting a glance over to Andrea's place.

Jane said, "Please reconsider. I have no idea what could have prompted them to act in such a manner, but it couldn't be further from the truth. Please don't do anything rash."

Stephen thanked her for her very kind words and casting a glance up the street he saw Andrea leaving Sandra's place with her dog in tow. Andrea kept her head down and walked directly to her home.

Walking back into the house Stephen relayed the conversation he just had with Jane.

Daniel said, "I'm withdrawing from the Board. This is bullshit! We've put so much time and energy into this place and this is the thanks we get. I'm done."

With that he drafted a quick and succinct resignation note and sent it off. In the meantime, Stephen's inbox was quickly filling up with emails from more and more people. One hundred percent of the notes were shocked and appalled, and all of them asked him to change his mind. What was conspicuous by its absence was that there was absolutely nothing from Andrea, and Stephen had not ever expected anything from Sandra.

And there was another shift. While Stephen had certainly felt good about their contributions and time dedicated to the community, there was suddenly a weight lifted from him he hadn't even known was there. It suddenly hit him their calendars were no longer full of committee meetings, community gatherings, or Board functions. The commitments had encroached so slowly, neither Stephen nor Daniel had realized to what extent all these activities had taken over their lives.

And suddenly it hit Stephen that it had been their anniversary that day. A part of him now questioned the timing of "the incident," as Andrea absolutely knew what the day was. They made plans to go to their favorite restaurant for dinner, but there was still a dark cloud hanging over the evening.

Returning from dinner, Stephen logged into his email and was flabbergasted to see more than one note from some of the committee members. They had all bcc'd him on an email Sandra and Andrea had co-authored and sent out late that afternoon. Nary a mention of Stephen stepping down or of Daniel leaving the Board, instead it proclaimed their stewardship of the "New Communications Committee" and included an entirely new, redesigned, and recrafted newsletter that was being sent out for committee approval.

Stephen alerted Daniel to this new development and they both bent over the larger screen to open the attachment. Gone was the custom header Stephen had spent weeks on. Stephen, having been first a Fine Arts major, then a Commercial Arts major, before going into Computer Graphics, had crafted a custom header, using original pictures taken around the complex along with a custom logo, to emphasize the uniqueness of Thornwillow Heights. Now in place of the logo was "Thornwillow Heights" in Palatino Semi-Bold in a beige box. And the articles were, at best, generic. Three columns, front and back, with incredibly cheap looking clipart adorning stories that looked like they had been scraped from local online news sources.

Stephen now had a clear image of Andrea and Sandra in their pajamas, or worse, as he didn't want his thoughts to go "there," staying up all night like two schoolgirls trying to get their midterms done in time. And thinking of schoolgirls, he realized Sandra's whole "someone said" thing was complete and total bullshit. If "someone" was truly offended, they would have spoken for themselves – no one in the community was shy!

And thinking about it a bit more, he realized she had made it sound like more than one person but hadn't spelled that out. The "only" incident Stephen could think of was when Daniel asked the new neighbor's daughter to have her friends move their cars. Was that really it? And Stephen realized there was even more of a "girls club" thing going there. The new neighbor was a single mom and Andrea had made no mention of or move to introduce them or make "that" inclusive.

Stephen was very encouraged to see many, if not 100 percent, of the committee members push back on the "new and improved" newsletter. Everyone bcc'd Stephen, and it was fascinating to see Andrea's replies.

Not once did she say, "It's unfortunate that Stephen has chosen to step aside," or even a weak, "We want to thank Stephen for all his efforts…," but instead defended their paltry generic offering with, "Well, I do not have access to all the Adobe programs Stephen uses, nor his expertise. This was the best we could do under the circumstances."

"UNDER THE CIRCUMSTANCES! THEY CREATED THE FUCKING CIRCUMSTANCES. WELL, FUCK ANDREA AND MOST CERTAINLY FUCK SANDRA! They so deserve each other!" he thought.

And after reading all the BCCs, Stephen turned to Daniel and said, "We need to move."

Daniel said, "Actually, I was beginning to think that before this all blew up, but I didn't think you wanted to. Okay, we'll get started on that first thing tomorrow."

Chapter 29 – After "The Incident"

Andrea sat there in the meeting space staring straight ahead after Stephen and Daniel had stormed out.

Sandra sat there staring at her. Glaring was more like it.

The silence had engulfed the building, and the room seemed to have taken on a life of its own. Sandra, drawing upon her time facing adversarial business meetings during her life, shut her eyes, willed her blood pressure to decrease, and tried to center herself.

But when she opened her eyes and saw Andrea just sitting there like a deaf-mute, she felt her face flush, her blood pressure rise again, and her anger reignite.

After waiting a few more minutes, mindful of her tone and volume, Sandra said, "What the fuck was that? Seriously? WHAT. THE. FUCK?!"

Andrea, blinking as if she had just woken from a nap, looked in her direction, but still remained quiet.

Sandra, finding it hard now to contain her rage, got up and began to pace in front of the stone fireplace. "WE agreed this was the best thing to do. WE agreed this was the best time and night to do it. WE agreed to do this together. Again, WHAT. THE. FUCK. Where the hell were you? Were you so far up your own ass that you were checking the weather report on CNN? Jesus. I have no idea what is going to happen now. I don't know if they'll just go home and this will blow over, or what? Are you even awake? Is anyone in there? Say something dammit!"

Andrea, still looking stunned, looked up and started to open her mouth, but shut it. Looking away, then back again she finally said, "Umm, I didn't expect it to go this way" and paused. "I know we discussed what we'd say, but…"

But before she could continue Sandra let out a harsh, brutal laugh, "WE?"

Andrea, licking her lips, exhaled, and continued, "I mean, I didn't think it was going to be such an abrupt ambush. I thought we were going to ease into this, sound them out, and take it slowly. You just rushed in front-and-center, and I was, frankly, I think I was just as surprised as they were."

Sandra gave Andrea a condescending glare and flared her nostrils. Trying once more to employ her time-honored techniques to reduce her stress, she stopped pacing and shut her eyes.

Lowering her voice, she said, "We have discussed this too many times to recount. We have created a lovely and safe social haven in our section of the street. Our new neighbor Iris has been amazing. Then those two, yes, I know it was Daniel who charged in there like a bull in a China shop, but it was both of them, upsetting her daughter Abagail unnecessarily. Iris is now seriously talking about moving when her lease is up! Christ knows what we might get in her place. Look at some of the undesirables that have moved up here recently!"

Continuing to fume, Sandra said, "Men ruin EVERYHING!" She had a flashback to her last meeting in the office. She knew the shit had hit the fan before going back that last time, but despite telling herself she was prepared for anything, the reality had still hit her like a gut-punch. The years she had invested into building the company up from nothing and burnishing her own career and brand at the same time were wiped away in seconds. And seeing the fake nod of sympathy from the company President had just pushed her over the edge. Sandra's whole world had spiraled out of control in a very short period. ENOUGH.

Andrea just sat there as Sandra paced some more.

Looking at Andrea, Sandra thought, "Jesus… Is this what my life has come to now? First, a carefully crafted career goes down the shitter, and now, I can't even gain control of a simple hayseed homeowners committee. Well, this one is NOT going to be yet another loss."

Clearing her throat, Sandra, modulating her voice to hide the tension and anger said, "I realize this seems hard for you. But this is really a great opportunity. I honestly had no idea they'd react that strongly, but if my senses are right, I suspect they're going to quit the Board and committee."

With that, Andrea's head shot up.

Sandra continued, "We need to pull an all-nighter and completely redesign that stupid newsletter and have it ready to send out first thing tomorrow. This will not only underscore how little either of them is needed but will also lay the groundwork for us to increase our influence and control."

Hearing "all-nighter," Andrea smiled, thinking to herself, "Finally…"

After leaving the clubhouse, Andrea dashed home and gathered up her laptop and a couple of good bottles of wine. Stopping in front of the hallway mirror, she stopped for a couple of seconds and fluffed her hair. Realizing the evening could become more *intimate*, she dashed back upstairs and did what she referred to as a "disco bath," running a warm washcloth under her arms and all points south, along with a quick gargle of mouthwash, and just a faint spray of lemongrass perfume. In looking down, she reached for her clippers, realizing she'd need to do some extreme trimming. The last thing she wanted to hear tonight was the sound of Sandra gagging or spitting out errant pubic hair.

Chapter 30 – Consequences?

Early one morning about a week after "the incident," Stephen was going to go out to water in the front. Upon opening the door, sitting squarely in the center of their welcome mat was a perfectly shaped pile of shit. For all intents and purposes, it was absolutely perfectly formed and symmetrical. It was like Foster Freeze had a machine that could deliver this perfectly formed swirl at a given notice. It seemed highly improbable that a raccoon or even a dog would have found their way to the front door and left such a perfectly placed deposit. It was like someone had whipped out a tape measure and zeroed in on the EXACT center point.

Far from being upset, Stephen was actually amused. He spent quite a while trying to decide if it could be human waste, or if someone had taken the time to lovingly transport something their dog had had done as a message. A very small part of Stephen wanted to take it in to be analyzed, recalling a news story about an HOA somewhere that actually analyzed dog waste and then matched it to their human owners in order to fine offenders for not picking up after their pets.

Stephen felt this was most likely Sandra, Andrea, or something both of them went in on together. Stephen could almost hear the conversation.

Andrea, "Sandra, I just can't squeeze one out. I really haven't had enough fiber lately."

Sandra, "Get me a bucket of KFC. I'll take care of it."

Shaking his head, Stephen stepped over the "offering" to shake it off into the trash and wash the mat out in the driveway. While going through the motions, and also after discovering the "present" was clinging tightly to the doormat, Stephen started to think about other areas of Andrea's behaviors. Many small incidents that weren't major events started to crowd into his thoughts.

While Andrea always came off so calm, peaceful, on the quiet and grounded side, there had been numerous times when her behavior belied the "nice" façade. Many times, doing community work someone would walk by and say hello and once out of earshot, Andrea would mutter something like,

"What an asshole! They actually think I LIKE THEM!" and then chuckle darkly.

But then other, more disturbing thoughts were coming forward to mind. He recalled her joking once, "Oh, we should bake some cookies and put ex-lax® and other things in it and leave it for the old Landscape Committee."

At the time, since it was so sophomoric and juvenile, Stephen chuckled, but dismissed it. Now, with everything that had happened, Stephen realized Andrea had recently presented them with an odd gift, lavender sugar.

When she brought it to the door, she said, "Oh, I've made this especially for you and Daniel. I hope you enjoy it."

What made it odd was Andrea knew they seldom (if ever) used sugar. More often than not they didn't add any sweetener to anything, but on the rare occasions they did, it was usually something like Truvia® or Splenda®. Stephen went into the kitchen, pulled the now ominous container out of the pantry, and poured the contents into the trash. While he didn't think she'd necessarily put poison in it, he felt she might have put something in there to cause gastronomical distress, and then he could see her nodding in sympathy and even saying, "Maybe it was something you ate?"

Another story she had shared in a rather off-hand manner now came back to Stephen. It wasn't long after they met, and Stephen had asked how she came to move to Thornwillow Heights. She mentioned she had been living in a condo in Union City and out of *nowhere* her immediate neighbors had taken umbrage with her for some unknown reason and things had escalated to the point where she said her car was keyed and her tires were slashed. More than once. So, she moved. At the time Stephen couldn't imagine ANYONE having that level of animosity toward such a "nice" person. Except, *now* he could.

And there was yet another peculiar story. She had invited Stephen over for wine one evening and said offhandedly, "I was downtown ordering coffee at Starbucks today, when my cousin and her family walked in. She saw me standing there and she immediately turned around and left with her family."

At the time Stephen asked, "What on earth would have prompted that type of behavior?"

Andrea only said, "Well, I don't really know…"

And then lastly, Stephen recalled a concert he and Daniel treated Andrea to. It was at a very small club in San Francisco. The majority of the club was standing room only, but there were a small handful of seats on risers on either side of the stage. From decades of concert going Stephen knew when to line up and how to snag one of these prized spaces.

Once inside and holding down three seats, people started crowding close to the stage, with one man, getting close to where Andrea's feet were resting. Not really in her space, but adjacent. Wearing her Doc Martin's, she landed a very hard kick into the center of his back. The man turned around, but then just shook his head and moved to another area. Andrea made no eye contact with Stephen and redirected her gaze back to the stage.

If Stephen had had any doubts about moving, they were gone. In amazingly short order, Daniel had constructed a spreadsheet encompassing the entire Bay Area and a bit beyond. He included general price range, home size, neighborhood safety, air quality, political affiliations, local taxes, access to health care, major shopping, BART, and absolutely the biggest and most important item on the list: NO HOA!

"The Incident" had happened on a Thursday night, and by Saturday morning they were driving up through Novato exploring options in North Bay. With an app that would ping when you were near any open houses, Daniel and Stephen discovered they were able to define what worked and what didn't work very quickly. Their initial inclination was to look for something in the same ZIP code, but they quickly realized, they really wanted to be far away from and completely rid of Andrea and Sandra's toxicity. And this would take more than a zip code or two of distance.

By this time, they had already engaged a local realtor to get the ball rolling on selling their place and had mapped out every weekend to search for a new home. Stephen was actually rather shocked to realize not only how quickly they made the decision to sell and move, but also, how right it felt. About a week or two after "the Incident" as Stephen was coming back from getting mail, Thelma was rolling a trash can in from the street.

She waved and beckoned Stephen over, saying, "So, you've shitcanned the committee work, and I hear Daniel has tendered his resignation from the Board. AND you're moving."

Looking over at Andrea's place, she said, "It was them, wasn't it?"

Stephen made a face and said, "Yup."

She lit her cigarette and as she exhaled, she said, "The clit-club. It won't last. That one" pointing at Sandra's place, "is unfuckable. Shit, anyone who goes 'down there' is going to get frost bite and freezer burn. And that one," now pointing to Andrea's place, "is a snake in the grass. She comes off all sugar and spice, with her low breathy voice, but she has no allegiance to anyone. In fact, having been here this long, I know she likes throwing everything into the shitter and screwing people over just for the thrill of it all. It's almost a compulsion. It's their loss, certainly not yours. Just know your efforts were appreciated, and you and Daniel will be missed."

She then went on, "I hear the ice queen lost her job. No idea why, don't really care. Couldn't happen to a nicer person. Maybe she thought taking over the newsletter was a career move?" And with a terse laugh and trailing smoke behind her, she left with Stephen feeling much better about things.

In less than two weeks Stephen had boxed up a good portion of their belongings in the house and was meticulously stacking them in the garage, for maximum space and movement. He had met with the staging specialist his realtor suggested, and she liked everything she saw. Her only two suggestions were throw-pillows, lots, and lots and lots of throw pillows, and also NOT to have their own towels out.

Stephen was very curious and asked about the towels.

She made a face and said, "You cannot believe the vile stuff people do in open houses. I found a dirty diaper under a hand towel once. Let me bring mine. I can always burn them if anything too horrid is there. Also, HIDE ALL YOUR PRESCRIPTIONS. Just remove them from the house if you can."

So, the second weekend after "the Incident," Stephen had just finished working out on the elliptical and was about to start packing a new box. Daniel was in the garage, working out, headphones on doing a Teaching

Company course when the doorbell rang. Stephen opened the door and standing there was Andrea.

Wishing he were attired in something other than a sweaty T-shirt and workout shorts, very coolly he said, "Yes?"

Andrea said, "Can we talk?"

Stephen stood there staring at her. His heart was racing a million miles an hour, but after a beat he said, "Come in."

Rather than sit, she just sort of stood by the dining room entry way landing. Stephen, arms crossed, turned to look at her.

Andrea said, "I wasn't sure you'd even let me in. Thank you for that."

Stephen remained mute, arching his eyebrows ever so slightly.

Andrea continued, "Well, I don't really know what happened. I mean, it just happened so quickly. I was speechless. I was just stunned. I didn't know how to react, or even what to say. I was just stunned."

Stephen stood there, silent. He was thinking, "She's throwing Sandra under the bus. Placing ALL the blame on her… let's see how deep she digs herself in."

Stephen said, "And?"

Andrea, not really focusing on anything but not really making eye contact either, continued, "It was so unexpected. I mean, you know, I think she (Stephen felt it interesting that she didn't use Sandra's name) had this all planned, and you know, there I am, suddenly caught up in the middle of things. Bottom line, I'm sorry and could you please come back to work."

Stephen's eyebrows rose and he thought, "Work. She doesn't view anything we've done as friendship, but only as work. Work she was trying to commandeer and control. And that was a spectacular fail, so she's asking me to come back? To WORK?"

White-hot rage overcoming him, Stephen, asked, "What are you sorry about? Sorry your coup didn't work? Sorry you got called out by all the other committee members? Sorry your grand plan failed to launch?"

She started to mumble and look away.

Stephen continued, "So blindsided you couldn't say a single word, yet you could just sit there and let her go on and on. And what's up with this junior-high 'so and so doesn't like you' bullshit? If there was a specific incident, have the integrity and balls to say what it was. Don't hide behind vague accusations and imply all sorts of people are or were unhappy with us. As it was, I felt very bad and apologized to several people if we had indeed overstepped, and you know what? Not a single person I spoke to have any idea what that could have been about. Ummm… that really only leaves you and Sandra. And c'mon, if you really felt SO BAD and were SO BLINDSIDED by what she said that night, why not a quick text that evening or even the day after to say what you're saying now?"

Andrea, looking a bit distraught, said, "I just… I just… I didn't know what to say or do. I mean, it JUST HAPPENED!"

Stephen, his rage leveling off now with an incredibly disgusted look on his face, snarled, "YOU. YOU WHO ARE SO SUPPOSEDLY GOOD WITH WORDS. AND YOU HAD NONE. NOT ONE. I'M IMPRESSED! LITTLE MISS I DIDN'T KNOW WHAT WAS GOING ON!"

Continuing, Stephen said, "I was blind copied on a lot of emails that went round the next day and beyond. It was abundantly clear to everyone that you and Sandra had been hatching this little takeover for a while and were more than ready to pull the trigger. In fact, judging from the speed with which you deployed your newsletter mockup, I'd say you were both probably ecstatic that I resigned and there wasn't going to be a prolonged battle."

Andrea, looking away, said, "Oh no, that was never the plan… that was…" and let the sentence trail off into silence.

Then, perhaps in defense of all that taken place, Andrea said, "Well, someone put poison under Sandra's garage door to try to poison and kill her little dog. This is how worked up people are over you and Daniel stepping down. Everyone HATES US!"

Stephen just stared at her, and then said, "Really? That's SO INTERESTING, as she just spent hundreds of thousands of dollars to have her place redone, and I noticed a brand-new roll-up garage door that, to my eyes, goes flush against the level cement garage floor. I doubt anyone could slide two pieces of paper underneath it, let alone poison."

Andrea had an expression on her face Stephen couldn't read, and after a long pause she said very quietly, "Do you think she made that up?"

Stephen didn't respond. After a long pause on his part, he then said, "Well, shortly after your coup attempt someone left a steaming pile of shit on our doormat. Someone who either has a large dog..." now arching his brows looking at Andrea pointedly, "Or ... or maybe they squatted down to leave their own personal message."

What was interesting was, Andrea didn't look surprised, stunned, or bothered. After another long pause, in a faltering tone she said, "Who do you think did it?"

Stephen sarcastically said, "Maybe the same person trying to poison Sandra's dog. And when did she get a dog?"

He then simply stated, "I am so disappointed, saddened and hurt, as I thought we had a real friendship. And it was all swept aside in a matter of minutes. I don't know what or who to believe, but we cannot live here any longer. We're putting the place on the market and moving."

Andrea looked startled and surprised. At that point when Stephen felt he had more than made his points, the garage door opened and Daniel walked in, soaking wet from his workout. Looking surprised, Stephen said dryly, "Someone came by to apologize."

Daniel, while nowhere near as worked up, still expressed his disappointment and dismay at such an obvious betrayal of trust and friendship.

With that, Andrea said, "Thank you for letting me in and listening" and turned and left.

Chapter 31 – The End

Very quickly Stephen and Daniel had put their place on the market. And very quickly they had two solid, competing bids and went with the one that gave them a few months to stay in their home while they found a new place.

Stephen had received a LOT of emails, calls, and visits from neighbors and friends, asking them to reconsider and not only stay, but to continue on with their Association work. Thanking each and every one, Stephen informed them the decision had been made, and there was no going back.

What was very illuminating to Stephen and Daniel was how many people expressed openly negative opinions of Andrea and confessed they had always had reservations about her. Most said the implied endorsement of both Stephen and Daniel allowed them to brush aside their questions or concerns. Unsurprisingly, absolutely everyone loathed Sandra. No one had warmed to her and never really understood why Stephen and Daniel allowed her into their circle. Stephen wished some of them had been expressed these views earlier.

Now that their home had been prepped for the open houses and the garage was filled to maximum capacity, the elliptical was no longer an option for working out, so Stephen started going for long walks in the neighborhood. It had never been a big walking community, and at the hour Stephen went out he rarely saw a single person. So, it was with some surprise one morning, while rounding the corner about five blocks away from the house, Stephen encountered Thelma, cigarette still firmly in place. What with her age and the smoking, exercise didn't seem like a likely grouping. Still, she was a hoot, so they walked along together for a bit. Stephen realized he was going to miss Thelma.

Rounding the corner, coming up the street straight at them was Sandra. Stephen's first inclination was to cross the street and ignore her. Thelma wasn't having any of it! As they met, Sandra's shoulder ever-so-firmly grazed Stephen's as she stared straight ahead and said in a very arch and sarcastic tone, "Hello."

Stephen turned and somewhat bolstered by Thelma's presence, yelled, "How is that passive-aggressive bullshit of yours working out? Oh, wait! I heard you got canned!"

Sandra kept walking, but Thelma, not one to miss a moment turned and said "Twunt!" in a very loud voice.

Stephen and Thelma turned, and once they were a few yards away, both started giggling.

Shortly afterwards, Daniel and Stephen attended the next Board meeting. Neither Andrea nor Sandra showed up. They didn't send notice that they would not be present. Carol and Timothy had very kind words for Daniel and also gave a shout-out to Stephen for his work.

In the almost ten years Stephen and Daniel had been at Thornwillow Heights, with people coming and going, they had never heard of or seen any farewell events. When Tom had moved, a large group had gone to the open house he held and had a make-shift BBQ, and when Roger left the Board, Rebecca had made a fuss and gave Roger an engraved pen and pencil set. But that was it. So, Daniel and Stephen were surprised when they were told there was going to be a going-away party at the clubhouse before they left.

Shortly after that, Stephen was getting items ready for a large trash pick-up date. As he was stacking the items trying to decrease the space they took, he suddenly smelled smoke. Coming towards him was Thelma, puffing away.

She asked, "Do you need any help?"

Stephen replied, "I think I have it all set up so it won't impact the shared driveway."

Thelma then smiled and said, "So, I was out watering when Andrea came by with her dog. I smiled and asked her, 'Oh, are you going to Stephen and Daniel's going away party?' and she looked kind of flustered and mumbled 'I don't think so' and walked away."

Smiling widely as she walked away, Thelma said, "You're welcome."

The party was MUCH larger than either Stephen or Daniel could have imagined. The entire clubhouse had been reserved and everyone outdid themselves decorating the place and providing an amazing amount of food and drink. More people were there than either Daniel or Stephen were expecting, and Stephen started to have twinges of regret about leaving. Having felt he was a part of something good had been quite wonderful, he realized there were more good people here than not. But even with the pangs of regret, he knew in his heart, it was time to leave and there was no way to undo what had been done.

Finding their forever home had happened surprisingly fast. No longer blindly going into whatever came along, they had their long list of what they wanted, and most definitely did NOT want with their new home. And no HOA was still at the very top of the list.

When the moving van had left and they were in their new home having a celebratory glass of champagne, Stephen stopped and said, "Can you hear that?"

Daniel furrowed his brow, straining a bit, and said, "No, I can't hear anything."

Stephen smiled and said "Exactly!"

Aftermath

Sylvia

Sylvia looked at the clock and was surprised to see it was later than she had realized. As upset and angry as she had been when the whole homeowner upheaval had taken place, and while she'd never admit it to a single solitary person, she was stunned to discover her stress levels had dropped dramatically and she now had time for things and people who really mattered to her. Fluffing her hair in the entryway mirror, she looked at her reflection. The henna-red hair was now replaced with a reddish-brown with blonde highlights. Also, gone the asymmetrical angles. A more conventional, but still stylish, cut now greeted her gaze.

Grabbing her wallet and keys she decided on the spur-of-the-moment to go to Whole Foods in Palo Alto to see what might be enticing for dinner this evening. She needed to drop off some papers with her accountant there, and she always enjoyed the ambience in Palo Alto. She had just had her Datsun 280ZX detailed and thought it would be a lovely day to open the sunroof and maybe see if that flower stand by the train station was still there. She thought some delphiniums might look nice near the fireplace.

Parking was a bit of a pill today, but once she found a spot, Whole Foods wasn't nearly as crowded as she thought it would be. The selection of cheeses was a bit overwhelming and for once Sylvia was having a very difficult time making up her mind. There was a lovely Beaufort d'Éte, but the Caciocavallo Podolico also looked quite good. And then there was always the Wyke Farms Cheddar. You could never go wrong with that, but for some reason, something French seemed like the right call today. Not in a rush, and not really ready to decide, she kept meandering around the plentiful choices, always spotting something else alluring.

At that moment a cart banged into Sylvia's cart. A flash of anger overtook her as she turned around to lay into whoever had rudely bumped into her, but Sylvia stopped dead in her tracks. Behind the errant cart was one of the loveliest women she had ever seen. A slightly older version of Audrey Tautou was standing there. She had on a maroon wool suit, and were those Tabra earrings she was wearing?

Before Sylvia could say anything, the woman said, "Excusez-moi!"

Sylvia, flushing just a bit, said, "Êtes-vous Français?"

Before either of them knew it, they were splitting a baguette at Pastis.

As they headed for their cars, Sylvia asked, *"Aimez-vous Duran Duran?"*

Roger

Roger sat in his living room taking in the view one last time. He was trying to recall exactly how long he had been at Thornwillow Heights. He thought, "Maybe, thirty years? Thirty-five years?"

He looked out across the street to where Rosemary had once lived. He was shocked when he heard she was packing it in after so long. Of course, she didn't tell him directly. He heard it from Terrance who came running over like a twelve-year-old girl who had just heard fresh gossip on the school playground. He still recalled that day with Terrance excitedly banging on his door.

When he opened it, Terrance didn't even ask if he could come in, instead he rushed past Roger, and said breathlessly," Did you see? There's a moving van at Rosemary's place! I ran over when I saw it and she told me she sold it last month and was moving to a seniors-only community up near Healdsburg. She said she can hardly wait to get up there."

Roger was stunned. Pushing past Terrance, he ran across the street. Making his way through the pile of boxes and moving men coming in and going out he found Rosemary sitting in her kitchen having a cup of tea with her two neighbors Phil and Margery.

Roger sputtered, "You're moving? To Healdsburg? When did this happen?"

Rosemary, unruffled, smiled and said, "Oh, I've been going up there off and on for years. Some dear friends have always lived up there, and on a whim, they took me to see a lovely community that's relatively new. I fell in love with it instantly. I pulled the trigger, and here we are."

Still smiling widely, Roger noticed a brochure on the table. "Villa Romano? It looks quite nice" Roger read out loud to himself. Without a lot of fanfare, Roger wished Rosemary well and said his goodbyes.

Once he was in the door, he fired up his trusty Bondi Blue iMac and searched for Villa Romano. The website looked quite nice, as he scrolled through the pictures. And the prices weren't that bad, considering all the services and accoutrements. The next day Roger drove up and asked for a tour and was very impressed.

As he was leaving, he asked the woman showing him around, "Oh, my very good friend Rosemary Stoddard is moving in shortly. She was the one that suggested I check it out. She mentioned the section she was moving to, but it slipped my mind. Would you know which section she's in?"

The woman smiled, pulled up her iPad, and scrolled a bit. She said, "Ah, here she is. She's moving into the newest section. Villa Rufolo. We do have some openings there. In fact, the unit whose front door shares a walkway with hers is available. Would you like to view it?"

Now, taking one last look around the place, he didn't have any regrets or sadness about leaving. Gathering up his paperwork and doing one last walk-through to make sure he hadn't forgotten anything. Stepping outside the front door, he locked the deadbolt and stopped. He bent down and plucked a large group of daffodils and carried them to his car. He could hardly wait to see the look on Rosemary's face when he presented them to her and announced he was her new next-door neighbor.

Durusha

Durusha realized it was lunchtime. She shut her computer down and headed toward the lunchroom. Of course, no one else would in there. No one ate in this place.

"My god!" she thought, "If someone had one extra carrot stick for dinner everyone would hear about it for days."

While it was a tad demoralizing to be the only person who wasn't striving to be a cover model for *Shape* magazine, she did enjoy the solitude and quiet of having the lunchroom to herself. Everyone else was either at the gym, out doing "a quick run, so I'm loosened up for tonight's big workout," in one of the isolation pods, or in the yoga room.

And it was always easy to locate her lunch in the refrigerator. Everyone else's lunch was in clear plastic Ziplock containers with veggies, some fruit, and the random yogurt container. Hers was the only brown bag, which held a decent sized sandwich, some chips, and a diet soda. No one ever stole her lunch. In fact, it seemed to her people very purposely placed their containers as far away from hers as possible, as if they'd catch "carbs" just being near her bag.

Settling in, Durusha pulled out her book, a romance novel she'd normally be too self-conscious to read in a crowded space, but since she almost always had the lunchroom to herself, there was nothing to worry about. She thought Delaney's *Desert Sheikh* was definitely a good read. She'd have to go back to Barbara-Ann's recommended reading list when she finished this one. Two bites into her sandwich and completely lost in the book, Durusha didn't notice the sound of the refrigerator closing but looked up when she heard the chair across from her was being pulled out.

Sitting across from her was Bryce from Accounting. She had noticed him at the main company meetings, but their departments had zero overlap. He had stood out at those meetings for probably the same reasons she did. He wasn't trying to look like the latest cover of Men's Health. His semi-curly brown hair, while not messy, never looked styled. It complemented his dark brown eyes. One of the very few men to who always wore a tie to work… that had always impressed her. Always nicely presented, but not coming off like he stepped out of the men's section at Nordstrom's. Nice looking, but certainly not that fake movie star look.

Suddenly realizing Bryce was staring at her intently, she tried to hide her book as quickly as possible and hoped she didn't have potato salad stuck in her teeth.

Smiling, but with her lips pressed together (for safety's sake), Durusha asked, "Bryce? Right?"

Bryce smiled back, and she noticed how much more attractive that smile made him. He said, "Durusha? Right? It's nice to finally see someone who actually eats in this place. My god, it's like everyone is competing for an eating disorder award."

For just a split-second Durusha wasn't sure if he was saying she was a glutton or if it was a compliment. Erring on the side of a compliment, she said, "Likewise. All the men here seem to only consume protein shakes mixed with powder to bulk up. Frankly, it's a bit exhausting being around those types all the time, feeling their judgment."

Bryce smiled and said, "Umm, aren't we doing the judging now?"

Durusha smiled back and feeling secure that not too much food could be stuck between her teeth, laughed out loud.

Looking around as if they were going to be caught doing something, they shouldn't Bryce said, "Umm, I don't want to be too forward here, but would you like to go out for dinner or drinks one night? Maybe Thursday?"

Durusha started to say, "Oh I have an HOA Board meeting this Thursday," but she suddenly realized, she didn't. And while leaving the Board had left a bit of a vacuum in her life, she had really come to appreciate not having the stress and time constraints.

Now she was very happy she didn't have those concerns, smiled, and said, "I'd love to. What time works for you?"

Looking down Durusha hoped Bryce didn't notice the marinara sauce spilled on her sweater.

Melva

As Melva slowly got out of bed, she realized she had absolutely nowhere she had to be, or anything she absolutely had to do that day. Slowly easing into an early retirement, first cutting down to thirty hours a week, then to twenty, and finally only working from home for ten or fifteen hours had been very effective. Coupled with no longer needing to attend endless meetings for the Homeowners Association, even though at first, she had been quite peeved at being ousted, now she was at a loss to figure out why they had all held on as long and hard as they did. It really had taken its toll, but no one seemed to recognize that.

And then meeting that lovely woman, Elsa, at the mall. Any other time, she'd get in and out with exactly what she wanted or needed without straying from her plans. But with work fading into the distance and the Homeowners work gone, she now found herself window shopping lingering around the main area of the mall and enjoying the unique experience. And then Elsa had come up to her.

Not recalling the last time she had encountered anyone with such an intense gaze, she stopped when Elsa said, "You have a mind, and this is the owner's manual," holding up a book.

Normally, Melva would have ignored the woman and moved on, but something about her gravitas gave her pause and she stopped to listen. They ended up moving to seats near the food court and before she knew it over an hour had flown by. After Melva and Elsa had said their goodbyes, she turned back and asked, "Have you actually met Tom Cruise? Is he as short as everyone says he is?"

Renaldo

Renaldo opened the vintage bottle of zinfandel he had been saving for a special occasion. After aerating it, he put his favorite gargoyle wine spout in the bottle and reached for a Riedel wine glass. He sat back and stared out the window at the planes taking off and landing at OAK. After a generous pour, Renaldo swirled the wine a bit, and lingered on the aroma. Taking a small sip, he sat back and continued to watch the planes.

He thought, "This time next week I'll be on my way to Portugal."

It seemed like he had friends in every country in Europe and he planned on taking several months to visit as many of them as he could.

Sitting on the table to his right was the latest newsletter from the HOA. In looking at the updates on reserves and the plans being rolled out for maintenance and repair, he took another sip of wine, balled up the newsletter, and tossed it in the trash. Taking a deep breath, looking at the planes, he closed his eyes for a minute or two. It sounded like someone was knocking at his gate. The gate that was always kept locked at all times.

Renaldo didn't care. Now that he was off the Board, he never saw or interacted with his neighbors. It appeared there was money in the reserves and things were being taken care of. There was nothing that needed his attention here as he wondered where he and his friend Phillipe would dine when he got to Portugal... Oh, and he needed to drop a note to the management company about that soft wood on his deck where the water had been overflowing from the potted palm.

Jon

Jon put his paper down and was suddenly very aware of how quiet and peaceful the house was. It was actually startling. He closed his eyes and listened intently. There were no drawers or doors being banged shut in anger. There was no cursing, or muttering, or any kind of upset being broadcast.

When did this actually start? While running up to the elections had been an absolute nightmare in the house, listening to Rebecca rant and rail against everything and everybody, afterwards was just so much worse. The phone never stopped ringing. Her walking back and forth venting, complaining, explaining, blaming... It was like someone had unleashed a hurricane in the house. And the visits... All the well-meaning friends, bottles of wine in hand... The women all around the dining room table, dissecting what had happened. And the trash-talk! Oh dear, the trash-talk! Taking each and every person down, one peg at a time. Their looks, their jobs, their personalities. It was so toxic Jon kept expecting the EPA to come in and shut them down.

And then somewhere along the way, things shifted. The trash-talk seemed to have exhausted itself. The vitriol seemed to have finally been exhausted. The calls decreased. And then Jon didn't recall hearing the phone ring for, what was it? Weeks now? And the visits from those Board women became less and less. It was SO NICE coming home and not seeing them gathered round the dining room table, several empty wine bottles lined up, hearing the same complaints restated over and over and over again.

And now? It was actually peaceful! And Rebecca seemed reborn. No longer wielding her anger like a weapon, she truly seemed happy. Or at least, not unhappy... In fact, being away from the constant grind of all the Association business seemed to have taken years off Rebecca. She was looking and acting like the woman she was when they had first gotten married. And they were interacting socially with people NOT in the HOA.

Jon sat back in the overstuffed chair, looked around, and realized he was actually able to appreciate their lovely home and the life he and Rebecca had together.

Rebecca

A glass of chardonnay in her hand, Rebecca peered out from underneath the cucumber slices covering her eyes. Looking about, she finally spotted the spa manager and waved her over.

Rebecca said, "I know I didn't book it, but would it be possible to get a seaweed wrap after my massage?"

Smiling the manager said, "No problem. Would you like a refill?"

Smiling Rebecca held up her glass, saying, "I really shouldn't, but… why not?"

Exhaling, Rebecca suddenly realized this was the most relaxed she had been in… ages! She couldn't believe all the bullshit that had gone down with the Homeowners Association, and yes, she'd fought tooth, fang, and nail. Nails? Her nails! Look at them now! The times she could never get in to have them done, the Association eating up each and every second of her life. And her diet. She had been grabbing whatever was at hand. Not good. And the stress. Oh, the stress.

And now? She'd made it to the spa four weeks in a row! And who would have thought the spin class would be enjoyable. It was fun showing those youngsters who still had it and who didn't. She never in a million years would have believed it would be something she looked forward to. And her weight. Some of her vintage couture actually fits again! And it's back in STYLE! And getting back into some of the political action committees felt good. Climate change and racism are both serious issues that need attention.

But the Association…

Rebecca thought, "The new Landscape Committee doesn't know their ass from a hole in the ground, but they're trying. But Andrea? Who the fuck does she really think she is? Was that really a Chanel jacket she had on at the last meeting? And sunglasses? Sunglasses at a nighttime Board meeting? I always thought she was more of a wash-and-wear dyke. Or Goodwill.

Granted, a Goodwill from Hillsborough. I never really noticed her until she proved to be so adept at quietly assuming pole-position with the Board.

Who saw that one coming? I most certainly did not. I always thought it was that uppity gay couple, what were their names, who were the instigators? It doesn't matter. They're gone.

They'll all be gone. Andrea drove them all away. She has the personality of a limp-fart, and a face to match. When she enters a room, it feels like three people left. Well, she can have it if she wants it that badly.

But… I'm still going to show up and throw my opinion at her from time to time. I could be wrong, but I sense her sphincter tighten anytime I get up to speak.

And Sandra. She's an odd duck. I swear ice crystals start to form when she enters a room. I read about the upheaval in her company, and from what a friend-of-a-friend said, they were well rid of her. I did love hearing her comment at the Board meeting when someone asked how her vacation skiing in Austria was. And her reply, 'It was delicious.' The look on Andrea's face was abject misery. Even Helen Keller could see Andrea was pining for that one. They both deserve each other."

And with that, Rebecca put the cucumber slices back in place, took a nice deep sip of the crisp chardonnay, and really hoped Janine would be her masseuse today. She did magic with the tension in her shoulders and neck. Feeling around for her phone, Rebecca lifted the cucumbers one more time and put in a reminder for her to book a couple's weekend up in Napa for her and Jon. Maybe they'd even drop by and surprise Rosemary?

Betty Jean & Stan

Betty Jean went upstairs to see Stan with his binoculars firmly in place.

Sighing, she said, "Stan, you know this is the final curtain call? Enjoy the last show. We are so out of here once the movers get the last items tomorrow morning."

Stan sighed, lowering the binoculars, and said, "Frankly, the show has gotten kind of stale. I mean, once you have more than five people, but less than ten, it's not really an orgy. And she could at least have ONE MORE female guest star."

Leaving the bedroom, Betty Jean sighed and cast a gaze out the upstairs landing window. She was certain Franny had HER telescope trained on their house. With that thought, she quickly shut the blinds.

She thought, "Our new place will NOT be in the direct sightlines of ANY of our neighbors."

Sarah

Sarah drained the last bit of gin from her glass, added another layer of bright red lipstick to her already painted lips, then put a bit more on her fingers and rubbed it into her lined cheeks. Squinting into the mirror, while she couldn't make out much without glasses, what she saw did the trick. Grabbing a bottle of wine someone had given her ages ago, she headed towards the door, when the slight breeze alerted her to the fact that she was still only wearing her paper-thin kimono, with nothing underneath. Pausing for a second, she thought about going back to change, but then thought about her new next-door neighbor, Liam.

She wasn't thrilled when she found out she'd be getting new neighbors. The previous tenant had abruptly moved out. She had rather fancied Anthony, but he made it abundantly clear he did not feel the same way about her. He had actually had the audacity to get a restraining order! The nerve. But after he had left, one day when she had gone out to water, Sarah noticed the garage door was open next door. She was curious about the new neighbor. Shirtless, his bulging muscles glistening with sweat as he moved furniture about, in her most coquettish voice said, "Oh, you must be the new neighbor? I'm Sarah. I live next door. If there is ANYTHING you need, please don't hesitate to ask. ANYTHING."

Sarah, decided the kimono was fine, letting the belt hang a little loosely, she headed over to welcome Liam to the neighborhood.

Sandra

Sandra was staring out of the living room window at her new view. Well, view adjacent. This view was significantly less than it had been at her previous place. Actually, you might call it a view-ette. Swirling the Scotch in its glass, she looked around her new living room. Sadly, even the really good bottle of Scotch wasn't going to change this.

Taking a deep breath, she looked at the sad living room and said out loud, "Jesus. A bowling alley bar in Toledo called and they want their raw-rock fireplace back."

She drained her glass and looked out the window again. If she stood in *just* the right spot and tilted her head, she would have a sliver of a glimpse of the San Francisco Bay. But only just.

And then she thought back to that one Board meeting. Christ, how long ago was that now? Two years? Not one of the knock-down-drag-out-blow-out meetings, but contentious enough. She had needed to get away from those people and step outside to get some air. It was a beautiful evening that summer. The sun was still out, the sky was a gorgeous shade of blue, and with the front door shut to the clubhouse, she could no longer hear the bickering and rancor. She exhaled and centered herself.

At just the moment Sandra was starting to feel grounded, she heard the front door open and close. Not wanting to engage with anyone, she stared straight ahead at the open sky. She felt someone standing near to her, and despite disliking having her personal space invaded, she turned her head. Rebecca was standing right next to her. This was long before Sandra was on the Board and might have been *just* before she joined the Communications Committee. She had never been introduced to Rebecca and felt it was a safe bet Rebecca had no idea who she was or her ties to the new Board and committees. Nodding to Rebecca she turned her gaze back to the open skies.

Rebecca, not really addressing Sandra, gazed up at the sky and said, "Everything was *just fine* the way it was. Why did they have to go and spoil it?"

Sandra, startled, turned her head to look at Rebecca, but felt the statement was rhetorical and not necessarily directed at her.

Not wanting to leave abruptly, Sandra and Rebecca both stood there gazing up at the sky. Rebecca's statement didn't warrant a reply, and after an acceptable amount of time had passed, Sandra nodded at Rebecca and then went back into the meeting.

And now, sitting in her "new" living room, Rebecca's statement was echoing in her head. "Everything was just fine the way it was. Why did they have to go and spoil it?"

And in looking around, so much had been spoiled, and no, none of it could ever go back again. Moving some boxes out of the way, Sandra reached for the bottle of Scotch, and filled her glass much higher than she'd ever do if anyone was around. Sitting back, she replayed it all.

Sandra's carefully curated world, where every aspect of her life from work to home had been meticulously fine-tuned to perfection. And then it wasn't. Did it start with that Schuster man? Maybe? Were the work issues Tiffany's fault? Maybe a little. Had she been in Tiffany's place, she might have played it the same way. Was it James' fault? Somewhat. He never would have become or held onto being CEO as long as he had without Sandra being the one to take care of the heavy-lifting and dirty work. Did she overvalue her contribution? Obviously. But still...

Sandra wasn't destitute. She had investments, but even with those, she really couldn't afford to maintain the newly remodeled home that wasn't the home she had envisioned or wanted. Then after the firebreak work, she felt exposed like every set of eyes on the walking trail were directly aimed at her. And the neighborhood had started to feel like a fish tank. And she was the fish.

Then there was Andrea. What a Pandora's box of dysfunction she really hadn't seen coming. First impressions are not always correct. The straw that broke the camel's back was Daniel upsetting the neighbor. Their new neighbor was EXACTLY what their part of the street needed. After so much discord, good energy, FEMALE ENERGY had settled in. And then Daniel goes charging in and upsets her to the point that she's talking about moving once her lease is up. Men ruin everything.

And at the end of the day, in hindsight the whole takeover of the Communications Committee was a mistake. But there was this void and

Sandra had really needed to grab the reigns in some part of her life, and the situation presented itself. It had started out innocently enough. Sandra, Andrea, a few bottles of wine. Both of them were displeased at the thought of losing a neighbor who fit in so well. And while Daniel wasn't incorrect in addressing a potentially dangerous situation, the way he handled it was a troubling sign of things to come. It was best to nip these things in the bud, versus letting them get too far out of hand. A lesson that she should have learned with Tiffany.

Things had been fine just the way they were. But Andrea… That night… WTF? They had both discussed addressing the issue in great detail and agreed on how to handle that evening. But that night? Andrea had just sat there like a piece of furniture. Sandra thought she might have stroked out or something. The lights weren't on AND no one was home. This left Sandra out on a limb by herself. It was NOT what they had discussed. The intent and hope were, Daniel and Stephen would listen, absorb what was being said, and then dial it back and there would be a modicum of normalcy restored.

But NO. OMG! Talk about an overreaction. The way they both carried on you would have thought their first-born was had been murdered. But it opened a door, and with absolutely nothing else happening, it was a door Sandra was ready to walk through. And that night… up all night with Andrea. The way she was behaving, you'd have thought it was her honeymoon.

Giggling like a teenager saying, "Why don't we get into our pajamas and completely redo this newsletter from the ground up."

And to be fair, compared to all the other bullshit going on in her life at the time, having a momentary diversion was a bit of fun.

But the blowback! Sandra was expecting some pushback, but the nearly unanimous negative responses were shocking. Sandra felt the newsletter Stephen had done was too folksy and not to her own tastes and styles. She preferred something more corporate and structured. But the naysayers had their way, and their all-night experiment died a quick and ugly death. And then the temperature in the community. You could chill wine by just walking into any of the meetings after that. The smiles couldn't have been any more forced if they had toothpicks jammed in their cheeks. Both Sandra and Andrea wisely laid low until Stephen and Daniel were gone and things could cool off.

Of course, that wasn't the end of it. Their neighbor DID move at the end of her lease, which made Sandra's place much less inviting. When she saw the older couple across the way had listed their place, she went over. The main floorplan was workable, but it hadn't been updated or touched in thirty years (or more). Dark, cheap cabinets, original flooring… it was a time capsule no one wanted to open. With absolutely no takers, they had pulled the listing. But thinking it over, Sandra had realized with the money she would undoubtedly make selling her place and the considerably lower price these people had listed their place for, she could cut her living expenses by more than half and also regain the privacy she lost with the firebreak work.

So one evening Sandra went over and asked if they had had any offers. Both of them, now in their late 70s, shook their heads. They lamented the fact they wanted to move closer to their daughter and grandchildren, but they knew the lack of updates was making it a hard sell.

Having already crunched the numbers, Sandra offered an all-cash deal with no contingencies if she could get it within the next month. To her surprise, they accepted and were out almost instantly. Sandra's place had an offer she couldn't refuse before it was even officially listed. While not ideal, it was the best move to make at that moment.

Then there was still Andrea. Sandra could still hear her whining, "You know you could have moved in with me. Why didn't you mention it or talk it over first?"

Ugh! NO. It took everything in Sandra's power to not backhand her on the spot. Taking a deep breath, she had said, "I really want and need my own space. But look on the bright side, we'll still be neighbors."

What Sandra left out was she was no longer in Andrea's direct line of sight, so she hopefully could come and go without being too closely observed. But probably not.

Finally emptying her glass, Sandra tried to decide what she wanted to get for takeout for dinner, when there was a knock at the door. When she opened the door, there stood Andrea, with a gift bag in one hand and a bottle of wine in the other.

In a too-perky voice Andrea said, "Welcome to the neighborhood. Again."

Sandra gave a strained smile and said, "I was just heading out. I need to run some errands."

Andrea, looking over Sandra's shoulder into the unpacked boxes and furniture scattered about said, "Well, it's getting to be dinnertime. Would you like to come over or maybe go out and grab something?"

The look on her face was like a retriever hoping its master was going to take them out for a walk or give them a treat.

Sandra tightened the smile and said, "Oh, that would really be lovely, but I'm meeting a friend from school. She'll only be in town for the night. Maybe another time?"

It was Andrea now who had the forced smile as she said, "Uh, okay, well, the offer still stands and we can do it another time. Have fun."

And she walked away, looking back over her shoulder.

Taking the wine and gift bag into the kitchen, Sandra looked into the bag. There was a canning jar with a bow on top and a note, "This is lavender-sugar that I made myself. Sweet dreams. Andrea."

Sandra looked at it, wrinkled her nose and immediately chucked it into the trash. Looking at the wine she saw it was a decent red. Maybe she'd have that with whatever she finally found for dinner. Walking out to her car, Thelma was taking the trash out, and was she humming? It sounds like the theme to *The Jeffersons…*

Andrea

"**FUUUUUUCCCCKKKKKKKKKK!**" echoed throughout the entire house. Andrea's dog's ears pricked up and it immediately ran up the stairs and hid under the bed in the guest room. Down in the kitchen blood was now smeared all over the counter as Andrea ran to the sink to turn the water on.

"Shit! Shit! Shit!"

Taking a deep breath, she found a rag and applied pressure to the spot where she had let the newly sharpened kitchen knife pierce the skin on her hand. Tonight, of all fucking nights. SHIT. The Board meeting was going to start in forty-five minutes. Why on earth had she thought cutting the chicken up at this point was a good idea?

She knew why she wasn't paying attention. Rebecca. That afternoon, just before she was going to start dinner, she saw the email. Rebecca said she knew it was late but requested time to speak at the meeting regarding a pressing landscape issue. Andrea always got thrown off when Rebecca attended a meeting. And it was always even worse if she was slated to speak. This got Andrea thinking back to how things used to be. She remembered when she felt safe and supported at the meetings. The recaps with Stephen, Daniel, and Sandra. It had been really fun. And with a couple of years of hindsight, Andrea wished things would have gone a different way.

WHY did she think things with Sandra were going to get more serious then? For a time there, when Sandra lost her job, it almost seemed fated that they'd finally get together. But they didn't. If anything, things became even more strained and formal after *the incident.* Had it been worth throwing the friendship with Stephen and Daniel away for it? At the time, it had. But the cold slap of reality came soon enough. Sandra couldn't afford her place, but instead of discussing it with her, Sandra had bought that museum piece of a home a few doors down. Her message was delivered loud and clear. But still, Andrea had clung to hope.

Andrea had also hoped going round to all the committed players on the Board and on the committees doing a one-on-one PR campaign would put all the ugliness and rumors to rest and allow them to get on with things. And it had. Up to a point. But the support she had started to erode quickly. But to her surprise, despite the stress and social anxiety of now having risen to be President of the Board, she enjoyed the power and prestige. In fact, she had raced to update her LinkedIn page the second she won the seat. She found she derived a fair amount of pleasure dismissing complaints, denying payments, pushing off requests, and gazing imperially at people from behind the dais.

But Andrea also hated surprises. And this afternoon she had had a doozy. Stephen and Daniel's car was parked in Thelma's driveway. Andrea had just rounded the corner to water when she saw them getting out of the car. She darted back quickly; certain they hadn't seen her. But it threw her off. Why were they here? What did they want? Shit, they weren't thinking about moving back, were they? Before a meeting, Andrea would normally have a couple of drinks, skim the meeting documents, and ground herself by sitting out back in her patio. But now, she was thrown off balance. And then the note from Rebecca. Shit! It's a wonder she didn't sever a finger.

Knowing Rebecca would be there this evening, Andrea went upstairs and started digging through her closet. She started going through a large selection of clothes. Some clothes that weren't even hers. She had never said anything to Sandra, but in all the time Sandra had stored her clothes there, Andrea had gone through and pulled out select pieces; a blouse here, a skirt there, a jacket she knew Sandra would never wear again, and even select pieces of lingerie. She didn't think Sandra noticed. Or if she did, she never said anything. Pushing past her own clothes, she stopped and looked at the jacket she was looking for. Louis Vuitton? Could she fit into it? Gently tugging on the arms, she felt some pull, but she very gently poured herself into it. If she didn't wave her arms around too much and didn't exhale fully, it should work. Ummm, maybe, just maybe Rebecca would notice tonight? And who knows… grabbing a canning jar, she started making her special lavender sugar…

Raul

Raul walked in his front door, dropping his bag and cooler loudly on the floor. Drenched in sweat from working on the shrubs of the HOA across the road from Thornwillow Heights, he was exhausted. He peeled off the shirt that was clinging to his torso and tossed it onto the floor. He called out, "I'm home" and went into the kitchen.

Fumbling around he found a cold beer. Before uncapping it, he held the bottle up to his forehead and stood in the open refrigerator door for a minute or two to cool down. Looking around, he called out, "You home?" hearing a couple of thuds and a mumble from the end of the house, he uncapped the beer and took a deep swig.

Walking into the bedroom, and pulling his work boots off, he said, "Those crazy women at Traviata Estates. They all think I'm doing their Board president, and I'm pretty sure their Board president thinks I'm doing everyone else. There are some days I can't even get out of bed thinking about dealing with all those crazy people."

At that moment, a dazzlingly handsome man in his mid-30s entered the room. A soaked tank top and gym shorts clinging to his torso indicated he had just gotten back from a run. Swallowing the last bite of the apple he was holding, he said, "Oh, if they only knew what was lurking underneath that gardening uniform, they'd never let out you of their sight."

Raul, taking off his pants, said, "As crazy as the new place is, it has NOTHING on Thornwillow Heights. I felt like I needed police protection from that old bat, what was her name? Sarah? And then that other woman… can't think of her name. I'd get a request for something near her door, she'd ALWAYS answer in only a towel, drop it in mock-surprise and say, 'You caught me'. Ugh!"

They both smiled and putting an arm around each other's shoulders they headed out back to the hot tub.

Ryan & Trevor

Ryan shut the door at their new place. The moving van belched a lot of black smoke as it pulled away. He could hear Trevor rummaging around in the kitchen for glasses so they could have the celebratory glass of champagne. The move had seemed to take forever. Exhaling, Ryan looked around and felt like he could finally relax. There had been SO MANY hurdles to jump through to get here. Beating everyone else out in a red-hot bidding war, getting pre-qualified, finally being able to sell their old place, but that was all behind them now.

They got the place they wanted. It had amazing light, all the windows south facing, with views of San Francisco all the way down to South Bay. While it was listed "with original flooring," this stuff was from another century and would need to go. And the front door! Someone had just put some oil or varnish on it when it definitely needed to be refinished or replaced. It needed work. White carpets. Who puts stark-white carpets in? And a marble countertop in the kitchen. You breathe on it, and it stains.

But still, a big upgrade from the one-bedroom condo they had been in for the last five years. That whole area they had moved from just exploded with construction and went from a funky downtown to clogged high-rises almost overnight. The congestion, the noise, and the lack of space was wearing on both of them. Finding this place and being able to get it was definitely a new beginning.

As Trevor was still opening boxes searching for the glassware, Ryan looked through the large folder of closing materials, getting them in order so he could file them away once the office was set up. One smaller envelope slipped out and a bunch of newsletters spilled out onto the table. Everything was so fast when they finally were ready to close Ryan had never really looked any of this over.

He thought to himself, "Interesting. It looks like several years back the Association didn't send out much in the way of newsletters or updates, and then suddenly they had very nice newsletters, ones sent out monthly for a couple of years."

As he looked those over, he saw they were informative. really keeping people updated so they could see the work the Association was putting into the community and where expenditures were going. And then, it just stopped. They were back to the sporadic, generic ones that really only admonished people for infractions.

He wondered, "Ummm, it looks like this Andrea person has been on the Board and been Board President forever. And it doesn't look like they've done too much the last couple of years..."

As Trevor came into the room holding two champagne glasses, Ryan said, "why don't you put some music on?" Trevor pulled up Apple Music, opened his library and pressed play.

Walk.
Away.
I walked. Away.

I saw you, the other day.
I kept on walking there was nothing to say.
You went your way. I went mine.
I hope you're doing well, because I'm doing fine.

We knew each other, a long time ago.
When the dust had settled there was nothing to show.
You weren't the person, I thought you to be.
And in the end you never knew me.

I saw you, turned and walked away.
There is nothing left, nothing more to say.
You go your way. I'll go mine.
I hope you're doing well, because I'm doing fine.

I walked.
Away.

You made your decisions. So did I.
There's no lament. No tears to cry.
No going back, even if we could.
Things landed just like they should.

I saw you, turned and walked away.
There is nothing left, nothing more to say.
You go your way. I'll go mine.
I hope you're doing well, because I'm doing fine.

I walked.
Away.

Listening to the music, while still going through some of the older newsletters Ryan looked around and said, "You know, maybe when we get settled, I might just throw my hat into the ring and try and shake up this board that's been in place forever. Who's the artist that did that song?"

Trevor looked at his phone and said, "Uh, they're called Munich Syndrome. It looks like it's just one guy. They have a HUGE discography."

Mittens

After time-sharing Michael and Brenda's home as well as Carol and Sam's place and Phil and Margery's home, Mittens escaped Thornwillow Heights when she got trapped in the back of a moving van and was discovered the next day at a palatial mansion up in the Berkeley Hills. Her new owners were delighted to find her and treated her like the queen so Mitten's days of terrorizing that vapid woman and her sloth of a husband are now over.

The End?

Thanks!

We want to thank everyone who made the Kickstarter Campaign a success allowing the book to be published:

Sydney Baker   Anna Love
Sharon Bennett: Queen of Disco Art   Tom McIntire
Emma Bonar   Catherine Moran
Brenda Burhance   Gretchen Nelson
Anthony R. Cardno   Karen Nierhake
Robert Chamberlain   Jeffrey & Patty Norman
Joanna Cole   Maria Puentes
Darren Faragher   Pype720
Alex & Susan Fields   Lawrence Rhodes
Joyce Gorham   Stacy Shuda
David L. Hatt AKA D3   Leanne & Steve Sims
Suzanne & Brook Isola   Julianna Sockol
Jake   Gretchen Ward
Arn Johnson: Longtime Friend &   Nicole Warmerdam
Fellow Synthesizer Plugin Addict   Randall Watkins
Marilyn Kanes   Fusae & Jack Wicks
Matt Knepper   Michael Wright

(Mittens is currently in a witness protection program.)